CORDELIA CODD

CORDELIA CODD

FRANKLY, RUBY, I DON'T GIVE A DAMN!

CLAIRE O'BRIEN

ORCHARD

ORCHARD BOOKS
338 Euston Road, London NW1 3BH
Orchard Books Australia
Level 17/207 Kent Street, Sydney, NSW 2000

First published in the UK in 2013 by Orchard Books

ISBN 978 1 40831 402 9

A CIP catalogue record for this book is available from the British
Library.

3 5 7 9 10 8 6 4 2

Printed in Great Britain

Orchard Books is a division of Hachette Children's Books,
an Hachette UK company.

www.hachette.co.uk

To everyone who ever wanted

REVENGE

I needed to find a quiet place to get over the
HORRIBLE SHOCK I'd just had, so I pretended
to need a wee and headed for the toilets. I was
only out of the art room for a few minutes but
THAT'S when it got WORSE. That's when
DISASTER STRUCK.

I'm at Wellminster Community College,
which will be my new school from next week.
It's still the summer holidays but I'm here early
because I've joined something called the Scrap
Design Project. This is like one big long art lesson
for keeping bored kids like me busy until term
begins. It stops parents going BONKERS WITH
STRESS because they can't think what to do
with us. Mum was very enthusiastic when she
saw the leaflet. It said:

Don't throw your old things away!
TRANSFORM THEM
into something lovely at the

SCRaP DESIGn PRojEcT

Bring along your ideas and your scrap materials.

Monday 29th August –
Saturday 3rd September
9.30am – 4.00pm each day

in Wellminster Community College's
award-winning art block

OPEN TO ANYONE AGED 11–18

Call this number to enrol or for more information
01987 68745

I LOVE doing arty stuff and, MOST IMPORTANTLY, I thought it would be a BRILLIANT chance to meet some DESPERATELY NEEDED FRIENDS. We moved here when the summer holidays had just started and I haven't met ANY girls my age for the ENTIRE, LONG, DISMALLY DULL five weeks since then.

Eight of us turned up for the start of the Scrap Design Project this morning, including a boy called Joe. I'd met him once because he lives in the same village as me, Heckaby, about five miles from Wellminster at the BUM HOLE END of the KNOWN UNIVERSE.

Joe gave me a little wave and a smile when I arrived, and I waved and smiled back, but there hasn't been time to chat yet. The teacher, Mrs Allen, seems friendly and jolly – SO jolly that she almost BOUNCES. She got us to introduce ourselves and describe our project ideas. I'd been thinking about mine REALLY hard and I was all knotted up inside with nervousness about sharing it.

There are two girls here, Ruby and Becky. They'll be starting year eight next week, same as me, so I was REALLY looking forward to making friends with them and finding out all about my new school. In fact I was almost EXPLODING with excitement because AT LAST I'd found some other girls to talk to. But that idea has just been **SERIOUSLY STAMPED ON**. Everything has suddenly turned **SOUR** and **SCARY** right ON THE VERY FIRST DAY.

As soon as Mrs Allen sent us off to our tables to start work I got ready to smile at Ruby and Becky and say hello. But when Ruby walked past me she didn't smile. Instead she looked at the old curtains I'd brought along to make something out of and whispered, 'That is *disgusting*,' with her nose screwed up. '*You* are *disgusting*.'

How UNBELIEVABLY HORRID!

And that was just the START of her NASTINESS. I had to escape in here, to the toilets, but she FOLLOWED me.

I'd just had a quick wee, washed my hands and was drying them in the whizzy-whooshy hand-drier when I turned around to find Ruby standing about a metre away from me, blocking the door. The sound of the drier was so loud that I hadn't heard her come in. She was GLARING at me with a face like a STORMY MONDAY.

'You're a right flirt, aren't you?' she said, looking at me like I was a nasty stain on the floor. 'I saw you looking at Joe.'

I screwed my nose up. What on EARTH was she talking about?

'No you didn't. You're making that up,' I said.

I turned my back on her and pretended to dry my hands again because her expression was so TOUGH and HARD that I was too frightened to look straight at her – I needed to GATHER MY THOUGHTS and BREATHE DEEPLY. The whizzy-whooshy drier was pretty loud but her voice was even louder.

'Oh, I *made it up*, did I?' she yelled. 'Well, if you're going to start chasing all the boys at this school before term even starts you're going to get a bad reputation! I'll make sure of that!'

I finished drying my hands for the second time and turned back to face her – there was no escape. I was SO scared by then that I wasn't sure my legs could hold me up much longer. My knees were DEFINITELY shaking and I think I might have been on the brink of a HEART ATTACK because I couldn't breathe properly – only little pants and puffs came out.

'Leave me alone, Ruby,' I managed to say. 'You've never met me before. Your life must be really boring if you have to invent stupid lies about people you don't even know.'

Before I could dodge her, she swung her arm wide and **SLAPPED** the side of my face. It *REALLY* hurt and nearly knocked me over. I was so upset that I couldn't react.

'I don't like you. **Got it?**' she shouted. 'And I'm going to make you wish you'd never come here. You'll be sorry you ever saw that **thief** Joe Grover.'

Just before she walked out of the toilets, she spun back. 'And if you **dare** tell anyone I hit you, you'll be in **hospital** next time.'

So I'm just staring at myself in the mirror now, making sure that I'm still the same girl. Yes, I'm still there, still me, but I've NEVER been slapped before, not by ANYONE. I can't even cry – the tears are stuck. I think I'm actually, really having a genuine TRAUMA. Today was supposed to be the end of my TERMINALLY BORING and LONELY summer and the start of my new life full of friends.

Instead it's plunged head first into a scary CONFUSION SOUP of sick-making FEAR.

WHAT is her problem with me and how on earth am I going to SURVIVE here?

To understand just how **_CATASTROPHICALLY AWFUL_** this feels you need to know more about my summer so far.

2

We moved here on a hot, sticky day in July. Mum, Dad and I went for a walk along Heckaby High Street as soon as the removal men had left. It was IMMEDIATELY obvious that we'd moved to a place that was mostly

CLOSED DOWN.

The post office was CLOSED DOWN,

the primary school was CLOSED DOWN,

the library was CLOSED DOWN,

most of the shops were CLOSED DOWN

and the church was DERELICT. It should be ILLEGAL for parents to make their children live somewhere like this.

Our new home is an old pub called the Jug and Monkey. Mum inherited it from her Great Auntie Deirdre when she died. The front of the pub has an old wooden porch and a sign that swings and creaks in the wind like a pub sign in a ghost story. At the back there's a big stone yard with some little brick buildings called outhouses where people used to keep animals and store barrels of beer. Then there's the paddock. It looks like one of those battlefields from the First World War that you see on television – just a big space full of churned-up mud and stones with weeds growing in between. There's an ENORMOUS old barn, too, but the roof is partly missing.

The whole place is a complete WRECK and there's a constant CRASH-RACKET going on – drilling, hammering, builders shouting and RUBBISH music BLASTING out of the radio while they work. Nothing is cosy or tidy and everything is covered in brick dust and paint splashes. The building work starts at eight in the morning EVERY DAY except Sundays. We had to stop the builders from working on Sundays because the neighbours complained – they complain A LOT.

To make matters worse, I'm in constant danger of WHACKING my head on beams and scaffolding because I can't seem to stop growing. I'm nearly as tall as Mum's shoulder and probably DESTINED to be taller than my dad. This is a problem because we don't have ANY spare money at the moment to replace the clothes I keep growing out of. Every penny Mum and Dad have is going into the building work. On SEVERAL OCCASIONS I have dangled my arms in front of them, pointed to the gap where my sleeves don't reach my wrists any more and said, 'This is getting serious. Could you PLEASE prioritise my SHRINKING WARDROBE SITUATION?'

They're usually looking at bills when I do this and don't even glance up, just mutter something like, 'Not if you want a carpet in your new bedroom,' if it's Dad, or, 'The only new clothes you can have are your school uniform. Anything else will have to wait until Christmas,' if it's Mum. Either way, I am NEGLECTED.

Because of this neglect, I walk around looking like my clothes have shrivelled up in the wash, which is EMBARRASSING and gives me a ZERO glamour score. To hide my CLOTHING SHAME I've started borrowing Dad's jumpers and tucking my TOO-SHORT jeans into wellingtons (borrowed from Mum because mine don't fit any more).

I expect I sound like a complete MOANING MAGGOT and I know that ONE DAY our new home will be BEAUTIFUL and I'll get some decent clothes but at the moment it's all DULL and DREARY and HARD WORK. Mum says things like, 'Nothing worth doing is easy,' and, 'Rome wasn't built in a day,' and, 'Every mountain climb starts with one step.' I wish I was a bit more like my mum.

Dad isn't quite so patient. He has a lot of arguments on the phone with people who are supposed to deliver things but don't – fridges, tiles, wood, tools, you name it, it'll be late for one reason or another. He's very lucky that he has Mum to keep him calm or his hair would probably all drop out with worry – what's left of it.

Dad is turning the Jug and Monkey into a gastro-pub and Mum is going to make the barn into a cinema. Dad's a chef and he makes FANTASTIC food. He used to have a restaurant before but he had to sell it because it didn't make enough money – this is his BIG CHANCE to start again.

Having her own little cinema is Mum's DREAM PROJECT. It's going to be called HECKABY PICTURE PALACE. People will come here from the villages all around to watch old films. There'll be a big chandelier hanging from the ceiling and little tables next to every seat so that you can have tea and cakes or a glass of wine while you watch the film.

Mum and Dad know a lot about films because they studied something called Film and Television History at university together, years and years ago. That's where they met. There are boxes full of films all over our house but I can't unpack most of them yet because of the building mess, which is another HUGELY annoying problem I have because I should NOT be expected to live without old films to watch.

I suppose it's because of Mum and Dad that I love old films. I'm ESPECIALLY obsessed with the clothes that the actors wear. That's one of those CRUCIAL things you need to know about me. Some girls want to be doctors or teachers or singers but one day I, Cordelia Codd, am going to be **the** *˟˟ **GREATEST** ˟˟* **costume designer in the history of cinema.**

My favourite film stars are mostly dead now. I like Audrey Hepburn, Ava Gardner, Grace Kelly and Rita Hayworth – and lots of others, too. If you've never heard of them you'll have to look them up on the internet or in a library book, or you COULD just ask an old person.

At the moment my favourite film is *Gone with the Wind*. The star is called Vivien Leigh and she wears those dresses with big hooped petticoats underneath that swing and bounce. It's a REALLY long film so I sometimes skip through to the scenes with lovely dresses in. I watch the same scenes over and over and draw the costumes in my sketchbook. I have to keep pausing the film to do this, which Mum says makes me the MOST ANNOYING PERSON IN THE WORLD to watch films with. But she doesn't mind REALLY.

♥

There have been PLENTY of deeply UPSETTING and ANNOYING things about this summer, like:

a) having no friends

b) living in the **dullest** village on planet Earth

c) having sawdust and nails and the smell

of damp plaster everywhere

d) wearing **too-small** *clothes*

e) not having enough films to watch

But BELIEVE ME, life at home is a MASSIVO-MASSIVO improvement on last year.

Last year my parents had a GIGANTIC bust-up because Dad behaved like an IDIOT and went off to London with someone called Janet. THE EVIL JANET. Mum and Dad are both living here now and THE EVIL JANET has disappeared FOR EVER but Mum hasn't completely forgiven him for being a STUPID TWIT and leaving us, so they're still NOT QUITE TOGETHER. That's why Mum and I are going to live in the flat above the pub when it's finished, and why Dad is CURRENTLY sleeping in a caravan in the back yard.

Until our flat is ready Mum and I are squeezed into a MICRO-TINY cottage that's built onto the side of the pub. It's like a little cereal box glued onto a big cereal box. When we move into the flat Dad will have this tiny cottage but at the moment Mum says he must stay in his caravan next to the outhouses. NO ONE must EVER know that my Dad lives in a caravan. It's not like a film star's trailer or a romantic

gypsy cart pulled by a horse. It's just a BIG GREY
TIN on flat tyres with rust around the bottom. He
pretends he likes it, as if he's a six-year old boy living
in a den he's built for himself, but I can tell by the
way he looks at Mum when he says, '*It's lovely and
cosy,*' that he doesn't mean it. I KNOW he'd rather be
with us in the cottage.

Sometimes I feel sorry for him and suggest that
he could sleep on our sofa but Mum won't EVEN
discuss it. I USED to think my mum was a bit of a
softie but she's SCARY-STRICT with Dad these
days. He's like a naughty puppy that got sent to sleep
outside in a kennel.

I wake up some nights feeling frightened in case
Dad DISAPPEARS again. I cried when Mum got
cross with him the other day because he accidentally
broke a window when he was moving a ladder. It
would be HORRIBLE if she told him to go away
and not come back. I think I'd die of SADNESS if
that happened. Losing Dad again is SUCH a scary
thought that I TRY not to let it creep into my brain.

♥

Mum and Dad are so BUSY-BUSY organising the builders that I don't get the chance to chat to them for more than five minutes a day. There haven't been any picnics or bike rides or walks in the woods this summer – not even a visit to boring relatives! The only trip I had this holiday was to the CARPET SHOP! And that was a NIGHTMARE because:

a) Most of the carpets were too **ugly** to even **look** at.

b) I can't **stand** the smell of that rubbery green stuff they put underneath. It gets right up my nostrils and I was very nearly **sick** out of the car window on the way home.

c) ~~After~~ **all that time** spent **stressing** and arguing about **colours** and **patterns** Mum *and Dad decided to have varnished floorboards instead!*

What a complete waste of half a day of my life THAT was!

It feels like Mum and Dad are under some sort of DEMON SPELL that makes them only able to talk about roof tiles and plastering and wiring and plumbing and carpets and floorboards. If I was accidentally taken away in the builders' skip one Friday evening I don't think they'd even NOTICE that I'd gone until the following Wednesday or Thursday.

3

There is ONE person I can tell when I get worried
about things. She's my ONLY friend. Her name is
Dru and she lives in Seattle, which is a QUILLION-
TRILLION miles away on the other side of the
world, in the USA. She was at my last school for a
while but her family went back home at the end of
term. When I think about the day I said goodbye to
Dru it still gives me a horrible, sad feeling. I miss her
like BONKERS.

Dru has a genius-sized brain and is always
SENSIBLE about things – AND she helped me
to get Mum and Dad ALMOST back together.
Because of that I WILL LOVE HER FOR EVER,
even though she's so far away that we only get to
talk on the computer now.

At my last school Dru was the ONLY person
who would still speak to me by the end of term. I
fell out with my old friends – I couldn't help it. It
was because when Dad went off with the EVIL

JANET and Mum had a broken heart my behaviour went a bit LOOPY because my head was completely MUDDLED and WEIRD. I lost my temper a lot and got stroppy with people I'd NEVER argued with before. I still lose my temper sometimes, but I'm not nearly so grumpy as I was.

Since Dru went back to Seattle my only company has been Mr Belly, our ginger tom cat, but he disappears for AGES to get away from the noise of the building work. Poor Mr Belly! Whenever he finds himself a cosy corner to curl up in it gets filled with paint pots or wood or tools, so it's not SURPRISING that he runs off to find a peaceful spot. It's been very good for his waistline, though. He used to be a PLUMPO FAT-CAT but now he's a **_LEAN, MEAN MOUSE-EATING MACHINE_**. Actually, he just chews the mice a bit and then brings them to me as a sort of present. I try to look pleased and say *thank you* to him but it's hard to feel delighted when you've just accidentally trodden in mouse guts.

Then there's Joe, who I don't really know at all yet. His stepmum, Jenny, and my mum got chatting in the queue at Akbar's Newsagent one Saturday morning. Jenny invited Mum round the following weekend. I tagged along because there was NOTHING ELSE TO DO.

It was only what Mum calls 'a good stretch of the legs' to Jenny's house at the other end of the village. We passed all the

CLOSED-DOWN shops

and the CLOSED-DOWN primary school

and the CLOSED-DOWN Post Office

and the CLOSED-DOWN library.

I stopped to look in the window of the Copper Kettle Tea Room – which isn't closed down but SHOULD be. It's owned by Mr Clench, who deserves a prize for putting the UGLIEST things POSSIBLE in a window display. He has crammed it full of HIDEOUS teapots. There's a teapot shaped like the Queen and one that looks like a red London bus. There's a cottage teapot and a Dalek teapot, a telephone box teapot and a dog-shaped teapot. He also has two stuffed parrots on perches, which make me itch. Feathers do that to me, even if I just look at them, even if they're on something DEAD AND STUFFED.

I was just looking at the parrots, scratching my

arm and screwing my face up when Mum suddenly gave a little shriek and started running towards the corner near Mike's Bikes. I ran after her, but I didn't really know WHY I was running at first. Then I saw her bend down and talk to something pink and frilly on the edge of the pavement.

'Hello, Mina, what are you doing out alone?' Mum asked very calmly.

The pink frilly bundle was Mr and Mrs Akbar's little daughter, Mina, who is only three years old. Mum had spotted that she was about to step into the road and ran to stop her. Mina started screaming even though Mum was ever so gentle and sweet and didn't even TOUCH her.

'I'll get someone,' I said, because baby screams PIERCE MY BRAIN and I HAVE to move away from them.

I dashed into the newsagent's, where the Akbars live, and came back with Mina's big sister Maryam. She looked a bit embarrassed.

'Come on, Mina,' Maryam said quietly, 'you're supposed to be upstairs with Mummy.'

She thanked us and disappeared back inside with her squealing baby sister.

'That Mina is such a handful,' said Mum. 'She's

always wandering off. She'll have an accident one day.'

Joe only stayed for a few minutes when we got to the Grovers' big posh house. He was stuffing things into a bag in the hallway. His dad popped into the room where we were sitting to say hello, but he was too busy cooking to sit and chat.

Jenny told us that Joe was Mr Grover's son from when he was married to another lady. Joe looked a bit like his dad, tall and sporty-strong, but I guessed that his mum must be black because he was a different colour from his dad, who had whitey-blond hair and white eyelashes and very pale skin. Joe had the same shaped body and face as his dad but he had black hair with ginger bits that he wore in plaits.

There were little Grovers, too, namely Sam and Ben – twin boys aged about two. The Grovers also had a dog. The dog was the colour of pale toffees and was shaped like a BURP – round and short, and poppy-eyed.

I had to hold back a giggle when Jenny Grover

called the twins her GORGEOUS PUMPKINS. I
suppose she HAD to like them because she's their
mum, but I found them a bit of a PAIN IN THE
BACKSIDE for several reasons:

a) They had bits of dried food stuck to
their fat little faces.

b) They tipped **everything** onto
the floor.

c) They tried to climb up **anything**
they stood next to.

Meeting Sam and Ben that day was when I
decided that I'm probably NOT going to be a mum,
it's just too MESSY.

Joe finished filling his bag and called, 'I'll be off
now. Nice to meet you. Bye!' from the doorway.
He gave me and Mum a smile – a really handsome,
friendly smile – and a little wave. He was dressed like
a scarecrow, in what looked like his dad's old clothes.
'I'm off to my allotment,' he told us, which explained
his outfit.

Jenny and Mum mostly ate cake and talked about diets, and how they really shouldn't be eating cake at all. Why do grown-up women do that? Why don't they just ENJOY THE CAKE?!

Mum didn't look very relaxed. Not because of the messy babies crawling all over the place – she seemed to ADORE them, but she was sitting up straight, not flopping back into the sofa cushions like she did at home.

Jenny's clothes were a bit TOO SMART for weekends but Mum was in her usual jeans and sweatshirt. Even Jenny's plates and cups and cakes were posh. I felt sorry for Mum. She needed friends, too, but I wasn't sure that she was going to get on with Jenny very well.

Still, I managed to scoff two of her big DELICIOUS posh cream cakes and drink a HUGE glass of orange juice – the fresh kind with bits in. But I was soon BORED, as usual, so I peeked inside a sketchbook that Joe had left on the table. He'd drawn what looked like a bunk bed without any mattresses. It had numbers and measurements written very neatly all over it.

'What's this?' I asked, showing Jenny one of his drawings.

'It's a project Joe's working on,' she explained. 'He's building a greenhouse for his allotment out of an old bunk bed frame.'

I liked the idea. It was brilliant and his drawing was the NEATEST I'd EVER seen. Joe was obviously VERY CLEVER, but STUPID ME said the first thing that came into my head.

'You must have lots of money if you have a posh house like this, so why don't you just buy him a proper greenhouse?'

Mum choked on a cake crumb, went red as a beetroot and glared at me, saying, 'Coco!'

I knew I've been rude but, thankfully, Jenny laughed and said, 'The idea is to make everything out of *scrap materials*. It's part of a design project that the school are running for the holidays. You could join in if you like. It sounds quite fun.'

'I don't really know anything about greenhouses,' I said.

Jenny waved her hand, like she was brushing flies away. 'Oh, it's not just greenhouses,' she said. 'You can make *anything* you want as long as it's from things that are being thrown away.'

I thought about all the stuff piled up in our outhouses and in the skip in the back yard – junk that we hadn't got rid of yet. I thought especially about the old curtains.

'Can we make costumes?' I asked.

'I don't see why not,' said Jenny. 'Let me get the leaflet about it and you can find out.'

Then the phone rang in the hall. Jenny went to answer it and we heard her say, 'Oh dear, *not again*. I'll be right there, Mike. He won't have meant any harm.'

Her face was bright red when she came back.

'I'm sorry,' she said, stuffing things into a big, glossy handbag. 'I have to pop out. That was Mike from Mike's Bikes. Joe has been taking people's rubbish, just junk they leave out for collection – anything he can use on his allotment. *Apparently,* it's illegal unless you ask first and Mrs Driscoll from the corner shop is *a bit upset* because Joe took some old shelves that she'd left out. Mike says she's threatening to call the police. I'll have to dash down there and see if I can talk her out of it. Here's the leaflet about the design project.'

Mum took the crumpled piece of paper from Jenny's hand.

'Joe will be fine, I'm sure,' she said. 'You mustn't worry.'

'I hope so,' said Jenny, shaking her head. 'But bad reputations spread very quickly in a gossipy little place like Heckaby. I'm *so* sorry to chuck you out like this. You *must* come again.'

I'm not sure she meant that bit. She didn't look at Mum when she said it.

Then she opened the living-room door – a signal that we had to leave IMMEDIATELY – and shouted down the long hallway to Mr Grover in a sudden SERGEANT MAJOR voice.

'Tony! Another Joe emergency. I'll handle it. You stay with the pumpkins.'

Jenny looked different then. She looked like she could invade a small country and take it over single-handedly.

As we walked back past The Copper Kettle Tea Room (*scratch, scratch!)* and the closed-down shops and the closed-down EVERYTHING we looked at the leaflet and talked about the Scrap Design Project. Mum used her chirpy, ENTHUSIASTIC voice, so I knew that she REALLY wanted me to go to it – probably because I'd be out of the way. When my parents are ENTHUSIASTIC about something it makes me NOT want to do it straight away. I think this is because I like things to be my OWN idea. But I didn't resist this time because I NEEDED something TO DO and it would also be the PERFECT place to find some friends – HOORAY!!

When we got home I managed to grab some time on the computer before Mum needed it to search for bathroom-ish things like wall tiles and taps and a new shower. I sent a quick chat message to Dru.

She was online, which was REALLY surprising because it must've been RIDICULOUS O'CLOCK in the morning over in Seattle.

★ **Cordelia** to Dru

Hi Early Bird!

How come you're up? It must be about 4.30am over there!

★ **Dru** to Cordelia

Hi Cordelia

It's **SO** hot that no one can sleep.

We're all super-crabby with each other and have huge eye-bags.

I tell Dru that I might be joining this Scrap Design Project thingy and about Joe and his idea for a greenhouse, and that he is in trouble for recycling.

★ **Dru** to Cordelia

Never mind the recycling, more about the boy, please.

★ **Cordelia** to Dru

Nothing else to tell, yet.

★ **Dru** to Cordelia

Well, is he cute?

★ **Cordelia** to Dru

Cute as in good-looking, handsome, beautiful?
Yes, very.

★ **Dru** to Cordelia

And...

★ **Cordelia** to Dru

And **NOTHING**. I can't become a great costume
designer and bother about romance at the same
time. Gotta go! Being called for lunch!

Love you lots. Don't melt!

C x

Mum rang the school while I was chatting with
Dru and signed me up for the Scrap Design Project
straight away.

Hooray! The end of BOREDOM was in sight.

4

The next day I started beating dust out of some old green curtains. This caused SERIOUS coughing and gave me pink eyes. When I'd swallowed about a desertful of dust and couldn't stand any more, I RUMMAGED like a mad squirrel in the skip and the outhouses for other stuff to use. I found several old bamboo hoops, the kind that were used for hula-hooping before plastic was invented. This got my imagination working.

Late in the evening, when it was too dark to be a rummaging squirrel, I sat in the kitchen and went into a drawing and thinking FRENZY, making LOADS of sketches and watching scenes from *Gone with the Wind* a zillion times over on our tiny telly. There was still almost a week to go before the Scrap Design Project started but I had to have an idea ready to show to the group on the first day. Mum saw me frowning and chewing my pencil.

'Relax, Coco,' she told me. 'That way the

inspiration can FLOW into your mind SLOWLY. You didn't even hear me ask if you'd like one of these chocolates.'

If I am DEAF to an offer of CHOCOLATE then I know I'm seriously OVERDOING IT. So I forced myself to take a break each day after that and kept tagging along with her when she had things to do in the village.

A few days after we'd visited Jenny, I went with Mum to Driscoll's Discount for bread and milk. The shop was empty apart from us and when Mum went to the counter to pay, Mrs Driscoll gave her a LONG lecture about who she should 'watch out for' in the village.

'Mr Akbar at the newsagent's will overcharge and their goods are dodgy,' she told Mum. Mike from Mike's Bikes 'leaves greasy fingerprints on my packets'. Vera from Hair by Romano 'drops trails of hair clippings and couldn't trim a poodle properly'. Lily from the chip shop 'gives very small portions of mushy peas', and the Kwan family from the takeaway are 'foreign and not to be trusted'.

Then she started going on about Joe Grover and his ACCIDENTAL RECYCLING HABIT, although she called him a 'brazen thief' and a 'no-good'. HONESTLY! You'd have thought we were living in a big steamy city full of gangsters and terrorists instead of a muddy village at the abandoned end of the planet. We were both glad to get out of there.

Mum drove me to Wellminster on the first day of the project. It was another cloudy, sticky-hot day like it had been for weeks – as if thunderstorms were waiting to break and the sky was almost too heavy to hold itself up, but I didn't mind – who cared about the weather when there were six full days of art to look forward to!

I had my idea ready. Everything I needed was crammed into a big suitcase on the back seat of the car.

I was a nervous JELLY-WRECK but I was excited, too. I didn't know if I was more excited about making the costume or about finding new friends. No, wait, yes I did, new friends were going to be the BEST bit. I wasn't going to be an isolated SADDO any longer. Today I would start meeting girls who might be my friends ALL the way through school.

We arrived WAY too early. Mum is ALWAYS early for things and Dad is ALWAYS late. Mum insisted that we use the extra time to make a mini-tour of the school, even though I was dragging the heavy suitcase on squeaky wheels behind me. It had the ENORMOUS pair of old green curtains inside as well as dress patterns, costume books and my sketch pad. I also had the four bamboo hoops tied to the outside with washing-line rope. I'd done my best to clean these up but they still had specks of black mildew on them. I must've looked like a mad old BAG LADY pulling this behind me while Mum pointed at things and chirped like a canary, going, 'Oh, Coco, look at this,' and 'That's good, isn't it?' and 'Ooh! That looks a lot better than at your last school, doesn't it?'

There was a basketball tournament going on in the sports hall and a rock band practising in the drama studio. Some people were learning Holiday German in Room 1C and French for Beginners was next door, in Room 1D. The tennis courts were busy, and the canteen was packed with people having tea and sandwiches. They weren't all schoolchildren. There were grandparents and mums and dads, and toddlers, too. Mum was beaming. 'This is great, isn't it?' she said.

And it WAS great, it was the most lively place

I'd seen since we moved here, but my arms felt like they were getting longer and longer from pulling the suitcase so I just grunted, 'Yes, it's OK.'

Mum left me and my suitcase outside the art block because I REFUSED to let her come with me all the way to the door.

'I'm not still seven years old and I don't have a special need,' I told her.

THANKFULLY she understood and LUCKILY for me that's when Jenny tapped her on the shoulder.

I said hello to her very quickly then escaped into the art block and soon found a door with

SCRaP
DESIGn PRoJecT

Tutor: Mrs Polly Allen

stuck to it on a sheet of printer paper. I peeked in and relaxed a bit when I saw Joe. Even though we hardly knew each other, at least he was someone I recognised. Joe was talking to a woman about the same age as Mum but a bit fatter and taller and with short, spiky blonde hair and MASSIVE earrings. Joe was concentrating on explaining his drawings to her. The woman saw me peering in through the glass and waved me into the room.

'Hi! Come in! Come in!' she called, all gushy and friendly. 'This is Joe, I'm Polly Allen. Make yourself comfy. Be with you in a tick.'

Joe and I nodded to each other. He gave me a quick, friendly smile and a wave.

As soon as I parked the suitcase and sat down, more kids came through the door. Although there were only eight of us everyone had brought boxes and bags full of stuff and it took several minutes of noisy settling down for us to spread ourselves out at the tables. I watched carefully, ready to smile at anyone who might become my new friend. I hoped I didn't look desperate but I couldn't help it, I was just so PLEASED to see other human beings my age.

The tables were big and wide apart, and the room was full of light. It was SO different from the messy, tiny space we had at home – much better for working on new ideas.

Eventually, Mrs Allen gathered us together and introduced herself again.

'Hello all, I'm Mrs. Allen. Welcome to the Scrap Design Project. Some of you know me already because I teach Art and Design here at Wellminster. I see you've all brought plenty of things along to show. That's splendid.' She introduced us to Mr Carter, another teacher from Wellminster. He shuffled over from the woodwork area at the far end of the room.

'Mr Carter will be helpful if you need advice on metal and woodwork,' Mrs Allen told us. 'Saws, hammers, nails, drills, bolts, welding and sanding. Those are his specialities and he'll be around each morning to lend a hand.'

Mr Carter was quiet and a bit worn-out looking. He was probably ready to retire, or perhaps being a teacher just makes people get old more quickly.

'So!' said Mrs Allen, slapping her huge palms onto her big, trousered knees. 'You will all be expected to work very hard, every day, all day, for the next six days. That includes Saturday.'

No one grumbled about this. Everyone listened and concentrated. I could feel myself getting nervous. My tummy was fizzing and my heart was beating fast. If everyone's drawings were as brilliant as Joe's perhaps I wasn't good enough to be joining in and my idea would look like A BIG FAT JOKE.

'At the end of the project,' Mrs Allen went on, 'your work will be put on display and at the start of term a panel of judges will award a prize for the best design.'

I hadn't realised until then that there was a PRIZE. I wondered what it was but I didn't DARE ask. I didn't want to look GRABBY. Prizes aren't supposed to be important, are they? Still, it's GREAT if you get one.

'We're going to plunge straight in,' Mrs Allen said. 'I'd like you to introduce yourselves and show the group what ideas you've come up with. So step forward one at a time, tell us your name and let's hear your plans.'

Joe was first up to share his idea. He'd brought some photos of his allotment and of the bunk bed he was going to convert into a greenhouse. I was impressed – from the photos I could see that Joe's allotment was much tidier than I'd ever managed to get my bedroom! There were neat rows of cabbages and beans and some fruit trees and a great long row of raspberries, which are my favourite fruit in the WHOLE world. Mr Carter leaned forward and nodded.

'That's a lot better than my allotment, lad,' he

said. 'I'd better come to you for some tips.'

Joe looked shy and proud for a second, then carried on. 'I don't need to actually change the bunk bed frame to make a greenhouse,' he said. 'I just need to add these.'

He held up a pile of plastic, see-through sheets the size of a piece of printer paper.

'These are transparencies,' he explained. 'I found them in a skip at the back of Marshall's Printworks near the petrol station.'

I couldn't help wondering if he'd asked permission before he took them.

'I want to fix them together like big fish scales,' he continued. 'They need to be overlapping, so that it gets good and hot inside for the plants, but I want to be able to slide them open sideways to let the heat out if it gets too much, so if anyone's got any ideas…'

Several people threw in suggestions but I couldn't think of one. Joe listened and nodded and noted a few things down.

Next, two girls from year seven called Janna and Emmy told us their idea. They wanted to make bookshelves for their bedrooms from old wooden crates. When the crates were turned on their sides they were just the right size and shape to stand books in. 'We've just brought one crate each today,' Emmy explained, 'so that we can show you how it will work.'

'Yes, we've got six more at home, said Janna. 'My dad got them from the depot where he works.'

The wood looked a bit splintery to me. But they'd already thought about that.

'Could we learn how to use an electric sander, please?' Janna asked.

'And a drill,' added Emmy, giggling with excitement, 'so that we can fix the crates together with big bolts?'

'And if anyone has any leftover paint at home, please bring it in,' said Janna. 'We'll use it up. It doesn't matter what colour.'

Janna had her long hair tied up in big, mad, messy bunches and Emmy's curls were like a beautiful red bird's nest – they made me think of the girls in the old St Trinian's films who caused accidents and explosions. I hoped Mr Carter was going to supervise their drilling and sanding carefully. He looked a bit scared at the thought of them using power tools.

Gregor and Lennox were two boys from year

ten. That made them a year older than Joe and two years older than me. Gregor was going to make new lampshades out of old ones. He showed us his PROTOTYPE – that's just a fancy word for a practice try at something.

'I bought a few hideous old lampshades from charity shops,' he told us. 'Then I stripped them down to the frames.' Gregor held up the skeleton of a lampshade. 'I'm going to weave different coloured wool onto the old frames to make something much more interesting.'

'Where did you get so much wool,' asked Mrs Allen, peeking into an ENORMOUS bagful on the floor next to Gregor, 'and so many *fabulous* colours?'

'I was visiting my auntie in Bradford,' Gregor explained. 'There are loads of big wool shops up there and her local one was throwing this lot away. They were happy to let me take it.'

'Brilliant. What a great find!' said Mrs Allen.

Gregor was very confident about his idea. In fact, Gregor looked confident and clever and stylish in EVERY WAY. He looked like the sort of boy whose clothes always fit perfectly and are never dirty. His drawings were SO good that an art teacher could've done them. As well as drawings, he'd put together a whole scrapbook of ideas from magazines then added snippets of fabric and wallpaper and odd, beautiful bits and pieces, like feathers and shells and chips of bark. I decided RIGHT THEN that I MUST start my own scrapbook of LOVELINESS.

'I want to weave some of these different textures in between the wool,' Gregor explained.

I guessed that he was PROBABLY one of Mrs Allen's star pupils. No one said anything about Gregor's idea because we were all GOBSMACKED by how perfect it was.

Lennox was Gregor's friend. He was a bit more jokey than Gregor and his shirt was a bit crumpled. He was very tall and skinny and had LOVELY hair – it was the colour of conkers and long and shiny. His idea was to make cushion covers from a load of old shirts.

'These belonged to my granddad but he died last year,' Lennox told us.

'Was your granddad a bit of a hippy?' I asked, because most of the shirts were a mad mixture of psychedelic coloured flowers.

'Totally,' said Lennox, with a big, wonky-toothed smile. 'He told me that he thought it was "groovy" that I was into sewing. He would've loved me making his old shirts into cushions.'

Lennox showed us a cushion cover he'd already made on his sewing machine at home and it was BRILLIANT. Mrs Allen held it and turned it over and over, admiring it.

'Beautiful, Lennox,' she said. 'Fantastic.'

I was getting SERIOUSLY worried about sharing my idea now. Everyone else's looked SO good. I was sure mine was going to be the RUBBICULOUS (RUBBISHY AND RIDICULOUS) one!

5

Next to speak was Ruby, and then Becky. They looked the same age as me, so I was DESPERATE to get chatting with them at break time. Ruby seemed a bit shy about showing her idea at first.

'It's OK, Ruby, we're all friends here,' said Mrs Allen.

This must've helped because Ruby started to speak up. She told us that she wanted to recycle jewellery by taking old strings of beads apart and carefully re-threading them onto very thin fishing line. She had a box full of old necklaces and bracelets and earrings ready to take apart. Her drawings of how she was planning to string them back together were fantastic. I didn't know why she was shy. I would've been really proud if it was my idea. But, of course, now I know it was just an act to make people think she was sweet and innocent.

Becky had a TOTALLY different plan to Ruby's.

'My little brother needs a Roman soldier's outfit

for a play he's in at school,' she said. 'I'm going to make him some Roman armour out of these.'

She held open a GIANT carrier bag full of supermarket loyalty cards, the plastic ones that they always ask for at the till when you go shopping.

'They were in a box at the back of Tesco,' she told us. 'I asked a lady if they were going to be thrown out and she said, "Yeah, probably, 'cos they don't work properly," so she let me have them.'

Becky had a picture from the internet of a Roman centurion's armour.

'I need to find a way to fix all the cards together and make them into a sort of skirt,' she explained. 'They've got to be loose and move around when they're joined together.'

Emmy's hand shot up. 'You could make a hole in each of the cards,' she said, 'then loop them together with string or something.'

'Good idea,' said Mrs Allen, nodding in agreement.

Mr Carter joined in. 'I've got the perfect hand drill for making very small holes in those,' he added.

'And I've got a box of fasteners and threads that you can experiment with,' Mrs Allen said. 'We'll find just the right thing, I'm sure.'

Then it was my turn. My tummy jumped about.

I caught Joe's eye. He must've been able to tell that I was scared because he smiled and nodded like he wanted to say, 'Go on, you'll be fine.' That helped my legs to stop shaking enough for me to get up and start talking.

I said my name and then held up my sketchbook and explained my idea. I talked a bit too fast because of the NERVOUS NIBBLERS at work in my insides.

'I'm interested in costumes for films and the theatre and I want to make a sticky-out petticoat from these old bamboo hoops that I found in the outhouse at home.'

Mrs Allen laughed, but in a nice way, not like she thought it was stupid, and said, 'What a *marvellous* idea.'

That made me feel a bit braver. I slowed down my talking and was less like a JABBERING JUMPSTER.

'And then I want to make a skirt to go over it from those old curtains.' I pointed to where the faded curtains were laid out on the table.

'I see,' said Mrs Allen. 'And where did you get your idea from?'

'I've been watching a film called *Gone with the Wind*,' I explained. 'It's about the American Civil War. That was in the 1860s. In those days, big, hooped underskirts called CRINOLINES were the fashion. There's a woman in the story called Scarlett O'Hara and she uses old curtains to make an outfit after she has lost everything because of the war.'

'I know that film,' said Mrs Allen, her eyes twinkling. 'How's your sewing?'

'I can do straight lines on a sewing machine,' I told her, 'and I'm starting to understand about using a paper pattern, so I think I can do it but I need space to spread the curtains flat so that I can cut things out.'

'No problem,' said Mrs Allen, 'and we've got some excellent sewing machines you can have a go on.'

I showed the group a photograph from *Gone with the Wind* in my big costume book. It was really heavy and turning it round was difficult but I wanted them to see Scarlett O'Hara in her huge, hoopy skirt so that they'd understand what I was trying to do. It worked because they all started nodding and Emmy said, 'Oh, I get it.'

Then I put the book down and held up my drawing again of how I thought I could build the petticoat from the bamboo hoops.

'The real hoops were made from steel that was bendy and springy,' I told them, 'so my petticoat won't be QUITE so good, but it'll be the right shape.'

Joe was laughing. 'I bet women were always knocking the furniture over wearing those!' he said.

Then Lennox started laughing too, and chipped in with, 'I can't believe women ever wore that stuff. It's like wearing a tent.'

'And they had to wear these underneath,' I said, and showed them all a picture I'd found on the internet of some long, baggy bloomers. That set everyone off giggling, including Mrs Allen and Mr Carter.

'Women and girls had to wear bloomers that reached their ankles,' I explained, 'in case the wind blew their skirts up, because showing your ankles was considered VERY bad manners in those days.'

Then I held up another drawing. This one was of my idea for making the bloomers from Mum's old pyjama trousers and a strip of lace I'd cut off some ANCIENT, tatty net curtains that were left in the cottage.

Ruby was the only person not smiling or giggling. Perhaps she's shy, I thought, or perhaps she thinks bloomers are rude. Becky looked interested, though.

She was just about to say something when I noticed Ruby dig her in the ribs with an elbow. Why would Ruby stop Becky from joining in? Was she a bit jealous because people liked my idea? They liked hers, too, didn't they? Never mind, I thought. It will all be fine when we get a chance to make friends at break time.

Mrs Allen sent us off to our separate tables. 'You've got ten minutes to do a bit more work on your ideas before break,' she announced.

It was HEAVENLY to be able to spread my drawings and the curtains out and have lots of room. All this space was BLISS.

Ruby's things were on a table next to mine. As she walked past me I was ready to smile and tell her that I liked her idea but she didn't look at me, she looked at my curtain fabric first and ran her finger over it, with her nose screwed up. Then she pushed her face **REALLY** close to mine.

'That is *disgusting*,' she whispered, so that Mrs Allen wouldn't hear. '*You* are *disgusting*. Who wants to wear a pair of old curtains and some manky pyjamas?'

I was **SO** shocked that I wanted to burst into tears. I could feel my eyes starting to prickle and burn. My nose was probably turning red – it always does just before I cry. I breathed in hard, to push the tears back. It worked, JUST, but instead of staying cool and calm, or just laughing at her, I let a furious red feeling boil up inside me because I haven't QUITE learned to control my temper yet. If she could be horrid about my project then I could be the same about hers, I thought. My face might've looked tough and brave but my knees were shivering with fear at the same time.

'You need to use your brain if you're going to make a costume,' I said, keeping my voice to a whisper. 'It's not something **THICK** people can do. But even a trained MONKEY can thread a few beads.'

Ruby puffed out a breath. Her nostrils stretched wide and her eyes narrowed into mean little slits. 'It's very difficult, actually,' she said.

'Only if you're a **SIMPLETON**,' I snapped back, but I was still whispering. I didn't want Mrs Allen hearing my temper on the first day.

IMAGINE HOW I FELT! I hadn't spoken to another girl my age for weeks and when I did she turned out to be **THE MOST UNFRIENDLY HUMAN BEING IN THE UNIVERSE**. How unlucky was **THAT?** It was **NOT** a good start, and the Scrap Design

Project would last a whole six days! Was I going to have six days of **FOULNESS** from HER? Ruby went back to her table muttering, 'You'll be sorry, you stuck-up little goody-goody.'

I was still trembling. I really shouldn't try and PRETEND to be tough because I'm a softie underneath and now my insides were like blancmange and my hands wouldn't do what I wanted them to. I tried to get on with my work but I was feeling sick and I couldn't concentrate properly.

'OK, everyone take a break for twenty minutes,' Mrs Allen called at last.

I stayed in the room when the others went out to get snacks because I was frightened of what Ruby might say next and I didn't want to blub out loud in front of everyone. I thought I'd be safe in the art room with Mrs Allen. But – **CATASTROPHE!** – Mrs Allen went to get a coffee and Ruby came back in. She stood in front of my table with her arms crossed and a face like a storm cloud. Becky was hanging behind her. My heart was crashing, like someone hitting a dustbin lid with a hammer. I didn't look up but pretended to ignore her and work on scraping more mildew off the bamboo hoops.

'You think you're a bit special, don't you?' Ruby said, obviously wanting to start an argument. I tried **DESPERATELY** hard to keep my mouth shut this time, hoping that she'd get bored and go away. But she didn't.

'You think all the boys like you just because they laughed when you showed them your idea for your stupid baggy bloomers.'

This was so completely **NOT TRUE** but I still didn't look up or say anything, even though my ears were boiling and my teeth were grinding together.

'I expect you think you're going to win the competition, too, don't you?' she said.

THAT'S when I looked up and my mouth started moving before my brain could stop it. 'I don't **EVEN** know what the prize is,' I said, trying to sound like I didn't give a **FROG'S FART** whether people liked my work enough to give it a prize.

Ruby snorted out a laugh. 'You mean you don't even know why you're HERE?' she said, with her nose screwed up again like before. 'Now who's a *simpleton*?' She grinned a nasty, sideways grin, saying, 'Well, *I'm* here for the prize money. Why else would any of us bother coming?' She tapped her chest with her thumb and leaned right into my face-space again, so close that I could smell the liquorice she'd been chewing. 'That prize is *mine*, d'you understand, *dumb-girl*? That is *my* one hundred pounds! *Got it*?!'

This was absolutely the first time I'd heard what the prize was. ONE HUNDRED POUNDS! Wow! I didn't let Ruby know that I was impressed. I just pretended that it was SO UNIMPORTANT that I must've forgotten about it. I deserved an Oscar for my acting.

'Oh, that!' I said, flipping my hand like I was batting a fly away. 'Who cares about THAT? I'm here because I want to make something interesting. I don't have to be BRIBED with prize money. You're obviously just motivated by cash. That makes you really **SHALLOW** and **PATHETIC**, don't you think?'

Luckily for me, the others came back in at that moment, followed by Mrs Allen. Ruby glared at me like an EVIL GOBLIN and went back to her table. But **WHY** hadn't I just kept my mouth SHUT? Ruby would get me back for what I'd said, I just knew it.

I made an excuse and came into the toilets to try

and PULL MYSELF TOGETHER…and THAT'S when Ruby followed me and landed a *WALLOPING SLAP* on the side of my face.

So now I'm just staring at myself in the mirror, TRYING not to BLUB.

6

There's a red mark on my cheek where Ruby's hand caught me. I splash cold water on it to take the sting away then dry my face with the hand drier and make myself look as normal as possible. I take a few deep…slow…breaths and go back into the classroom. Cordelia Codd is **NOT** going to be **DEFEATED** by one slap from a bully, but she IS feeling VERY WOBBLY.

'Cordelia, you're back!' says Mrs Allen, as if I've been on holiday for a week.

Ruby is smirking, sitting up straight like a little princess, threading her beads.

'Sorry I took so long. Couldn't find the loos,' I lie, doing my best to sound normal.

I go back to my table silently, thinking over and over about Ruby's slap. Did it really happen? Did it? How **DARE** she hit me! How **DARE** she call Joe a thief, just because he took a few old things out of skips. I **HATE** her so much that it makes my cheek sting all over again.

Everyone is busy. Janna and Emmy are with Mr Carter, discussing their bookcase idea. Gregor is tying lengths of wool onto the top and bottom of a lampshade frame, threading beads and buttons onto the wool as he goes. Lennox is over by the far window, getting the hang of using one of the fancy sewing machines. Joe is sharing a table with Becky while they experiment with clips and pins and bits of wire to find the best way of fastening things together for their projects. Ruby is still UNCOMFORTABLY close to me, right on the next table. I can feel her RADIATING nastiness in my direction.

As soon as I see her again all my courage MELTS into a puddle and I feel sick. My hands won't do what I ask them to so I can't get on with ANYTHING. My fingers trip over each other and I drop the hoops and can't get my thoughts clear. All I can think about is that Ruby might hurt me again. I **HATE** her for making me feel like this. But I can't WIMP OUT of the project on the first day, can I? Even though I want to run a MILLION miles away – I want to run SO FAST that I get right back to the beginning of today and start all over again.

At lunchtime I wait to see which way Ruby leaves the art room and I go in the opposite direction. This means going outside and sitting on the wall near the staff car park. I'm just about to let my tears out because I think I'm alone when Joe comes bouncing up, so I sniff them back in.

'Not eating anything?' he asks, chewing on a carrot.

I shake my head. I've got an amazing pastrami and Swiss cheese sandwich in my bag that Dad made for me but I feel like **PUKING** at the thought of food. Joe sits down next to me. I think he senses that something's wrong. And suddenly I can't stop myself from blurting it all out. I tell him everything that's happened. I don't mean to but the words won't stay in.

I start with, 'Ruby hit me. Really hard. What was THAT for?'

I can't hold the tears back, either. They squirt out in all directions. Joe just sits there and lets me get it all off my chest. I don't suppose he was expecting to sit down next to a BLUBBERING FOUNTAIN OF MISERY but he hands me a packet of tissues that he pulls out of his bag and just listens and nods.

After a good five minutes of sobbing I manage to look up at his face. He's frowning and I can't help noticing that he has beautiful eyebrows. They are completely symmetrical and have just the right amount of curve to them. When he frowns they come together exactly in the middle. He waits until I've blown my nose about four hundred times before he says anything.

'Just try and keep away from her,' is all the advice he has for me.

'But she came looking for me, she's HUNTING me,' I say. 'And I **HATE** her. I hope she catches a disease that makes her vomit until she dies of exhaustion from puking. AND she called you a thief.'

Joe gives a little laugh and shrugs his shoulders. 'Everyone calls me a thief since I got in trouble for tatting.'

'Tatting?' Now it's my turn to frown. When I frown my face looks like a piece of chewed gum, not beautiful and symmetrical like Joe's. I know this because I caught myself in the mirror once when I was in a DEEP FROWNING MOOD. It was a nasty surprise.

'What's tatting?' I ask again, wiping my nose one more time and starting to calm down EVER SO SLIGHTLY.

'Tatting is when you pick up stuff that people have left lying around,' Joe explains. 'You pick up useful old tat.'

He's smiling, like he hasn't any worries in the whole world.

'I'm not bothered what people think of me,' he says. 'Especially not people like Ruby. But it was **proper nasty** of her to slap you.'

Joe touches my cheek where she hit me. He runs his thumb over the red patch and looks right into my eyes.

Now, I don't know MUCH about boys but I do know that if I liked Joe in a boyfriend-snoggy sort of way I'd feel something fluttery in my tummy right now, or I'd blush, or my toes would curl up. But I don't feel any of that. I just think how gentle and sweet he is and how much better I feel now that I've told someone as kind as him about Ruby.

'You stick close to me,' he says. 'She won't bother you if you're with me.'

'Why not?'

'Because she's a coward,' he says, 'like all bullies.

She won't hit you if you're with someone bigger than her.'

I somehow think she MIGHT but my chances of survival will certainly be better if I have a tall, strong friend like Joe. The trouble is, I worry that my being friends with Joe might be EXACTLY what makes her WANT to hit me again.

After lunch, Mrs Allen gathers us all together again. I make sure I'm standing close to Joe and as far away from Ruby as I can manage.

'By the end of the afternoon,' says Mrs Allen, 'I'd like you all to have your plans complete. I'll come to each of you in turn and have a chat about any equipment you need.'

We go off to our tables and the whole group works quietly for the entire afternoon. Janna and Emmy are already getting started on their wooden crates. Mr Carter isn't here after lunch to be able to supervise them with an electric sander, so they have to use sandpaper and work by hand to start with. All we can hear are scrapes and scratches from the woodwork area. Everyone else is in a BIG HUSH of DEEP THOUGHTS. You can almost feel the buzz of our brains ticking over.

Joe carries on experimenting with different clips and wires. He sits on his own by the window, instead of with Becky – I don't think he likes to have any distractions. Mrs Allen walks around giving advice. She sits with me for a long time asking questions about my petticoat. I was feeling better about my idea after I'd shared it with the group this morning but now I'm **STRESSING** again. It's as if Ruby has slapped all the confidence out of me.

'Have you thought how you might fix the hoops together, Cordelia?' Mrs Allen asks.

I show her my diagram again. I'm biting my bottom lip. Is she going to decide that the whole idea is STUPID and impossible after all?

'I thought I could join them together with pieces of elastic so that they bounce,' I tell her.

Mrs Allen nods and studies my drawing.

'Do you think I'll be able to do it?' I ask her.

'Oh yes, you must never doubt that, Cordelia. Bits of it will be tricky but you mustn't be a DOUBTING DILLY. If you believe a way can be found to make an idea work, then you'll find it eventually, even if it takes a lot of tries. But if you don't believe a way can be found, then it won't be. It just depends how hard you are prepared to work.'

It's really obvious to me then that all the stress and worry about whether I'm good enough to be here is inside MY head, not Mrs Allen's. I just have to CONTROL the thoughts that whizz around in my brain – which isn't as easy as it sounds, especially when someone like Ruby is trying her best to make you crawl away into a hole and be MISERABLE.

'I've got miles of elastic you can use,' Mrs Allen tells me, 'and you can make a belt from scraps of material for now, but you need something to hang the whole thing on while you put it together.' Her eyebrows spring up, like she's just remembered something, and she lifts a chubby finger. '*This* could be a job for Griselda.'

I must look BAFFLED because she smiles and adds, 'Just wait a tick.'

Mrs Allen disappears into her big storeroom. I hear her huffing and clattering things around and swearing a bit. She comes out three minutes later covered in dust and carrying a life-sized body on a stick. Of course! I should've guessed. Griselda is a dressmaker's dummy. That's what they look like,

in case you've never seen one. It's a life-sized body
with no arms or legs and it's on a big pole. You put
your dress or skirt or shirt onto the dummy to make
sure it will fit, like dressing up a real person. Mrs
Allen puts Griselda down next to my table, along
with a bag of elastic and a pile of scrap material.

'There. See what you can do with that lot,'
she says.

I spend the first half of the afternoon dusting
Griselda off, making her a belt from scrap fabric
and then working out how long my lengths of
elastic need to be. This is MIGHTY TRICKY and
I'll need a stronger belt to hold the weight of the
hoops. Then I'll need to sew a proper waistband.
I have to concentrate because it's all much more
complicated than I imagined it would be but I'm
enjoying it so much that I ALMOST forget about
Ruby, and she is so busy threading beads that I
begin to think she might have forgotten about ME.

At afternoon break I sit with Joe on a bench outside.
We have what my mum calls a 'good old chinwag',
about living in Heckaby and how boring it is and

how my mum and dad are annoying the whole
village with their building noise. I start to feel safer
and more relaxed but I keep half an eye open for
Ruby. Joe's right though, she doesn't come near
when I'm with him. When she comes out of the art
room and sees that we're sitting together she throws
me a nasty look then heads back inside.

We hear her say to Becky, 'C'mon, we're going to
get a drink from the machine.'

'We've just had one,' says Becky. 'I'd quite like to
sit outside now.'

'No you *wouldn't*,' Ruby snaps back, and Becky
follows her like a dozy sheep.

Joe sees the look of fear on my face. 'Stay cool,'
he says. 'She won't touch you while I'm here. I
promised, didn't I?'

I breathe out and relax a tiny bit. He changes the
subject back to us, to take my mind off Ruby. 'I've
only lived in Heckaby for a year,' he tells me. 'I was
in London before, with my mum.'

'Why did you move HERE when you could be
in LONDON?' I ask. 'I want to live in a big city
SO badly.'

He shrugs. 'I like it better here, even if it is a bit
boring sometimes.'

But I have the feeling that there's a story behind Joe coming to Heckaby. Maybe he emptied all the skips in London and got into trouble too many times. When I know him a bit better I'll ask about the details but I don't want him to think I'm a NOSY-FALOSY.

Mrs Allen leans out of the art room door just then and waves to us, her signal that it's time to start work again.

'If she had a flag and a whistle she'd look like a train driver,' I whisper.

Joe laughs. 'Are you getting the bus home later?' he asks.

'No, my mum's picking me up. Would you like a lift?'

'Great. Yes, thanks,' he says.

By four o'clock we all look completely EXHAUSTED.We leave things tidy and ready for the morning. Joe and I nod to each other as a signal that we're ready to go and that I haven't forgotten that I've offered him a lift home. Mrs Allen's voice suddenly sounds different.

'Cordelia, can you stay behind for a moment, please?'

It's the first time I've heard her being strict. I freeze.

'I'll wait outside,' says Joe.

Ruby is watching. She throws me another nasty look as she leaves.

Mrs Allen is holding a pair of super-sharp scissors. They are the same pair that she let me use for cutting the elastic. They're better than any I've tried before and I know they're VERY expensive to buy.

When everyone has left the room she says, 'Cordelia, these were found in your bag.'

I feel sick.

'WHAT? But I put them back on the shelf, like you showed me. I PROMISE I did.'

'There were also these.' She holds out three reels of lovely silky sewing threads that Lennox was using for his cushion covers. My voice will only come out dry and crackly.

'I wouldn't **STEAL** things, Mrs Allen.'

'Can you explain why I found them sticking out of your bag, then?'

'No, no, I **CAN'T**. But I promise you I **WOULDN'T, I COULDN'T**, I just don't **DO** that sort of thing.'

I can feel the hot tearful-taps starting behind my eyes again. I am **MORTIFIED!!** (Mortified =

embarrassed and humiliated all at the same
time.) I might drop dead of **SHAME** on the spot
but I think Mrs Allen sees that I am **HIDEOUSLY**
shocked and telling the ABSOLUTE truth
because she puts the scissors and threads on the
table and her voice changes back to soft and
friendly.

'OK, Cordelia, I believe you,' she says. 'I'm not
sure what's happened here but I'll be asking the
others some questions. Meanwhile, keep your bag
close to you at all times, please.'

'Yes, yes, I will,' I say, picking up my bag and
clutching it tight. 'Do you think someone else put
them there?'

And OF COURSE, I've answered my own
question in that MILLISECOND. It's OBVIOUS!
Ruby put them there! She didn't dare bother me
when I was with Joe so instead she set me up for
STINK-SWAMPING trouble with Mrs Allen.
But I can't PROVE it and THAT is NUCLEAR-
EXPLOSION-SIZED-FURY-MAKING!!

'I know who it was…' I start to say, but Mrs
Allen stops me.

'Let's not go pointing the finger of blame just yet,
Cordelia,' she says. 'I'll be keeping an eye out for

the culprit. Off you pop home now and don't worry about it.'

I am too cross to speak to anyone. Joe runs after me as I stomp down the corridor to the main doors. 'Whoa! What's happened?' he calls, following me out into the fresh air. I look around for Mum.

'That Ruby MacPherson put some stuff in my bag so that it looked like I was nicking it!'

Joe nods slowly. 'Don't let Ruby bother you. She's always giving **someone** a hard time. Just let it go.'

I gasp. What IS he talking about? 'Let it *GO*... *LET IT GO??*' I'll boil her in oil and feed her to the vultures if I get the chance. I am *FUMING*. 'How can you *SAY* that?' I am close to crying *YET AGAIN*. 'She just made me look like a *KLEPTOMANIAC!*' *(Kleptomaniac = someone who can't stop stealing stuff.)* 'She very nearly *WRECKED* my reputation with Mrs Allen but LUCKILY she could see that I was innocent and about to die of shame ON THE SPOT otherwise I'd be the NUMBER ONE SUSPECT every time something went missing from now on.'

Joe shrugs again. 'So Ruby didn't succeed, did she? Don't worry about something that hasn't happened. Reputation is only people's opinions, anyway. **You** know the truth, **that's** what matters. Let it go. Ruby's a brat.'

'**NO WAY** will I let it go,' I say. 'I'm going to have revenge on her for this.'

'Revenge is a stupid waste of energy,' says Joe. 'Wanting revenge is how wars start. It's just not what **intelligent** people do.'

But I don't get time to argue with him any longer because Mum arrives. I bend down to the car window and act like I'm cheerful because I don't want to tell Mum about Ruby in front of Joe and sound like a blubber-baby AGAIN.

'Can we give Joe a lift?' I ask with a fake smile.

I let Joe sit in the front seat. He chatters away with Mum, being polite and charming, but I hardly speak all the way home. Joe tells her how great the Scrap Project is and describes everyone's ideas. Mum loves hearing what we are all doing and because she is concentrating on driving and listening to Joe she doesn't seem to notice my **SOUR** face.

After we drop Joe off I tell Mum that I'm a bit tired and lie down on the back seat with my eyes shut, trying to block out my HORRIBLE day. She carries on muttering about HER day and then gets on with BUSY STUFF as soon as we get home. I WILL tell Mum, but not today. Not on my FIRST DAY. This is a job for SUPER DRU.

7

No one is on the computer when we get home so I send a quick message to Dru before dinner. Maybe she'll be awake and online – staying cool before the sun gets too hot.

★ **Cordelia** to Dru

Hey Dru

One day I **PROMISE** to send you good and cheery-making news. Today is **NOT** that day. I hope it isn't still baking hot there because I need your brain to be fully functioning right now.

I tell her all about Ruby making my first day at the Scrap Project a DISASTER. I ramble on and on to her, my fingers bashing the keyboard like hammers to get my anger out. Every time I go online to chat with Dru I seem to be COMPLAINING. Sometimes I worry that she might decide I'm too much of a MISERY GUTS to bother with and just unplug our friendship. But good-old, lovely-old Dru comes straight back with her words of wisdom.

★ **Dru** to Cordelia

Hi Moaning Mouth

This Ruby MacFearsome, or whatever her name is, sounds like what my Aunt Zillah calls **A PIECE OF WORK**, which means she is **TO BE AVOIDED**. Meanwhile, I have four important questions.

1. Do your mom and dad know about her?

2. How many kids will there be in your new school?

3. How is your design going?

4. Have you told your cute friend Joe and, if so, what does he make of it?

It's still crazy-hot here but I will put ice on my head so that my brain can help you.

★ **Cordelia** to Dru

Answer 1. No, I haven't told Mum and Dad yet. They're too busy to listen anyway.

Answer 2. There are 1,400 kids at Wellminster. That's **MASSIVE**.

Answer 3. The costume is going really well. I think I might be going to make something altogether **EXCELLENT** and **FAN-DABBY-DOO-DI-LA-LA**.

Answer 4. Joe says I should let it go and not try to get my own back. He thinks I'll start a mini-war if I do.

And your reason for these questions is? Oh mighty iced-brain!

★ **Dru** to Cordelia

Answer to answer 1:
Make your parents sit down and **TELL THEM**. Parents have their uses.

Answer to answer 2:
There'll be 1,399 other kids in your new school and they won't all be like **HER**, they'll be mostly great. School will go on for another five years but

this project is just six days. This
is not your whole, entire life, just a
tiny bit of it.

Answer to answer 3:
You're there to make a fantastic
costume. Right? So the most important
thing is going really, really well.

Answer to answer 4:
Joe is completely right and that
temper of yours could get you into
trouble.

★ **Cordelia** to Dru

But **I HATE HER!!**

I want to make her **GO AWAY!!**

Then the computer crashes and throws me off
the internet, as if it is bored with listening to me
and is saying, 'For goodness' sake pull yourself
together, CORDELIA CODD.' That's the end of
communication with Dru until the internet comes
out of its sulk.

Mum calls up the stairs, 'Could you pop to the
shop for me, Coco?'

After Dru's advice, I was just thinking that I
should speak to Mum and Dad while they're both

in the kitchen and tell them about Ruby but Mum's voice is tight and stressy. It *squeaks* a bit, which is a sign that she's too overloaded with things to listen to my problems just now and that going to the shop is not really a request but an ORDER. Besides this, when I get downstairs and see the dark circles under Mum and Dad's eyes from working all day I feel like I have to MAKE MYSELF USEFUL, so I take the money and the shopping list Mum gives me.

It's raining, which means that I have to put on Dad's HIDEOUS bright-green waterproof because, as I said, mine is too small – I'm in danger of being a freaky giraffe-girl by Christmas. I have to borrow Mum's wellies, too, which are covered in silly pink flowers – I am NOT especially into PINK. Girls who wear too much pink are the TRAGIC VICTIMS of someone else's COMPLETELY WRONG idea about the purpose of girls.

Dressed like a luminous frog with pink feet, I set off to Witchy Driscoll's Discount.

By looking at the shopping list Mum has given me I can guess what we're having for dinner. SCROMLETTES – YUMMO! My dad's scromlettes are the BEST thing if you like eggs and cheese and need a bit of cheering up. The eggs and cheese are mixed up with lots of herbs and tasty leftovers and served with brown sauce or tomato ketchup.

When I push open the door of Driscoll's Discount an electric buzzer sounds somewhere in a room behind the shop. Witchy Driscoll shuffles out. She always appears IMMEDIATELY, as if she's a robot that is activated by the electricity from her own doorbell. I've never seen her wearing anything except a blue nylon housecoat over baggy old clothes, and big, wide shoes.

The shop is dusty and cluttered and some of the packets of food are a bit sticky. There's a funny smell in the air that I think is a mixture of mouse poison and mothballs, and the lights are those harsh, bright strips that flicker.

Witchy Driscoll doesn't stay behind the counter, like a normal shopkeeper. Instead, she comes right up to you and follows you around, asking what you want and pretending to be helpful when she's really SPYING on you. Adults don't realise it but shopkeepers behave very differently towards young people when we aren't with our parents. Most of them are quite unfriendly towards us but the EXTRA-MEAN ones like The Dreaded Driscoll are HORRIBLE. Witchy Driscoll PATROLS when young people are in her shop, looking like she wants to chase us out with a broom.

Sometimes I wonder if perhaps Mrs Driscoll really wanted to have a flower shop or a hat shop but instead she got stuck with margarine, toilet paper, breakfast cereal and thousands of gloopy things in tins. PERHAPS if she'd had a flower shop or a hat shop she might've been happier and smiled more. Or perhaps she's the sort of person who will be miserable WHATEVER she does.

As I look for the things on Mum's list Witchy Driscoll shuffles after me. I can't get up the aisle to the eggs because she's blocking my path. She's shorter than me and quite skinny but she still manages to fill the ENTIRE shop with her GENERAL GRUMPINESS.

'Can I help you, young lady?' she says, her eyes narrow and squinty.

'Yes, I'd like some eggs please, a dozen,' I say.

Mrs Driscoll turns sideways and lets me go past. 'At the back. You'll have to fetch them yourself, I'm not traipsing all the way up there.'

I walk up the aisle, past cans of soup and packets of instant sauce and sultanas and tins of treacle.

When I get to the shelf at the back I lift down a big box of eggs, using both hands. I open the lid to check that they aren't broken, the way I've seen Mum do. There is a crack in one egg so I put that box back and take another one. These have a few feathers and a bit of chicken poo stuck to them, but they aren't broken. I know that chicken poo and feathers aren't a problem if the eggs are free range, so I feel happy with these. When I turn around Mrs Driscoll is REALLY close behind me and I jump **OUT OF MY SKIN!**

'*OOH!*' I shout.

The eggs fall and SPLATTER-CRASH all over the floor.

'*OOH!* I shout again, flapping my hands. 'Sorry! Sorry! You made me jump.'

Mrs Driscoll looks down and tuts loudly. 'You'll have to pay for those.'

'But you made me jump. It wasn't my fault,' I say, my eyes popping out with **OUTRAGE** and SURPRISE.

'Cheeky young madam!' snaps Witchy Driscoll, folding her arms across her skinny chest. 'You'll *pay* for them. You should've held onto them properly.'

I don't dare argue with her but I'm not going

to offer to clean up. I take another box of eggs without checking them, step over the yolky-squish on the floor and find the herbs and cheese quickly. Mrs Driscoll follows me all the way back to the counter, floppity-shuffling in her big old shoes, like a bad-tempered penguin.

She pokes the buttons on her till VERY hard. 'That's two dozen eggs, a dozen *broken*...thyme and cheddar. We'll call it ten pounds exactly.'

She holds out her bony hand for the money but doesn't offer me a bag to carry things in, and I daren't ask for one. It's not eco-friendly to use plastic bags anyway, but I don't think eco-friendliness is Mrs Driscoll's reason for not offering me a bag, I think it is just total UN-FRIENDLINESS. I pay her and leave very quickly without saying goodbye.

When I get outside I feel like I've been holding my breath all the time I was in her dingy little shop. I scurry home, hunched up over my shopping, taking deep sniffs to get some air back inside me. There hasn't even been time to recover from my sob-a-thon about Ruby and ALREADY I have Witchy Driscoll causing me *MAJOR DISTRESS* as well, just over a few stupid eggs. I'm not sure that even a massive scromlette will make me feel cheerful just now.

When I get home Dad is in the hall, arguing with one of the builders over the telephone. Mum is in the kitchen, chopping onions to go in the scromlette. I put the shopping down on the kitchen table and burst into tears…AGAIN.

Mum gives me a quick cuddle, hands me some kitchen roll to blow my nose on, then tuts a lot and shakes her head as I tell her what happened in the shop. She finishes cutting up the onions and then starts cracking the eggs I've brought back with me into a big plastic bowl.

'She *is* a bit of a scary one, that Mrs Driscoll,' Mum says, 'but she *has* had problems with young people stealing from her recently, so she's a bit touchy. Don't take it personally, and don't worry, you won't need to go in there very often.'

'NOT VERY OFTEN is the same as SOMETIMES,' I say, shouting a bit. 'I'm not going in there on my own *EVER AGAIN*.'

Mum sighs and beats the eggs with a big fork. 'You'll have to toughen up a bit, Coco. If you're frightened by a grumpy old lady what will you be like when you're a costume designer and you have to deal with bad-tempered film directors and fussy actors?'

I want to tell her that becoming a costume designer and Mrs Driscoll being horrid to me are not in the LEAST BIT connected but Mum knows EXACTLY how to join things up that seem to have nothing to do with each other. She says it's all TRAINING to toughen me up for the big, bad, grown-up world. She's probably right but it's a bit HARSH and I don't want to hear it so I flounce out of the kitchen and bump into Dad just as he finishes on the phone. He looks FURIOUS about something the builder has told him.

'Out of the way, Coco,' he says, not noticing my VERY UPSET FACE and stepping straight past me. He starts telling Mum about his phone call and at the same time chopping tomatoes and generally taking over the cooking – he wouldn't EVER let someone else be in charge of scromlettes – that's his department. I sit on the bottom of the stairs, just outside the kitchen and blow my nose, waiting for dinner to be ready.

The smells of cheese and herbs, onions and garlic are soon wafting up from the big frying pan. Mum and Dad are jabbering on about the builders. I want to interrupt and make them listen to MY troubles but they're soon talking at FULL STEAM

POWER – cooking and moaning, complaining and stirring things at the same time. They wouldn't listen properly, so what's the point?

At dinner time they only stop talking long enough to chew their food. That's when I grab the chance to tell Dad about Mrs Driscoll, to see if I get a more sympathetic reaction from him than I did from Mum.

'She frightens me, too,' Dad says. 'I feel sorry for her when I hear that kids have stolen things out of the shop but that's no reason not to be polite to customers.'

I feel a tiny bit better knowing that at least one of my parents understands that Mrs Driscoll is a UNIVERSALLY RECOGNISED SCARY PERSON and I'm thinking that this might be the moment to move the conversation on to telling them about the much more important business of Ruby and her slap. But Mum suddenly remembers something and I lose my chance.

'I nearly forgot,' she says to Dad. 'We have to decide when we want the dishwasher delivered.'

She and Dad start discussing dishwasher delivery. They're so SERIOUS and INTENSE about this that you'd think we had a family of

TRAUMATISED REFUGEES arriving, not just a piece of kitchen equipment. I decide that it's HOPELESS trying to mention Ruby tonight. I don't want Mum saying that it's just another bit of TRAINING that will toughen me up for the grown-up world. I can JUST ABOUT cope with this theory when it's applied to Witchy Driscoll but Ruby Macpherson is ANOTHER MATTER ALTOGETHER. She actually hit me! She has also made me want to **KILL HER**. Ruby is a much more serious problem. I couldn't BEAR it if they didn't listen PROPERLY so I have to choose just the right moment to tell them.

8

The clock next to my bed suddenly says four-thirty in the morning! I have **EXPLODED** awake with my heart banging as if I've just run all the way from Wellminster.

In the middle of a fairly nice dream about eating breakfast, Ruby MacPherson suddenly popped up from under the table. She'd turned into a MAD-EVIL-ZOMBIE with electric eyes that drilled into me like bright orange killer-laser beams. She just stared and stared. It would've woken ANYONE up. It was **BEYOND FRIGHTENING**.

Outside, the birds are already singing and daylight is peeking in through the little gap between the curtains. I screw my eyes shut TIGHT, like they are sticky-taped down, and try to sleep again but every time I nearly nod off THERE is Ruby again, popping up with her laser-beam stare. In four and a half hours I'll be back in the art room with her, the girl who whacked me across the face and then dropped me right in the DOO-DOO with Mrs Allen. How **DARE** she stop me from sleeping!

When the clock says nearly six, I give up trying to go back to sleep. Instead, I lie there plotting a GRISLY revenge on Ruby, ignoring Joe and Dru's advice to just AVOID her and LET IT GO.

I have to get the bus to Wellminster that morning, the second day of the Scrap Project. The weather is hot and wet again. Drizzle is whirling around in the sticky air. Mum can't find where we packed the umbrellas when we moved house so I have to choose between going out in Dad's bright-green waterproof jacket again or Mum's boring blue one. I choose the blue one but refuse to wear her silly pink wellingtons. She finds a black pair that are her old ones. They're cold and hard on the inside and a bit too big for me, but I'd rather wear these with some extra socks than the others. It's a good job I'm not particularly bothered about fashion because I must've looked MEGA-EXTRA UNGLAMOROUS. I can hear you saying

'WHAT??!! You? Not interested in fashion?
But you're obsessed with film-star frocks!'

Really, trust me, honestly, it makes sense. I love
gorgeous clothes, but only for films, I wouldn't
be stupid enough to try and look like a film star
in real life, it would take up FAR too much time
to decide what to wear every day and then get
my hair right and fuss about with make-up. I
need my time for drawing and watching films
and thinking up gorgeous ideas for OTHER
people to wear. So, if you're a fashion follower
and find it COMPLETELY HORRIFYING and
INEXPLICABLE that I would step outside the
front door dressed like part of a campsite, that
should explain it a bit.

Mum says I'm 'focused'. That's me, focused on
what I'm going to do in the future. But on this
particular morning, being focused doesn't stop me
feeling like a MESSY DOG'S BREAKFAST that
has been chewed up, spat out and SCRAPED into
the bin.

I went to bed FAR too late for a girl who has
important things to do the next day because Mum
and Dad forgot to remind me when it was bed

time and I was watching films until nearly eleven
o'clock! Then I was woken up FAR too early by
those nightmare visions of Ruby and thoughts about
how to **MURDER** her. Hating people takes a lot of
energy, I've noticed.

By the time I had to get up I didn't even have
the strength left to clean my teeth properly or find
a hairbrush. So when Joe strolls up to the bus stop
looking fresh and healthy and frowns at me, saying,
'Wow, you look *really* rough!' I'm VERY surprised
that I don't BITE HIS HEAD OFF. But there's
something about Joe's cheeky expression that
makes me laugh at myself and not get in a NARKY-
PANTS TWIST.

We sit together on the bus but pretty soon
I start to nod off because I'm still so tired and I
HONESTLY don't realise that my head has flopped
down and is resting on Joe's shoulder. This is a
NEAR-FATAL ERROR.

When Ruby gets on the bus, just over the little
river that separates Heckaby from the other villages,
I'm fast asleep. She 'accidentally' knocks me **VERY
HARD** with her bag as she goes past and wakes me
up, then stomps right to the back of the bus.

'Ignore it,' Joe whispers.

But all the scared, angry feelings from yesterday come RUSHING back and knot my insides up. At first I wish I could go back to sleep and wake up somewhere else but then I think, 'No, hang on a minute, I WANT to go to school and make my costume. Being frightened of Ruby is just getting in the way.' I've got to be strong or she'll stop me doing things I like, she'll start **CONTROLLING** me and **NOBODY** is going to do **THAT** to Cordelia Codd, even if I do feel sick and wobbly-at-the-knees while I'm being brave.

Mrs Allen gathers us all together before we get on with our projects. She looks healthy and full of fresh air and jolliness. Some people are like that in the mornings, I've noticed.

'As a bit of an incentive today,' she begins, clapping her hands together like big, dry loaves of bread, 'I want to remind you that all your work will go on display in the school foyer from the start of lessons next week until the half-term holiday.'

Everyone except Gregor looks a bit nervous at the thought of their work being seen by everyone in time and I was watching films until nearly eleven o'clock! Then I was woken up FAR too early by those nightmare visions of Ruby and thoughts about how to **MURDER** her. Hating people takes a lot of energy, I've noticed.

By the time I had to get up I didn't even have the strength left to clean my teeth properly or find a hairbrush. So when Joe strolls up to the bus stop looking fresh and healthy and frowns at me, saying, 'Wow, you look *really* rough!' I'm VERY surprised that I don't BITE HIS HEAD OFF. But there's something about Joe's cheeky expression that makes me laugh at myself and not get in a NARKY-PANTS TWIST.

We sit together on the bus but pretty soon I start to nod off because I'm still so tired and I HONESTLY don't realise that my head has flopped down and is resting on Joe's shoulder. This is a **NEAR-FATAL ERROR**.

When Ruby gets on the bus, just over the little river that separates Heckaby from the other villages, I'm fast asleep. She 'accidentally' knocks me **VERY HARD** with her bag as she goes past and wakes me up, then stomps right to the back of the bus.

'Ignore it,' Joe whispers.

But all the scared, angry feelings from yesterday come RUSHING back and knot my insides up. At first I wish I could go back to sleep and wake up somewhere else but then I think, 'No, hang on a minute, I WANT to go to school and make my costume. Being frightened of Ruby is just getting in the way.' I've got to be strong or she'll stop me doing things I like, she'll start **CONTROLLING** me and **NOBODY** is going to do **THAT** to Cordelia Codd, even if I do feel sick and wobbly-at-the-knees while I'm being brave.

Mrs Allen gathers us all together before we get on with our projects. She looks healthy and full of fresh air and jolliness. Some people are like that in the mornings, I've noticed.

'As a bit of an incentive today,' she begins, clapping her hands together like big, dry loaves of bread, 'I want to remind you that all your work will go on display in the school foyer from the start of lessons next week until the half-term holiday.'

Everyone except Gregor looks a bit nervous at the thought of their work being seen by everyone in the school for a WHOLE HALF TERM. We've GOT to make sure it looks good or we'll be totally HUMILIATED. Mrs Allen might sound a bit soft but she has clever ways of putting the PRESSURE on you.

'And I should also remind you,' she continues, 'that the Parents' Association will be judging your ideas and are offering a prize of £100 for the best design. So, any questions before we get to work?'

Ruby sticks her hand up. 'Will it be hard cash or just book tokens, like the painting competition last year?' she asks.

I can't BELIEVE she said that. What a little money-grabber! What a VULGARIAN! *(VULGARIAN = lacking sophistication or good taste.)* And you can call me a snobby-chops if you want to but asking if the prize is *hard cash* is DEFINITELY 'lacking sophistication or good taste'.

Other people laugh a bit. That's what people do to cover up their embarrassment when someone says something CRINGE-MAKINGLY awful. Gregor doesn't laugh, he rolls his eyes to the ceiling and folds his arms.

'Well,' says Mrs Allen. 'I can see you'll do well

in business, Ruby. As far as I know it will be, as you say, *hard cash.*'

I think Mrs Allen is being kinder to Ruby than she deserves. Besides, I wouldn't mind winning book tokens instead of money because I've seen some AMAZING costume books that are WAY too expensive for my pocket money.

And THAT'S when it strikes me! The perfect revenge on Ruby! The way to squash her AS FLAT AS A PANCAKE without doing anything that might get me into trouble. I **HAVE** to make such a brilliant costume that I WIN the competition. I'll SNATCH the prize money from under her greedy little nose.

As soon as Mrs Allen has finished talking we all get on with our work again. I keep one eye on what I'm doing and one on Ruby. I don't trust Becky, either. Ruby seems to be IN CONTROL of her, so I'm not going to try and make friends with her JUST IN CASE she turns out to be Ruby's SPY.

I don't dare go to the loo or to get a drink because I know that if Ruby catches me on my own

I'll be ROADKILL. Something else is bugging me, too. Not a MASSIVE thing, but it's buzzing around like a fly at the back of my brain.

I'd spent so much time trying to get back online to Dru this morning – and failing – that I had to rush about like a MAD MONKEY after breakfast. It was time to run for the bus so I just BORROWED the leather belt out of Dad's jeans while he was in the shower. I hope he won't mind – it's bothering me that I didn't ask first.

The belt is now on Griselda and the lengths of thick elastic are tied onto it. I'm working on getting them all the right length and springy-ness, which is MUY COMPLICADO – that means 'very complicated' in Spanish. My Dad says it when he's doing a tricky recipe. By the middle of the morning all the hoops are hanging evenly and it's looking TRÈS IMPRESSIONNANT – that means 'very impressive' in French. Dad says that when one of his recipes turns out well.

My next job is to pin the paper skirt pattern onto the curtains that are spread across the table. Mrs Allen helps me with this.

The pieces of the pattern are big sheets of flimsy tissue paper and they need pinning onto the curtains very carefully. Mrs Allen shows me how to use special chalk to make little marks on the fabric. These marks will show how the pieces fit together once they're cut out. It's a bit like a 3D jigsaw puzzle and the chalk marks will stop me getting in a muddle and being lost for ever in a DEEP JUNGLE of green fabric.

For more than two hours I concentrate so hard that I forget about Ruby, and about how I'm going to explain Dad's missing trouser belt. I haven't noticed what the others are doing at all, and I barely heard the noise of the sander and the drill that Emmy and Janna were using. By the time all the pattern pieces are pinned into place and ready to cut out it's almost lunchtime. Concentration is a fantastic way to calm a fuzzy-problem head, even if it doesn't stay calm for long.

It's still hot and heavy outside. A thunderstorm MUST be on its way. I sit with Joe near the car park at the back of the art room again. While we eat, he tells me some of the good stuff about Wellminster, like the art gallery visits they do and the trip to Paris that Year Eight have in the spring.

'I went last time,' Joe tells me. 'It was fantastic. They've got so many art galleries that you nearly trip over them.'

I'm grinning MASSIVELY at the thought of this.

'Paris! Yes, please!' I say. And I make a note to start BEGGING Mum and Dad very soon to let me go, so that they have plenty of time to save up the money.

I had to make my own sandwich this morning so it's only one of my cheese and pickle THROWTOGETHERS – no salad with a fancy dressing like Dad would've done. But at least today I can eat my lunch and not feel sick with fear… or so I thought, until Joe says, 'I've got to go over to the allotment this afternoon to do some more measuring for the greenhouse. Are you going to be OK?'

My sandwich turns over in my stomach. The thought of him not being around to stop Ruby from hammering me on the bus is TERRIFYING, but he can't be there all the time, can he? So I just nod and say, 'Don't worry, I'll be OK.'

The end of lunchtime comes quickly and we are soon all back inside, working hard. By half-past two in the afternoon I've already cut out the first big piece of skirt from the curtain fabric – going slowly, slowly around the pattern with Mrs Allen's huge, heavy dressmaking scissors. It's a lovely sweepy-swirl of material, just the right shape and length.

When Mrs Allen is busy helping Ruby I grab my chance and run to the loo because I can't concentrate any longer. I didn't **DARE** go for an FW (Final Wee) after lunch in case Ruby was there so now I'm **BURSTING**. Ruby won't break off from her chat with Mrs Allen and follow me, will she? That would mean her missing an opportunity to be a creep and stay in Mrs Allen's good books. She drivels on, saying, 'Oh, thank you, Mrs Allen, that's a good idea. Yes, I'll try it that way,' and, 'May I use the special pliers to bend this piece of wire? May I? Please, thank you *so* much, these tools are *so* lovely.'

YUKKORAMA! She's so *slimy* – I don't know how she stays sitting on her chair without slithering under the table.

When I get to the loo I feel like my wee will go on for EVER, just when I want to hurry back to the classroom where it's safe. I hardly wash my hands at all, which is a bit disgusting but this is a DESPERATE SURVIVAL SITUATION. I glance in the mirror and see a scared, messy-haired girl with quite a big nose and absolutely no sign of a bust. That just about sums me up. Then Mrs Allen comes in.

'I'll just pop in here,' she says, all chirpy. 'I can't be bothered traipsing all the way to the staff toilets.'

I give a nervous laugh and just say, 'OK.'

What EXACTLY do I mean by OK? Well, HONESTLY! What are you supposed to say to a teacher who wants to use the pupil toilets? I can't yell GET OUT, YOU MAD WOMAN! THIS PLACE IS A BACTERIA PARTY, can I? But there's a much worse problem than disease, namely – I do NOT want to hear a teacher peeing! What if she does a fart? I'd NEVER be able to look her in the eye again without thinking about THAT TEACHER-FART. My education could be seriously held back. Instead of staying and taking that risk I go very slowly back to the classroom so that Mrs Allen will be just behind me when I get back to the art room. This means that if Ruby decides to launch an attack on me as soon as I arrive she will get caught in the MURDEROUS ACT – with her hands around my throat or something – by Mrs Allen returning from her trumpety-farting session in the pupil toilets.

When I get back to my table everything seems OK, except that stupid me had left my bag under the chair, so I check to make sure nothing has been planted in it – no expensive scissors or other school equipment. Ruby isn't going to catch me out that way again. It looks like I've managed a trip to the loo without any trouble, until I see Griselda. All the blood in my head suddenly *whooshes* up to scarlet-red boiling point and my teeth clench tight together.

When I left the art room, Griselda was happily standing there with my dad's trouser belt around her middle and the hoops bouncing neatly on six lines of elastic. It took me HALF A DAY to get those elastics all exactly the same length but SOMEONE has CUT three of them in the time it took for me to have a wee. The hoops are drooping down to the floor on one side.

If Ruby Macpherson wants WAR, she can *HAVE IT!* I take a deep breath and turn to look at her. My face is probably bright red and my fists are screwed up so tight that my knuckles are white. She pretends to concentrate on threading her beads. I look over at Becky who also has her head down, drilling holes in loyalty cards. Gregor and Lennox are so deep in conversation about their work that they probably didn't see what happened.

Mrs Allen comes back from the loo at this

point and sees me standing in front of Griselda and the lopsided hoops looking like I'm about to **SPONTANEOUSLY COMBUST** – that means 'burst into flames'. She bustles up to me and uses her ever-so-calming voice. 'Oh, Cordelia, what's happened here? You had that all balanced out beautifully before.'

I **MUST NOT CRY**! That's just what Ruby wants.

I manage to reply in a tight, squeaky voice that would be **LUMINOUS ORANGE** if voices had colours. It comes out like the first hot squirt of lava from a volcano. 'I think someone has cut the elastics,' I say.

Mrs Allen looks FLABBERGASTED, 'Well, really! We must get to the bottom of this.'

She claps her hands and waves everyone over. 'Meeting, everyone! Now, please! Janna and Emmy, too. Come on!'

The class put their work down and slowly gather around Griselda.

'So,' says Mrs Allen. 'I think we can all see that someone has damaged Cordelia's work. I cannot **imagine** what would make **anyone** act in such a callous and unkind way and we will now all stand silently and **wait** to see if someone is brave enough to admit to this.'

We stand...we wait...we wait...we stand. Everyone looks at the floor except me. My eyes are drilling into Ruby's skull. She doesn't flinch. After about thirty seconds I see – out of the corner of my eye – Becky nudge Ruby, like she's trying to get Ruby to own up to it. Becky's face is red. I can tell that she knows the truth but she DAREN'T say it. Ruby nudges her back quite hard. No one speaks. Emmy and Janna look at each other sideways. I feel sorry for them because they seem a bit frightened by the whole thing – their eyes are wide and their cheeks are pink. But it was nothing to do with them. Gregor looks calmly at the ceiling and Lennox keeps staring at his shoes. Finally, after about two minutes, the longest two minutes in the HISTORY OF TIME, Mrs Allen sighs and says, 'I see that no one is brave enough to admit to their actions. Well, whoever did this can be sure that I will be *making investigations* and, when I find the person responsible, they will be disqualified from the design competition. Now, get on quietly please and let's hope that someone's conscience is bothering them enough to come and tell me that they did this. Cordelia, I'll help you restore Griselda's petticoat.'

Is that **ALL** she is going to do!
OUTRAGEOUS! Two things are now clear.

1. Mrs Allen cannot be relied on to deliver justice.

2. I will have to take action myself!

Mrs Allen could've done something about Ruby yesterday, when she planted things in my bag, but she didn't. I don't believe she will MAKE INVESTIGATIONS or do ANYTHING. She isn't tough enough.

Well, Ruby MacPherson is not going to get away with this.

Even evil goblin-girls have to use the toilet sometimes. Ruby and Becky ALWAYS go at the same time.

When they leave the art room I grab my chance. Mrs Allen can't come to help me straight away because she has to check on what Janna and Emmy are doing at the back of the room with a jam jar full of bolts and a spanner.

Behind the table where Ruby sits there is a metal cupboard full of expensive craft materials like fancy beads and ribbons. It is a YUMMY treasure chest if you are into making stuff. The door is open because Mrs Allen is STILL being a softie and trusting us.

I double-check to be sure that her attention is fully taken up with Janna and Emmy, then I take the two tiny steps I need to get a good look inside this cupboard. I pull out some slim, pointed pliers for bending jewellery wire, the sort that Ruby has been using and saying how great they are. I also take a packet of beautiful beads made from little blue pebbles with holes drilled through them, some silver wire for making earring hoops and, just for luck, I also grab a special punch-tool for making holes in leather. I stuff the whole lot into the side pocket of Ruby's huge white handbag – she has really TERRIACKY (TERRIBLE + TACKY) taste in bags. I make sure that some of the wire and the handle of the punch-tool are sticking out enough for Mrs Allen to spot them and get back to my table JUST in time, before Ruby and Becky come back from the toilet.

When Mrs Allen comes over to help put my hoops back together I pretend to be adjusting Dad's trouser belt around Griselda's middle.

'Now, then,' says Mrs Allen, being gentle and comforting. 'Let's start again here, shall we?'

I nod and fiddle with the belt a bit more. 'I think it would be better if the belt was tighter,' I suggest. 'Do you have one of those gadgets for making another hole in a leather belt? This one's my dad's and it won't go quite small enough.'

'Oh yes, I know what you mean,' Mrs Allen nodded. 'I've got a punch-tool for that. Hang on a minute.'

Mrs Allen goes over to the cupboard-of-yummy-treasures behind Ruby's table, opens the doors wide and peers in. She looks up and down the shelves, rummages a bit, then steps back and scratches her head. The handle of the leather punch-tool is sticking out about fifteen centimetres from Mrs Allen's left foot. Ruby is arranging her beads. She has no idea what's coming. Mrs Allen turns to me, looking puzzled.

'That's strange,' she says, 'I'm sure there was a leather punch-tool in here.'

Instead of looking back at her I stare at the pocket of Ruby's bag and say quietly, 'Err, Mrs Allen, is that what you're looking for?'

Mrs Allen's eyes follow mine. She sighs with disappointment and tuts. I feel REALLY bad for tricking Mrs Allen – she is clearly a bit stupid about how DEVIOUS kids can be. How has she survived as a teacher up until now? And I KNOW that dumping Ruby in the POO like this is NOT the answer to my problem. It has nothing AT ALL to do with JUSTICE. It isn't suddenly going to make Ruby a nicer person, is it? And it makes me a slightly MORE HORRIBLE person than I was five minutes ago. But I just COULDN'T stop that spiky red demon inside me getting in the way of my common sense.

Mrs Allen bends down to Ruby and whispers in her ear so that the rest of the class don't see that she is about to get SPIT-ROASTED. 'Ruby, would you come with me for a moment, please? Bring your bag with you.'

Ruby jumps up with her fake smile on full beam. She probably thinks she's going to be given some reward or special treatment for being *oh-so-sweet-and-lovely*.

'You carry on getting those new lengths of elastic ready, Cordelia,' says Mrs Allen. 'I'll be back in a moment.'

I get on with my work and practise looking like I know nothing about what has happened, the same way Ruby did after she'd cut those elastics! But doing this hasn't made me feel like I've beaten her at something. It hasn't made me feel good AT ALL – I feel like a **SNEAKY LITTLE FAKE**, just like her. I'm **FURIOUS** with Ruby but, right now, I think I'm even **MORE** angry with Mrs Allen. If she wasn't so **DOPEY** and **WEAK** I wouldn't have to do this, would I? But I can't BURST OUT and tell her that or I might get chucked off the project for being so cheeky to her. I'm having to resort to **DRASTIC MEASURES** because she's not taking Ruby's CRIMES against me seriously.

When Ruby comes back into the art room her face is TOMATO JUICE RED. She doesn't look at me for the rest of the afternoon. She doesn't look at ANYONE. Mrs Allen puts the things back in the cupboard and comes over to help me. Nobody speaks much for the rest of the day. There's what you might call A BIT OF AN ATMOSPHERE.

I have to get the bus on my own that afternoon. I think about hanging around until Ruby and Becky have gone. Should I miss their bus and get the next one? But that would mean waiting a whole HOUR because there aren't many buses out here in the MIDDLE OF NOWHERE. I'll just have to be brave.

As soon as I'm in my seat I see Ruby get on and my heart starts pounding. I WISH I could become invisible but anyone with half a brain knows that THERE IS NO SUCH THING AS MAGIC. Girls do not become invisible just by wishing it.

So I hide the carton of orange juice I've just opened in case she tries to grab it and slide down in my seat, hoping it will make me smaller. This idea is against the rules of science. I just look CRUMPLED. I have long legs and big knees and there is NOWHERE to hide such things in a bus seat.

Ruby checks each face as she walks slowly up the centre aisle, like a fox deciding which chicken to have for breakfast. Becky is behind her but she sits down near the front instead of following Ruby. When Ruby reaches my seat, she stops.

'Not sitting with your boyfriend, then?' is all she says.

I ignore her. She knows Joe wasn't there this afternoon so it's a stupid thing to say. She leans RIGHT into my PERSONAL PATCH OF SPACE…AGAIN and screams in my ear.

'I'm **TALKING** to **YOU**, **DEAF-HEAD!!**'

A few grown-ups tut and shuffle and mutter about the noise, but do they actually DO anything? NO! We are just silly kids to them, and ALL kids are a problem, right? They seem to think that we are all as bad as each other. It wouldn't occur to them that one of us is nearly POOPING HER PANTS with fear and the other one is an EVIL

BULLY. They just hear kids being GENERALLY annoying. I am **SO** tense and frightened, and she is just so **LOUD** that I can't keep my cool. Ruby is still standing up and she's in just the WRONG position. When she glances behind her to see where Becky is I pull the straw out of my orange juice carton, reach up, turn it upside down and *squeeze* the sticky liquid over her head. It is just TOO tempting…and now I am probably going to DIE!

Ruby grabs my arm, the one that's holding the juice carton, but she's too late to stop the orange stickiness running down her carefully blow-dried hair and onto her pale pink T-shirt. Luckily for me she doesn't have enough room to swing a slap in the bus and at that moment the driver notices that there are school kids messing about behind him. He pulls up at the next stop and shouts.

'Sit down *now* or the bus stays here.'

Ruby looks around for a seat and THANKFULLY the only spare one is up at the front near the driver so I guess I'll probably live a bit longer. But before she sits down she bares her teeth like an ALIEN-PSYCHO-GIRL, and hisses at me, 'You're going to hospital, *juice-girl!* You just *wait!*' and I'm pretty sure she means it.

When Ruby and Becky get off the bus a few stops further on Ruby makes a REALLY rude sign at me from the pavement.

Now I DAREN'T tell Mum and Dad about Ruby because I've made the whole thing worse by planting stuff in her bag and squeezing juice on her head. And I REALLY DO BELIEVE that I'd end up in hospital, like Ruby threatened. I DO NOT want to go to hospital. Apart from the fact that I would have broken bones and bruises from her GRUESOME TORTURES, I've heard that you have to share a room with loads of other kids and they make you get up HIDEOUSLY EARLY so that they can disinfect everything around you… AND the food is terrible.

The other thing is this. I KNOW people say you should tell an adult as soon a bully starts on you but you have to think about it first, don't you? What I mean is, Mum and Dad MIGHT be brilliant. They MIGHT make sure that Ruby is exiled to a desert island with no hair straighteners or mascara for TEN LONG YEARS, like she deserves, or they might be RUBBISH, like Mrs Allen, and not do anything about her until she HAS put me in hospital.

Dad was going to cook dinner for us in the restaurant tonight. I was looking forward to that but when I get home Mum tells me he can't because the gas fitter didn't turn up to put the pipes in behind the cooker. I hear Dad being cross with someone down the phone about this.

Then Mum is on her mobile telling someone that they have sent the wrong shower head for the new bathroom and asking them to come and change it. She's using her ***THAT'S-AN-ORDER-AND-I-WANT-IT-DOING-VERY-SOON-SO-DON'T-MESS-ME-AROUND*** sort of voice. People let Mum and Dad down and muddle up their plans ALL THE TIME. No wonder they look WHACKPOOPTED (whacked, pooped-out and exhausted).

I don't mind MUCH that we aren't having dinner in the big restaurant, though. I like us all being cosy in the cottage at meal times. It feels safe. Ruby seems a million miles away, and Dad's cooking is just as good on our tiny cooker as on a big fancy one.

After dinner I want to get online to Dru but Mum and Dad need the computer. They are shuffling papers around and searching on the internet, and discussing how they can turn our scruffy outhouses into extra storage space. It isn't very interesting so

I plug myself into my headphones and watch *The King and I*. It's a musical where Deborah Kerr plays a teacher who goes to stay in a palace to look after the king's children – about a HUNDRED of them. She wears ENORMOUS hooped petticoats because it's the 1850s. It's a bit of a soppy story but the costumes are **unbelievably sumptuous**, and there are some good songs in it that I like to hum along to.

I am singing away and doing a pretty good drawing of the king's costume when Joe turns up on our doorstep out of the blue. He looks like he's just got out of the shower and cleaned himself up especially. I don't think a boy has ever washed just to come and visit me before.

'Who is it?' Mum calls.

'Just Joe,' I call back.

He looks a bit disappointed at being called 'Just Joe' and I INSTANTLY wish I hadn't said it like that. I bring him through to the kitchen and introduce him to Dad. Mum has already met him at Jenny's. Dad stands up and shakes Joe's hand. There are a few seconds of silence. Joe looks a bit fidgety, then he turns to me.

'Shall we walk to the bridge?' he suggests.

I look at Mum and Dad, to see if that's OK with them.

'Yes, of course,' says Mum.

'Be back in an hour, though,' says Dad, looking at Joe with a serious expression. 'It's getting late.'

Our high street is shaped like a horseshoe. At one end there's a little bridge over a stream. The stream runs along the bottom of the horseshoe, past the end of the primary school playing fields and the allotments and the woods before it comes out as a ford that trickles across the other end of the high street. A ford is a place where you just drive your car through the stream. It's never more than a few inches deep – we splash through it on the bus every day. The bridge is a short walk from the Jug and Monkey in the opposite direction.

We stroll past all the closed-down shops and Mr Clench's window full of teapots and itchy parrots. Even the places that haven't closed down are shut now because it's about eight o'clock and nothing is open here after six – except the Chinese takeaway and the chip shop. That will all change when Mum and Dad get the restaurant and the cinema open. Heckaby will have a nightlife!

'Have you told your mum and dad about Ruby yet?' is the first thing Joe asks.

I shake my head. 'Not yet. I'll sort it out myself and tell them when it's all over.' I'm lying because I have NO IDEA how I could POSSIBLY sort it out. It's a horrible mess and I've made it worse. I tell Joe about tipping juice over Ruby's head because I need to tell SOMEONE. He doesn't look impressed AT ALL. He doesn't laugh or say, 'I'm not surprised.' He doesn't say anything to make me feel better about it. He just listens and frowns his lovely frown, then says, 'Can't you see how she's dragging you down to her level of doing things? You're giving her a fight and that's just what she WANTS.'

'But she scares me into getting back at her,' I say. 'When people scare me I go **BALLISTO**.'

'Then you've got to stop being scared, Cordelia,' says Joe, like it was easy.

But he gives me such a kind, worried look that I promise myself I'll try harder not to RETALIATE. Retaliate means 'to make an attack in return for a similar attack', according to our big dictionary at home. When you read it on a page like that it's easy to see that retaliation is a stupid idea. It even SOUNDS like an idiot thing to do, doesn't it? You can just tell that RETALIATION isn't going to lead anywhere useful. So why can't I CONTROL my urge to do it? Perhaps I'm just a stupid person.

I don't tell Joe about slipping the things from the cupboard of treasures into Ruby's bag and dumping her in the DOO-DOO. If he's DEEPLY UNIMPRESSED about the juice episode what would he say if he knew about me planting stolen goods on her?

We reach the bridge. The drizzle that we've had all day has stopped but the air is still warm and sticky, like there's more rain on the way. The sky is still quite light, but only in the gaps between the dark clouds. We have to keep batting mosquitoes away to stop ourselves getting bitten.

Joe sounds serious. 'I thought I should come over to tell you something, Cordelia.'

'What's that?' I'm suddenly worried that he's going to tell me he's moving back to London. He's my only friend here. But it isn't that at all.

He sighs and explains. 'Well, I think Ruby might have dagger-eyes for you because she asked me to go out with her last year and I turned her down. I just don't fancy her, that's all.'

I hadn't expected THAT, so I just say, 'Oh.'

Joe has a lot more to tell me. It all comes tumbling out of his mouth. 'I tried to be nice about it but she's been **FUMING** with me ever since. I don't think she even *wants* to be my girlfriend any more, it's just that her **BIG FAT EGO** can't stand it when she doesn't get her own way. So now she **HATES** me and anyone who starts to be friendly with me gets a really hard time from her.'

I let out a big sigh and nod a lot. 'Well that certainly gives me an explanation for her ROCKET-POWERED NASTINESS.'

Joe looks at the pavement. 'I probably should've told you sooner.'

I sigh again. 'But then, if you'd said to me,

"I'd love to be your friend, Cordelia, but I must warn you that there's this lunatic girl who may try to kill you if you speak to me,"

I might've been too scared to be seen with you.'

'That's true,' says Joe with a little laugh, 'but...'
He leans onto the wall and looks down into the stream. I lean beside him and we watch a little pile of soapy froth float past, followed by a crisp packet.

He takes a big breath and reaches down to hold my hand. He holds it very lightly, just my fingertips. It's a big, warm, safe hand. His face has turned a bit pink when I look up at him.

'The thing is, Cordelia,' he says softly, 'I REALLY like you, and I'd love it if we could, you know, go out and stuff.'

Now, this is DEFINITELY one of those moments when I should feel a tummy-flutter, much more than when he touched my cheek yesterday lunchtime. But nothing like a flutter happens. I just keep thinking how sweet and kind and beautiful he is. And even I know that thinking a boy is sweet and kind and beautiful is NOT the same as wanting to fall madly in love with him.

About a TRILLION anxious ideas start spinning around in my brain all at once. I DEFINITELY want Joe as a friend, but will he still want to be MY friend if I say no to all that hand-holding, snoggy, romantic stuff? And if he DOESN'T want to be JUST FRIENDS will he fall out with me and leave me with no one to protect me from Ruby?

I can see that Joe has all the right ingredients for a boyfriend, but for SOMEONE ELSE. I can't go out with him just so that I'll have protection from

bullies, can I? That would be cruel, in fact it would be
THOROUGHLY,
> **COMPLETELY**,
>> **WRONG**,
>>> **WRONG**,
>>>> **WRONG**,

because what would happen when I don't need his protection any more? Then I wouldn't want to be his girlfriend any longer, and he'd be hurt that I'd been using him. So if I were a BRAVE person I wouldn't EVER pretend that I like him more than I do just so that he'll protect me.

But I'm not brave, am I? I'm TERRIFIED of Ruby.

So I DO pretend that I like Joe in a boyfriend sort of way. I let him kiss me and put his arms around me…but only a little bit. His kiss is gentle and dry and soft, like he's being ever so careful with me. It's exactly how I imagined a kiss should be when you're at the beginning of a big romance. Everything is there EXCEPT THE *tingle*. Joe just doesn't make me *tingle*. And all the time I know that I am only doing it so that I'll be safe from Ruby MacPherson. Being scared makes me do this terrible, COWARDLY thing. Poor Joe – UNBELIEVABLY HORRIBLE ME!

I sleep very deeply that night. I don't deserve to.
I deserve to lie awake TORTURED by my own
HORRIBLENESS but I'm so tired from the night
before, when I woke up with scary visions of Ruby
in my dreams, that I just ZONK OUT as soon as
my head hits the pillow.

In the morning I feel CRINGE-MAKINGLY
ASHAMED. What sort of girl am I? When Joe
finds out that I don't really fancy him he'll **NEVER**
be my friend again. I'll lose my friend AND my
protection from Ruby. **CORDELIA CODD**, **YOU ARE**
VILE, and you probably deserve whatever **HIDEOUS**
FATE Ruby is planning for you.

Mum is in the shower so I get online before
breakfast to tell Dru the DRAUMATICS
(DRAMATIC-TRAUMATICS) of yesterday. I am
too ashamed to tell her about putting all that stuff
in Ruby's bag and about the orange juice incident
but I tell her all about Mrs Driscoll and her stupid

eggs and about Ruby cutting my elastics and about Joe's kiss, and the LACK OF *tingle*, and I end by BEGGING her…

★ **Cordelia** to Dru

How am I going to get myself out of this boyfriend thing with Joe without him hating me **ETERNALLY?** That kiss should **NOT** have happened. It's going to make everything complicated and weird between us. **HELP ME!**

Your stupid friend.

There's no reply, even though I keep checking until the last possible micro-second before I have to get washed and dressed and have breakfast. I know that it's still around midnight over in Seattle and Dru is probably fast asleep, but my DOOMY-GLOOMY head tells me that she's given up on me in DISGUST at what I've done to Joe and will probably never contact me again.

When I get to the bus stop outside Mr and Mrs Akbar's newsagent's there's quite a crowd waiting for the number seventy-one to Wellminster. The newsagent's is a much smaller shop than Driscoll's Discount, and much busier and friendlier. Lots of people pop in to buy newspapers and sweets before the bus comes.

It's lucky that I'm watching them going in and out because I spot little Mina sneaking out and down the steps, still in her tiny pyjamas. She toddles off towards the same corner that Mum found her on last week. I drop my bag and run after her. As I catch up, a group of cyclists *swoops* around the corner really fast. I grab Mina JUST before she steps off the kerb. Phew!

Mina screams as if I'm kidnapping her but I ignore her and hurry back to the newsagent's, carrying her under my arm like a wriggling roll of carpet. I push my way through the customers, shouting, 'Excuse me! EXCUSE me! Can I get in please!' and plonk Mina down on a pile of *Daily Mail*s next to the counter, puffing and panting because I had NO IDEA that three-year-olds could be SO HEAVY.

'I just caught her before she stepped into the road,' I say to Maryam, who is serving a long queue of lottery-zombies wanting Euro Millions tickets (there's a £27 million rollover and the whole line of customers are looking a bit crazy and dribbly at the thought of all that money).

'I had to grab her,' I say, a bit louder, so that Maryam can hear. 'That's why she's screaming.'

Maryam looks embarrassed and takes Mina away quickly, through the back door of the shop. Her dad just nods to me and gets on with serving his customers. I've just saved your daughter's life, I think to myself. A 'thank you' might be polite. But then the bus comes and I have to run back for my bag and jump on.

Joe is already on the bus, sitting next to a woman called Mrs Tandy who runs Tandy's Teeny-Tiny Second-Hand Bookshop near the doctors' surgery. He is chatting to her about the weather. When I walk past his seat he looks up and smiles and gives me a little wave, then carries on chatting to Mrs Tandy. Seeing him being kind and sociable like that makes me feel even worse about myself. He deserves a much nicer girlfriend than me.

I find a seat a few rows behind him. It's better not to sit next to each other because I know I couldn't BEAR it if he held my hand again and looked at me all gentle and full of L♥VE.

Staring out of the window, I try to gather the fuzzy bits of my BRAIN-MUDDLE. How ON EARTH am I going to explain to him that last night

on the bridge was MORE THAN A BIT of
a mistake?

Becky gets on after we cross the ford and sits
next to an old man who is asleep. She's on her own.
There's no sign of Ruby. Perhaps she's too ashamed
to show her face after what she did to my elastics
yesterday. This seems unlikely so my BIG WISH
is that she's broken a leg in several places and will
be away for weeks! FAT CHANCE! She probably
just has a dentist's appointment and will be back to
terrorise me in the afternoon.

Joe sticks close to me as we get off the bus and
go into school. He doesn't try to hold my hand,
which is a relief. But in the corridor he gives me a
cheeky wink and smiles, like we have a romantic
secret, which is EVEN WORSE and I hate myself a
million times more.

Mrs Allen gathers us all for another quick
meeting before we start work so that we can tell her
what we intend to get done today. She asks Becky if
she knows where Ruby is. Becky shrugs. 'She's not
well, Miss. She had to go to the hospital last night.'

'I see,' says Mrs Allen, kindly. 'Well, if you visit
her, please give her our best wishes and we hope
she'll soon be back.'

'Oh yes, she'll be back, Miss,' says Becky, nodding. My heart sinks for a moment. But then I FORCE myself to stop thinking about THE RETURN OF RUBY and get on with my work. I **CANNOT** let Ruby Macpherson take up so much space in my head, there is FAR too much to do. I HAVE to get a grip on my brain.

We are all soon settled into our work again. I'm using the sewing machine. The curtain fabric is REALLY HEAVY. It takes quite a bit of concentration and all my muscle-power to stop it sliding off the table but after a bit of practice I'm soon whizzing along the SUPER-LONG seams up the length of the skirt.

Janna and Emmy have finished sanding down their wooden crates and Mr Carter has helped them to drill holes and bolt them together. Now they are getting ready to use some of the SEVENTEEN pots of leftover paint that Mr Carter and Mrs Allen found for them. Lennox has also brought some banana-yellow bathroom paint from home. I can't IMAGINE why anyone would want a BANANA-YELLOW bathroom but it was kind of him to give them the spare tin.

Mr Carter gets Janna and Emmy started on

trying out the different colours on odd bits of wood AFTER he's covered a large area of floor with a MASSIVE plastic sheet so that they don't get paint everywhere.

Becky is using another dummy, like Griselda, except hers is a man called Graham. (Who thought up these terrible names?) She's sprayed her supermarket loyalty cards silver and the top row of cards is glued onto a tape. Now she's getting ready to sew this tape around the waist of a short skirt that she's made from an old bed sheet. It will be a great costume, I have to admit.

Lennox has finished three cushion covers already and is working on number four, and Gregor has nearly completed his second lampshade. His work is perfect, OF COURSE. He has woven a million different colours and textures into each section of the lampshades. Bits of gold and silver wire and shimmering beads twinkle out from them as they catch the light. They are DEFINITELY works of art.

Now that the walls of his greenhouse are finished Joe is drawing up a design for a sloping roof to complete it. He works over by the big windows, stopping now and then to stretch his arms and scratch his head.

This lunchtime most of us, even Becky, sit together on a wall outside and have quite a laugh. I don't talk to Becky DIRECTLY because of my suspicion that she is under Ruby's CONTROL but I have to admit that she's much more NORMAL when Ruby isn't here.

Gregor stops being so super-cool and is quite jokey and Lennox tells us about the cafe his big brother is opening in Wellminster.

'He's got paintings for sale on the walls and these crazy lamps hanging from the ceiling that he bought in Morocco, and those proper candles made of beeswax so they melt all blobby and interestingly,' he tells us.

Everyone nods and agrees that blobby candles are the best kind.

'It sounds like the sort of place I should get my parents to go on a mini-date,' I say. 'I've got to get them to fall in love with each other again.'

Everyone nods again. Nobody seems to find this weird. Perhaps other people's parents are NOT-QUITE-TOGETHER, too.

Lennox pulls a little card out of his pocket and gives it to me. 'This is the place. It opens this weekend,' he says.

The card is a beautiful brick-red colour and the name 'Café Candela' is in chunky black letters across the middle. There's a tiny picture of a melted candle in one corner.

I say thank you to Lennox and immediately start thinking that I MUST find just the right place to put the card so that Mum and Dad will find it.

Emmy and Janna turn out to be REALLY clever. Janna can speak Italian and German as well as English because her family are from all over Europe and Emmy has just spent two weeks at a special maths camp for brainy kids.

I try not to sit TOO close to Joe, and I keep my fingers busy by sharpening all my pencil crayons while we're chatting just in case he tries to hold my hand again. I don't manage to eat my sandwich. Even if it was the most fancy, delicious sandwich in the world I wouldn't be able to swallow any of it because I can't stop thinking that I MUST have that IMPORTANT CONVERSATION with Joe as soon as possible – I have to tell him that kissing him was a sort of accident. The thought of telling him this fills my tummy with too much FEAR AND DREAD to fit lunch in there as well. That's

THREE sandwiches this week that have been spoiled by EMOIL (EMOTIONAL TURMOIL).

At afternoon break Joe comes to talk to me near the vending machine in the corridor. I've just bought a carton of juice and some chocolate because when I don't eat my lunch I get cravings for sugar all afternoon. Joe has an extra-deep frown between his eyebrows. He mostly eats raw vegetables so I am expecting him to be cross about my junk food habits but it's something much worse.

'I've just spoken to Becky,' he says, not sounding AT ALL like it was a cheerful conversation.

'Oh yes,' I say, hiding the chocolate bar in my pocket and feeling more than a little bit worried at what might be coming next.

'She told me that you put some stuff in Ruby's bag and got her into trouble.'

There's no point in denying it so I confess. Joe goes quiet for a second, like he's holding back a burst of temper. His frown has changed to a scowl.

'That was so *childish*, Cordelia,' he says, only JUST staying calm. 'I thought you were trying to rise above all that revenge stuff.'

I get flustered and try to make excuses. 'But she's **FOUL!**' is the best I can come up with.

Joe's cheeks flush red. 'Can't you see how *ridiculous* that is? Can't you see that the *cat-scratching* will just go *on and on, back and forth* between you, if you keep thinking you have the right to get back at her?'

He is SO right – I am the most despicable, wormy, micro-brained **IDIOT** in the universe but before I have a chance to say this Mrs Allen waves us back into the room. 'Come on, you two! Only an hour left before we have to pack up.'

When we've finished for the day Joe flies out the door without saying goodbye to me. I see him from the bus stop, waiting on the opposite side of the road to get a bus into Wellminster instead of going straight home. Why is life such a *MUY COMPLICADO* recipe?

The bus back to Heckaby is PACKED, and I have
to stand up most of the way. Drizzly rain sprinkles
the windows. People's faces are shiny with sweat
and they are fanning themselves with newspapers
and leaflets. I'm glad to get off when my stop comes
up and breathe some fresh air again.

When I get home I go online to Dru straight
away. She'll know how to unravel the *tangled
spaghetti* of my relationship with Joe, I'm sure.
But I'd better COME CLEAN first and tell her all
the facts. She'll know if I'm hiding something. Dru
is already writing to me. I calculate that it must be
around late breakfast time in Seattle.

★ **Dru** to Cordelia

Hey!

Fantastic thunderstorm here last night
so it's a **teensy** bit cooler.

★ **Cordelia** to Dru

I thought you'd abandoned me in disgust at what I did to Joe. I am **SO** relieved that you haven't but it's all got much worse and I have behaved **DESPICABLY**.

I tell her all about planting the things from the cupboard-of-yummy-treasures in Ruby's bag and about squeezing orange juice on her head and about Joe being ***THOROUGHLY DISGUSTED*** by my ***PRIMITIVE*** and ***BRAINLESS*** behaviour. When I've finished my long confession to her I stare up at the stains on the ceiling again and wait for Dru to ***PULVERISE*** me with words. But she doesn't.

★ **Dru** to Cordelia

There's no point being mad with you because you're clearly already mad at yourself. So I'll save my energy.

★ **Cordelia** to Dru

I don't want to lose him as a friend!

★ **Dru** to Cordelia

Whatever happens, promise me that you'll have a good talk with him to CLEAR THE AIR. Let him cool down overnight first.

★ **Cordelia** to Dru

I promise! I'll be brave! More later, I'm being called to help downstairs.

Love you!!! xxx

Mum and Dad have been working hard on the restaurant kitchen. I can't remember when I last saw them WITHOUT dark circles under their eyes.

The cooker and two huge fridges are in place, and the shiny metal worktops are ready. They've painted the walls in a fresh minty green and are mopping the floor.

'You can set the table, if you want to be helpful, Coco,' Mum suggests in her that's-an-order-voice that she's using too much these days.

I don't argue, even though I don't want to be useful right now but would prefer to flop in front of a film for a while. I've been thinking that it's a long time since I watched *The Barefoot Contessa* with Ava Gardner. She had some of the MOST glam dresses EVER, but Ava Gardner will have to wait because Mum is holding out the cutlery for me to take.

Dad winks at me. That usually means he has something planned that he knows I'll like.

'We can start work on the decoration for the

restaurant next week,' he says. 'You can help us choose some colours after dinner, if you like.'

GREAT! An interior design project. That's DEFINITELY my sort of thing, and ABSOLUTELY NOT the sort of choosing that should be left to parents like mine. They're fine on basic stuff, like fixing doors and windows, and painting a kitchen plain minty green, but they are CLUELESS about interesting colours and patterns, and fabrics and wallpapers. My involvement is CRUCIAL if we are going to avoid any STYLING TRAGEDIES.

We switch on the cosy side lights in the restaurant and I lay the table beautifully. We just put one table out in the middle of the BIG room because most of the furniture is still piled at one end of the restaurant, covered in plastic to protect it. Without any carpets or curtains, our voices echo off the ceiling and walls. Dad makes a yummy chicken stir-fry while Mum takes a quick shower and puts on a clean T-shirt and some earrings.

But the phone rings ALL the way through dinner. They don't pick it up but they can't resist stopping the conversation to listen to the voice messages, in case it's something important, which is very INTERRUPTING. Every time I think it might be a good moment to tell them about Ruby – despite the risk of being put in hospital – another message is left saying things like, 'Hello, Mr Codd, this is Jenson's the plumber here…' or, 'Good evening, Mrs Codd. Apologies for ringing so late, it's Dave the plasterer calling to let you know…'

Finally, Dad remembers how to switch the phone to silent so that we can have chocolate ice-cream without interruptions. But then we get straight on to talking about decoration for the restaurant and I find that having a creative idea to think about puts Ruby temporarily to the back of my brain.

We spend a long time DEBATING. First, Dad walks around telling Mum and me his ideas. I notice that he has to keep hitching his jeans up. It is now URGENTLY important that I sew a proper waistband for Griselda and return his trouser belt PRONTO-TONTO! I CANNOT let my dad walk around with a builder's bum cleavage. Bum cleavage is strictly NOT OK.

Mum takes her turn to say what she thinks would look nice in the restaurant, and then it's my turn. The evening starts to get very interesting, Mum and Dad and me around the table, discussing and comparing swatches of paint colours and fabrics, but then they go and RUIN it.

We have a little break so that we can try a bit more of the chocolate ice-cream Dad is thinking of having on the menu.

Mum puts down her spoon and says softly, 'Coco, we know you're quite friendly with Joe but we wondered if you'd made some other friends, yet…some girls?'

Now, I KNOW when my parents have been talking about me and are trying to LEAD the conversation somewhere but I'm not sure where THIS ONE is going until Dad gives a little cough and says, 'It's just that we've heard some things about Joe.'

'What *THINGS*?' I snap. 'Joe's lovely! What are you on about?'

Dad turns his spoon round and round in his fingers and stares at it. 'Do you remember us saying earlier that some things went missing from Mrs Driscoll's shop?'

I know what's coming next. My teeth clench together tightly as Dad finishes what he is saying.

'What if I told you that Joe might have taken those things?' Dad puts his spoon down and looks at me to see my reaction.

'Is that **ALL?**' is what I say. I am **DISGUSTED**. 'Just because he was in trouble for recycling things ACCIDENTALLY, now everyone suspects him whenever something goes missing. People probably blame him if they can't find their SOCKS in the morning. You've been gossiping with Mrs Driscoll, haven't you? How **COULD** you believe **HER**?'

Mum butts in. 'No, Coco, it's not just her. Several other people have mentioned Joe's name.'

I am clutching my ice-cream spoon in my fist and **REALLY** shouting now.

*'How can you be so **TINY-MINDED!**
You don't know **ANYTHING** about him,
or **ANYTHING** about **ANYTHING!**'*

I SLAM my spoon down on the table, and *flounce* off in my MOST dramatic way.

Up in my room, I sit on the bed hugging a cushion for a few minutes but I soon get fidgety and sneak down to use the computer while Mum and Dad are NO DOUBT discussing me as they tidy up. There's NO WAY I'm going to offer to help with the dishes. Not now. And I'm not helping them to decorate the restaurant until they apologise. Let it be a STYLING DISASTER! See if I care!

I write to Dru and tell her all about people gossiping and saying that Joe is a thief, and Mum and Dad believing them. She is still online. Once again, she comes back with a sensible response that calms me down.

★ **Dru** to Cordelia

```
I'm not making excuses for them but
maybe your parents are scared that
they won't fit into your new village if
they don't join in with the gossip.
```

★ **Cordelia** to Dru

You're probably right but why would they want to fit in with pea-brained, gossipy twits?

★ **Dru** to Cordelia

```
People will be fine with Joe when they
realise that they're wrong. And they
will realise what dumb-butts they've
been sooner or later. Something will
happen to change their minds, I'm
sure.
```

★ **Cordelia** to Dru

I **HOPE** you're right about Joe. But I **CANNOT** let my parents' brains shrink just because we live in a tiny-mind village. Why don't adults **NOTICE** when they start turning into fossils?

★ **Dru** to Cordelia

The tiny minds of some adults are an unfathomable mystery.

We're going camping for a couple of nights so I'll catch up with you as soon as we get back! Good luck! xx

I miss Dru SO much, and now she's off on a holiday with her big, happy family and I'm upstairs sulking and not speaking to mine.

12

The next day is Thursday. Including today, there are three days left of the Scrap Design Project. Joe is on the same bus as me but the seat next to him is taken by a toddler sucking on a piece of buttery toast so I can't sit with him and find out if he's still cross with me. I sit behind him instead but he doesn't say hello or turn around. What should I do? My head can't cope with emotional confusion so early in the morning so I just stare out of the window. Becky gets on alone again. Still no Ruby. I should probably start to feel a bit sorry for her but I just feel RELIEVED that she's not here.

But halfway through the morning, just as I'm finishing my last long seam on the skirt, Ruby walks in and my stomach turns over as THE FEAR returns.

She's wearing sunglasses, which is weird because the sun hasn't peeked through the stormy clouds for days. When she sits down and takes them off she doesn't look at anyone. It isn't until Mrs Allen goes over to help her settle back into her work that she glances up and I see the HUMUNGOUS black eye that she's been hiding. WOW!

It's a great big SQUASHED PLUM of a bruise – a green, red and purple MASH-UP. Mrs Allen looks a bit surprised. I'm still sitting close to Ruby's table so I can hear what they're saying.

'Goodness, Ruby, is that why you've not been here?' Mrs Allen asks, softly.

'Yes, I fell downstairs and had to have an X-ray,' Ruby whispers. 'It's OK though. Am I very far behind the others?'

SHE'S SO COMPETITIVE! I think to myself.

'Don't worry about that,' says Mrs Allen, being kind and reassuring to her. 'Each project is different so we don't need to race. Just pick up where you left off and I'll come and check on you again in a little while.'

Now, I must admit that I ALMOST feel sorry for Ruby, having a WALLOPING big shiner like that, but I suspect that she'll be on my case and bullying me again BIG TIME pretty soon, so I'm not going to try and be friendly towards her. Part of me, the spiky red demon part, wants to say something like, 'So, Ruby, someone gave you a good SLAP, I see. I hope it hurt,' but I manage to hold myself back, which is a good example of how I CAN control my temper if I REALLY try.

At lunchtime, Janna and Emmy are collected by Emmy's mum because they're being bridesmaids at a wedding soon and have to have a fitting for their dresses. Ruby and Becky disappear together, heading for the canteen, and Joe stays inside to get on with the drawings for his roof.

'I'm just at a crucial bit,' he calls to the rest of us. 'I can't stop yet.' He waves to Gregor, Lennox and me as we go out of the back door – at least I HOPE his wave is for me, too, because that means he's come out of his sulk and is ready to speak to me again. 'I'll be there soon,' he promises.

We leave Joe working and sit on the wall outside comparing our lunches. Lennox has a giant sausage roll and an apple, Gregor has something interesting and trendy in ciabatta with rocket and parmesan and I have a cheese and pickle throwtogether that I had to do for myself AGAIN.

Mrs Allen is chatting with two old people in the car park who have just finished a pottery class in another part of the art block. We can hear her laughing and joking with them and talking about how we are all working hard on some 'fascinating pieces'.

I watch Gregor and Lennox as they listen to this conversation, giggling together. Whenever I look at boys these days I can't help wondering what they would be like as boyfriends. I'm really not sure that I'll ever have TIME for a boyfriend and I'm not convinced that I need one, or even WANT one. Does that make me a freak? Why do people think it's so important to have a boyfriend or girlfriend?

And when I DO have a boyfriend, will it matter if we're not interested in the same things? How much time should we spend together? What's normal? I couldn't possibly stop drawing and watching films and wanting to be a costume designer so I couldn't see him more than once a week. And it won't work if he gets upset about films being interrupted – he'll have to be the most patient boy on the planet to put up with ME.

Joe joins us after about fifteen minutes. His eyes are pink from staring at his work but he looks pleased with himself. I don't care what anyone says about Joe, I think he's a bit special and there's NO WAY that he has the sort of SINGLE-CELL BRAIN that steals things from boring little shops like Driscoll's Discount.

For just a few minutes the sun shines, right at the end of lunchtime. We are all relaxing, soaking in this tiny peep of brightness between the clouds when Mrs Allen leaves her pottery people and walks past us, super-punctual. She is just in time to stop us all from nodding off.

'OK, here we go,' she calls, clapping her hands together and rubbing them into each other. 'Ready for round two, everyone?'

Ruby and Becky come back in through the opposite door – the one that leads to the corridor and the canteen – at exactly the same time that the rest of us trail in behind Mrs Allen.

Gregor suddenly swears VERY LOUDLY. A millisecond later Lennox bangs his fist on the table and swears EVEN MORE LOUDLY. Gregor is staring at one of his beautiful woven lampshades, or what's left of it. Straggles of wool are hanging off the frame. Glittering beads twinkle from the tabletop where they've rolled and scattered right across the surface.

Lennox is holding the torn pieces of his best cushion. The silky shirt fabric has been ripped from the back and the stuffing is spilling out like a burst of candyfloss. Mrs Allen sees immediately that their work has been wrecked and lets out one of her EXASPERATED sighs. Then Ruby chimes up.

'Please, Mrs Allen. We saw who did it. It was Joe.'

I see the words hit Joe like a thump in the chest. He lurches backward and shouts, 'Whoa! Hang on. This was *nothing* to do with me. I've got no idea who did this.'

But Gregor and Lennox are looking at Joe like they could kill him. Poor Joe! Oh poor, poor Joe! I know he'd **NEVER** do **ANYTHING** like this and I want to **SCREAM!** How **COULD** Lennox and Gregor believe Ruby?! They must both have gone **INSANE** because of their **PURPLE FURY**. People do that, don't they? They believe that someone is GUILTY because they NEED somebody to blame and be angry with. It was HORRIBLE watching how Ruby got them to turn on Joe. She was MANIPULATING them – which means 'controlling something cleverly'.

When people are angry and upset they can easily be MANIPULATED so that they can't see what is really going on.

Gregor slumps into his chair, puts his face in his hands and sighs but Lennox steps towards Joe and starts shouting **RIGHT** into his face. For a moment it looks like he's going to punch Joe! He **RANTS** and **SCREAMS** and lets off steam like one of those screechy train whistles in an old film where the sound goes right through your head and rattles your teeth. I want to jump at Ruby and black her other eye, but I also want to rush towards Joe and protect him from Lennox. I end up frozen, stuck, waiting, not believing what's happening.

'Joe stayed behind at lunchtime,' says Ruby calmly as Mrs Allen tries to quiet Lennox down. Ruby is wearing her FAKE angel face. 'We had to come back,' she goes on, 'because I'd forgotten my bag. That's when we saw him, didn't we, Becky?'

I can't stay quiet any longer. I start shouting, too. '**YOU** did it! Same as you wrecked my work. **YOU** did it! You **LIAR**, Ruby!'

Mrs Allen looks at me sternly and holds up her hand, showing the palm to let me know I should back off. 'Now then, Cordelia.'

NOW THEN? NOW THEN??!!! Is that all she can say?

There is **NOTHING** more **VOLCANICALLY FURY-MAKING** than knowing the **COMPLETE** and absolute **TRUTH** about something and not having any way to **PROVE IT!!**

Ruby is clearly having SUPER-EVIL FUN making all this up. 'That's what happened, Miss. Isn't it, Becky?' she says again.

I can tell that Ruby is MAKING Becky do this because Becky doesn't actually SAY anything. She keeps her lips shut tight and just gives a little nod.

Lennox is still calling Joe the WORST names I've ever heard. His voice has changed from a steam whistle to a machine gun. I want to cover my ears, it's so **LOUD AND SCARY**. It's a good thing Janna and Emmy aren't here or they'd be really frightened of Lennox. He is **SO EXPLOSIVE** that he can't hear Mrs Allen trying to calm things down, shushing him and waving her arms like a hopeless policewoman trying to control the traffic.

Joe stays sitting in his chair all this time, looking like he's calmly soaking in all the insults Lennox throws at him. I can't decide whether Joe is being INCREDIBLY strong or if he is just a BIG SOFT

SPONGY DUMPLING for sitting there and letting Lennox **ERUPT**. I can't work that boy out **AT ALL**.

Poor Gregor and Lennox. But most of all, POOR JOE.

Ruby is probably hoping that there'll be an ALMIGHTY punch-up so that Joe will get a good bruising from Gregor and Lennox JUST because he didn't want to go out with her. Well, she's seriously MISCALCULATED because, instead of laying into Joe with their fists, Lennox is having this **HYPER-HISSY-HEART-ATTACK-TANTRUM**, like he is desperate to win an Oscar, and Gregor is just sitting there, speechless and white as a sheet.

Eventually, Mrs Allen calms Lennox down and we have another of her two-minutes-of-silence sessions, standing in a circle waiting for someone to admit that they messed up Lennox and Gregor's work. NATURALLY, no one confesses. The whole thing is, **FRANKLY, RIDICULOUS** and is driving me **BONKERS WITH OUTRAGE**. Mrs Allen is **WORSE THAN WET**, she is *soggy*.

Once again, there is A BIT OF AN ATMOSPHERE in the art room and no one says much for the rest of the day. Mrs Allen concentrates on talking with Lennox and Gregor about how best to put their work back together. Gregor can't face the job of repairing his first lightshade so he carries on with the second one. Lennox has three other cushion covers completed and is working on number four, so he still has plenty for the display. When Mrs Allen goes into the big store cupboard to rummage for something I go over to Joe and whisper, 'I know you didn't do it, Joe. Gregor and Lennox will soon work out what's really going on.'

Joe shakes his head. 'Leave it, Cordelia. It doesn't matter,' he says.

'But it **DOES** matter,' I say, trying not to let my voice get any louder than a hush.

Joe snaps back in a hard whisper, 'I said *leave it*, Cordelia. I want to be on my own for a bit.'

I go back to my work feeling DESPERATELY sad for Joe. He stays silent, keeping his head down all afternoon. He must be SO UPSET. Who wouldn't be? I would've been churning over like a cheese machine on the inside if I was him. Being accused of something you haven't done is one of the worst feelings – it must feel especially GREY AND LONELY when your friends turn against you, too.

Gregor and Lennox have nothing to say to Joe after that. Joe doesn't get the bus home that afternoon, either. He leaves the art room quickly, on his own. I HOPE Mrs Allen is at least going to have a chat with him. She **MUST** know who really did it. **WHAT** is her problem?

I sit right at the front of the bus on the way home. That way, I calculate, Ruby won't be able to bully me without the driver seeing that something is going on. It seems to work and I decide that this will be my SURVIVAL STRATEGY every time I have to get on the bus alone.

As soon as I get in, I write and tell Dru all about the afternoon. While I'm waiting to see if she's online, I text Joe.

RU OK? DO U WNT 2 TLK?

Neither of them replies. Joe is probably down at the allotment doing some weeding to relax himself.

It doesn't seem a good idea to ring him, even though I'm tempted. He did SAY he wanted to be on his own for a while so I have to RESPECT that and try not to INTERFERE. At least if I send a text he knows I'm thinking about him. And then I remember that Dru is away camping for a couple of days, so she can't reply.

Mum and Dad are up to their eyeballs in paperwork again so I decide that this is a good time to put Dad's trouser belt back into his caravan, which I do with the speed and silence of a FOX. It also seems like a good time for one of my BIG, LONG soaks in a bubbly bath.

The bathroom in the new flat is ready and Mum and Dad say I can use it. I STRONGLY SUSPECT that they just want me out of the way while they talk about bills and they know that a bubble bath is something that will keep me busy for a while.

I find the fluffiest towels we have, fill the tub, put in gorgeous-smelling bubbles, slip into the steamy water and lie there, singing songs from *The King and I* and *The Sound of Music* to cheer myself up. I can watch the rain through the skylight above the bath and hear it getting heavier. I LOVE that sound but I hope Joe isn't out in it.

The hot water is VERY relaxing, and a long bath gives me lots of THINKING SPACE. It doesn't take long before I've worked out exactly HOW Ruby managed to wreck Gregor and Lennox's work and put the blame on Joe. This is my brilliant DEDUCTION *(deduction = thinking things through until you work something out).*

Joe came outside to join Gregor, Lennox and me for the last twenty minutes of lunchtime, or thereabouts, so the art room was left empty during that time. It LOOKED like Ruby and Becky came back to class at the same time as we did, but through the inside door. But what if they had ACTUALLY been back earlier? What if they'd had their lunch quickly, then come back and waited in the corridor until Joe went outside to join us before creeping back into the art room to mess up the boys' work? It would've been very easy to do the damage in just a few seconds: one snip of the scissors to Gregor's lightshade and one sharp rip-making tug on the back of Lennox's cushion cover. SIMPLE. Then they could've ducked back into the corridor and pretended that they hadn't been anywhere near the art room since the beginning of lunchtime. It was **GLARINGLY OBVIOUS** and I had to make sure Gregor and Lennox knew ASAP (as soon as possible).

13

Joe is at the bus stop the next morning but he isn't as bouncy and cheerful as usual. HARDLY SURPRISING after the day before. He seems to be speaking to me again, though. Maybe he's had enough time to cool off, or maybe it was because the AVALANCHE OF AWFULNESS that crashed down on him yesterday afternoon was so bad that it made our argument look tiny and pathetic and not worth continuing.

'Thanks for your text last night,' he says as we sit down – me by the window, him near the aisle. 'I didn't switch my phone on until really late, that's why I didn't reply.'

'I was worried about you,' I say, and I mean it. 'I woke up early this morning thinking how RUBBISH it would be if you dropped out of the Scrap Project because of yesterday.'

'I'm tougher than that, don't worry,' he says, smiling just a little bit, 'but thanks.'

The bus pulls away slowly. Wet raincoats are drying off all around us and the steam from them has misted up the windows.

'I've got a theory about yesterday,' I say, bursting to tell Joe. 'D'you want to hear it?'

Joe nods. 'OK.'

When I've finished telling him my PROBABLY SPOT-ON ACCURATE idea about how Ruby (and possibly Becky) crept back into the art room at lunchtime he is still nodding.

'You're probably right,' he says, 'but we can't prove it, can we?'

'But what are you going to do about Ruby?' I ask.

Joe just shrugs, which is ANNOYING. I huff a bit. 'Honestly, Joe. I don't understand you,' I say. 'Don't you ever want to get back at **ANYONE** for **ANYTHING**? Are you **SO FLIPPING SAINTLY** that you never feel like swinging a good hard kick at someone?'

Joe shakes his head slowly, looking down at his hands. He is picking at a scab on the back of his hand. 'Of course I feel like it sometimes,' he says, 'but, like I said, it's just *not very intelligent*, is it? It's just letting your feelings fly out and hurt people. Anyone can do that.'

He looks up at me. 'When you think about it,

most of the fighting in the whole world happens because people think they deserve revenge on someone. If we keep doing hurtful things backwards and forwards, everyone ends up hurt and everything ends up wrecked. I think the really brave people are the ones who stop throwing the hurt back. It takes a lot more courage to stop fighting than to carry on.'

He is ABSOLUTELY TOTALLY 100% RIGHT, of course. Who could argue with THAT piece of wizardly wisdom?

'You should be a politician,' I say. 'The world would be much happier with people like you in charge.'

He laughs. I begin to wonder if perhaps Joe is a bit more highly EVOLVED than me. For example, it had never occurred to my tiny, grumpy brain that I could actually CHOOSE not to try and get revenge on Ruby. All I had to do was to control my feelings, but THAT was the hard part.

'You're very old and wise on the inside, aren't you, Joe?'

'Not really,' he says, going back to picking his scab. 'I had a huge shock once and it made me decide *never* to have another fight.'

'What was that?' I ask. 'Maybe I need a big shock, too.'

Joe suddenly looks at me and his face is incredibly sad. 'No, you don't. Believe me. You don't need a shock like I had.'

His face seems frozen. It makes me shiver. I whisper, 'What happened, Joe?'

He gazes past me for a moment, out of the bus window, and then stares down at his hands again. His fingers are clutched together and his knuckles are pale.

'My brother got killed,' he says.

A little gasp rushes into my mouth, then a sigh comes out. 'Oh, Joe, I'm *so* sorry.'

'It was when I lived in London,' he explains. 'He just didn't come home one night. My mum opened the door at breakfast time and there were two policewomen outside. I never saw him again.'

My eyes are filling up with tears. I KNEW there was a story behind Joe being in Heckaby but I never expected it to be so sad.

'What happened?' I ask him very gently.

'He was in a fight. He got stabbed. It was just a stupid argument about a girl.'

'Is that why you came to live out here with your dad?'

Joe nods, then looks up at me again. 'I'm OK

though. I'm fine now. I miss him loads, of course, but it's Mum that came off worst. She lost my brother and then she sent me to live out here where she thought things would be better for me. She lost both of us and she's still there, in our flat, on her own, going to work and shopping and holding herself together. I don't think she'll ever be completely OK again.'

I reach out and touch Joe's hands that are still bunched together. I can't think of anything to say. His story makes my trouble with Ruby look like a big fat load of NOTHING.

'Anyway,' he says, sitting up straight and smiling again, '*that's* why I don't go in for revenge, d'ya see?'

'Absolutely!' I pause, then say – because I REALLY believe that it needs saying, 'But you've still got to stand up for yourself. That's different. That's not revenge, is it? That's…well, it's JUSTICE, isn't it? Making things fair. You can't be a doormat.'

And Joe just nods again and squeezes my hand gently. And I know that today is ABSOLUTELY NOT the day to have that IMPORTANT CONVERSATION.

The next village, Tollworth, is where Ruby always gets on the bus. Becky is with her but she sits away from her today, which is the first time I've seen Becky CHOOSE where she sits on the bus. Maybe she isn't under Ruby's CONTROL quite so much now. They've had to wait in the rain for the bus so they are SOAKED. Ruby's mascara is running and her hair has gone as frizzy as a mad sheep. She's probably far too vain EVER to wear waterproofs. I'm dry and warm inside Dad's old jacket and Mum's wellies. I might not look glamorous but at least I'm not in danger of catching pneumonia or winning a prize for being Miss Rain-Soaked-Mess-of-the-Year, like she is.

After hearing Joe's terrible story, I swear to myself that I'll try EVEN HARDER to control my feelings about Ruby but there is still a part of me, that spiky demon part, that is secretly VERY pleased that she'll be damp, uncomfortable and worried about her hair ALL DAY. SHAME ON YOU, CORDELIA CODD.

There are only two days left of the Scrap Project including today and we all have MASSES still to do. By halfway through the morning I've finished the long seams on the skirt and it is hanging over the bamboo hoop petticoat – it looks GREAT but I've still got the ENORMOUSLY LONG hemline to sew up and it has to be done by hand so that the stitches don't show.

Janna and Emmy are varnishing their bookshelves now. The shelves are all different colours and you'd never know that they started out as rough old crates from the back yard of a depot.

Becky is fixing the last few rows of loyalty cards around her Roman armour with fiddly bits of wire that she has to twist into place with tiny pliers.

Joe is mounting diagrams and photographs of his greenhouse onto a wooden board and Lennox and Gregor have nearly completed their latest creations. As for Ruby, she is obviously so DESPERATE to win that she's keeping her head down and threading beads at something approaching THE SPEED OF LIGHT. Her face is flushed pink, except for the bruise around her eye, and she looks like she would bite anyone who went near her.

After a little while I see Mrs Allen step outside with Joe. I hope she's reassuring him that she knows he didn't mess up Lennox and Gregor's work. She SHOULD be.

At morning break I follow Gregor and Lennox out into the corridor and catch up with them by the vending machine. Everyone else carries on working and there is still a PRETTY TENSE ATMOSPHERE after yesterday.

'You two have got Joe ALL wrong, y'know?' I blurt out.

'Oh yes? How?' asks Gregor, looking more interested in choosing something to drink than in hearing anything I might have to say on the subject.

'Well, firstly,' I say, holding up a finger. 'Can you really imagine him doing something so MORONIC as wrecking your work? Secondly...' I hold up another finger, 'what's his motive? Why on Earth WOULD he do it? And thirdly...' I put up another finger and check over my shoulder to make sure no one else is listening, 'Ruby hates Joe because he turned her down when she asked him to go out with her. She messed up your work and then blamed him because she was hoping that you two would beat him up.'

They both stare at me. Either they think I'm mad or else my BRILLIANT REVELATION OF THE OBVIOUS TRUTH is SINKING IN. While their brains are ticking over I tell them my idea about HOW AND WHEN Ruby did the damage.

'Come on!' I say, trying to speed up their thinking. 'It makes sense, you know it does. AND she wrecked MY work the other day because she's angry that I'm friendly with him. She thinks we're going out together…but that's a whole other story. You don't need to know about that bit.'

Gregor and Lennox look at each other. Gregor bites his bottom lip and nods. Lennox's nostrils have gone wide and flared, like a dragon breathing in before he INCINERATES someone with his fiery breath.

'I get it,' says Gregor.

Lennox's teeth are clenched, 'Yes, we get it,' he says, and it sounds like a growl.

'But don't do anything ACTUALLY physically violent to her, will you?' I ask, flapping my hands a bit, 'or she'll just claim that you beat her up RANDOMLY. And DO NOT tell Joe that I told you. I'll do that.'

'Don't worry,' says Gregor. 'We won't do or say

anything. We just needed to know the truth.'

Lennox looks like he DOES want to DO OR SAY SOMETHING but Gregor nudges him and adds, 'Didn't we?'

Lennox sighs. 'I suppose so. I'm going to win the competition, anyway, and that'll **really** punish her.'

Gregor and I both look at Lennox and frown.

'No, actually,' says Gregor, tapping his chest, **'I'm** going to win.'

'Hang on,' I say. 'I've decided that I'M going to win. It's the PERFECT revenge.'

'OK, OK,' says Gregor, smiling. 'As long as *Ruby* doesn't win, it doesn't matter who gets the prize. Are we agreed?'

Lennox and I nod. 'Agreed!'

At lunchtime Lennox and Gregor apologise to Joe. Helping to patch up their friendship is easier than I expected. My USEFUL INTERFERING seems to have been successful.

Everyone works through lunchtime and the afternoon is quiet – VERY quiet. Only Emmy and Janna whisper to each other and let out an occasional giggle. The rest of us are all so DESPERATE to snatch the prize from Ruby that we work like robots.

Ruby squints at her beads and hardly leaves her seat. Her black eye is fading to a mixture of snot green and the same banana yellow as the paint Lennox brought for Emmy and Janna.

I've finished all the machine sewing for the skirt, including a proper waistband, and I've put a black top with a low neckline on the top half of Griselda. It belongs to Mum but she was too busy to ask this morning so I borrowed it TEMPORARILY from her wardrobe. It goes REALLY well with the green skirt. Next, the hemline has to be measured to EXACTLY the same length all the way round. The bloomers will be easy. I just need to add the lace from the net curtains around the ankles. I am SO proud of how it's all turning out. By the end of the day I feel pretty happy.

But on the bus going home Joe plonks himself down next to me. His face is like thunder.

'Don't speak to me,' he says.

We sit in silence until Ruby and Becky get off. He is too kind to get angry with me where they can hear. But as soon as the bus pulls away from their stop he quietly **EXPLODES**. I've never seen him this cross before. He tells me that he worked out **IMMEDIATELY** that I'd spoken to Lennox and Gregor and he **ISN'T** pleased.

'I don't want you fighting my battles for me, Cordelia,' he says.

'But I was helping,' I explain, thinking he's being **VERY UNGRATEFUL**.

'You *shouldn't* have interfered,' he insists. 'It was up to me to decide how I handled Gregor and Lennox, *not you*. Just back off!'

My voice gets louder and angrier. 'Back off? But I was sticking up for you! I stick up for my friends. You stop Ruby from thumping me and I stop her from wrecking your friendship with Gregor and Lennox. Sounds like a fair swap to me.'

'Not if the other person doesn't *want* you to stick up for them,' he says. 'Not if the other person has their own way of handling things. OK?'

I start **PROPERLY** shouting. 'No, it's **NOT** OK. It's not **OK**, at all, Joe!'

People on the bus begin tutting and looking at us. Joe stands up and grabs his bag from the rack above the seats. 'Don't speak to me for a while, Cordelia. You've *really* annoyed me.'

And he jumps off at the next stop. I can't see which way he walks because the windows are steamed up again.

WHAT have I done wrong? I **REALLY** don't understand. And I suddenly feel like every good feeling inside me has been snatched away. I'm cold, even though the weather is humid and hot. This is the **WORST** feeling ever. I don't know if:

a) he's just dumped me, or

b) he's in another huffy-sulk that will pass, like before, or

c) he still thinks I'm his girlfriend, which means I still have to have that important conversation with him — except that I can't now because he's not speaking to me.

WHAT'S GOING ON? I just wanted to be his friend but SOMEHOW I've got it all COMPLETELY WRONG.

14

When I get home the noise is TERRIBLE. Another
big truck has arrived, delivering new roof tiles
for the barn. A team of people is scrambling up
ladders shouting instructions to each other, trying
desperately to get HUGE plastic sheets over the
hole where the old roof used to be, in case the rain
gets any heavier. If they don't, Mum explains, the
inside of the barn will be soaked and it could take
MONTHS to dry out such a big building.

Dad is in The Jug and Monkey. He has a dust
mask over his mouth and is waving instructions
to a woman with HUGE arm muscles covered
in tattoos. She's wearing a dust mask, too, and is
sanding down the floorboards with a MASSIVE
contraption that sounds like a MILLION-
DECIBEL vacuum cleaner.

An electrician is upstairs singing along REALLY
loudly to a
La La La La I Love Yoooou...

type of pop song on the radio while he twists bits of cable together. There are rolls of carpet stacked all the way up the stairs, wrapped in plastic and ready for the new flat. Every other space is filled with tins of paint and varnish and tool-boxes.

The only place to find a seat is in our tiny cottage where I find Mr Belly hiding under the table. He has brought me ANOTHER dead mouse. It is quite badly chewed. I just say, 'Thank you, Mr B,' and leave the little pile of mouse-squish on the floor.

Even from here the sound of banging and boot-stomping and sanding and the TERRIBLE singing comes through the walls. I can't put the lights or the telly on or use anything that has a switch until the electrician has finished for the day because the power has been turned off. So I sit in the gloom, staring out of the window, hugging Mr Belly.

We are there for AGES, and I've never felt so lonely in my ENTIRE life. All I can think about is how stupid I must be if I can't work out what I've done SO WRONG that it has made Joe storm off and not want to speak to me. Being tired and hungry isn't helping and I sink into a GENERAL GRUMP with life. I **HATE** Heckaby, I **HATE** not having any friends here, I **HATE** our house and The Jug and Monkey and the barn that is still a million miles away from being lovely Heckaby Picture Palace. I **HATE** the damp and the draughty windows and the noise, and the **TOTAL ABSENCE** of **ANYTHING GLAMOROUS** around me.

I tell all this to Mr Belly, who falls asleep on my lap. Life is much less complicated for cats.

After what feels like a million years sitting in the almost-dark staring up at fat purple thunder clouds, Dad pops in and announces that the builders have finished for the day. He asks if I'll go to the chip shop because he and Mum are too tired to cook dinner. Well, everyone likes fish and chips, don't they? So I jump up, even though it means a walk in the rain.

I'm not very PATIENT in queues, even when I'm in a good mood, which I clearly AM NOT, and it seems like HOURS before I get to the counter and ask Lily for haddock and chips three times and a large mushy peas. While I wait I stare out across the road through a little circle I've wiped in the steamy window.

Opposite the chip shop there's a Chinese takeaway, which isn't usually very exciting, but it certainly is tonight! I DON'T QUITE BELIEVE what I'm seeing at first. Ruby and Joe! Ruby and Joe are standing between the Chinese takeaway and Hair by Romano, having a **STONKING ROW**!

Maybe, FINALLY, he's giving her a good shouting at for her TOXIC IMBECILE behaviour. But Ruby lives in the next village, about two miles away, so why would she come all the way to Heckaby just to get a verbal battering from Joe? A huge wave of **MAXIMUM DREAD** washes over me. Perhaps they're on a DATE! Perhaps Joe DOES fancy Ruby after all. Perhaps he HAS dumped me, or else he's two-timing me. How confusing is THIS?! If they ARE on a date then it CLEARLY isn't going very well, but SOMETIMES people fight like two ferrets trapped in a sack and five minutes later decide that they're MADLY IN LOVE with each other again. What's THAT all about? I've seen it happen in LOADS of films. Joe and Ruby might stop arguing and start sloppy-cuddling at any moment! And if THEY become friends then I'll REALLY be on my own! THANK GOODNESS the chip-shop windows are too steamy for them to see my HORRIFIED FACE!

By the time Lily tells me my order is ready, Ruby and Joe have stormed off in opposite directions and I can get home without them spotting me.

Mum and Dad discuss the barn roof while we eat our chips so they don't notice how quiet I am. When they aren't jabbering they just pass the ketchup and vinegar in silence and get stuck into their food with blank, tired faces.

My head is full of BLEAK and GRIM visions of what life will be like if Joe, who a moment ago was a nearly-boyfriend I needed to gently dump, becomes friends (or more!) with my **WORST ENEMY**.

We have just finished eating when there is a RIDICULOUSLY LOUD knock at the door, like a police raid. We all jump, then Dad gets up.

SIGHS OF BOREDOM, it's Mrs Driscoll in what Mum calls *High Dudgeon*, which means she is having a MAJOR strop. Dad takes Witchy Driscoll into The Jug and Monkey to give her more privacy for whatever she wants to NAG him about. Mum rolls her eyes and gets on with the washing up. I sneak out of the cottage door and stand under the porch outside the pub so that I can hear what Dad and Witchy Driscoll are saying.

Mrs Driscoll is ranting on, telling Dad about a load of stuff that has gone missing from her shop. She is waving a piece of paper. I hear Joe's name.

'That seems a bit harsh, don't you think, Mrs Driscoll?' I hear Dad saying.

Witchy Driscoll shrieks back at him, 'Harsh, harsh? Stealing my profits is what's harsh, Mr Codd. Kids taking all that I've slaved for from under my nose.'

'I see your point, Mrs Driscoll,' says Dad, 'but I don't think an ASBO is what Joe needs.'

I give a little gasp of horror.

'No, I agree,' snaps Witchy Driscoll, 'a *flogging* is what *he* needs but they're too soft for that nowadays and the best we can hope for is an Anti-Social Behaviour Order. Now, will you be signing this letter to my solicitor or do you not *care* what sort of village this turns into?'

If Dad signs Mrs Driscoll's letter, Joe could end up getting some sort of criminal record. I **CAN'T** let that happen! That isn't **FAIR**. That isn't **JUSTICE**. I storm into the pub. Dad is holding a pen that Mrs Driscoll has passed to him. I **SCREAM** at him.

'IF YOU SIGN THAT I'LL NEVER SPEAK TO YOU AGAIN!! I MEAN IT!! YOU KNOW I MEAN IT!!'

Dad looks shocked as he realises that I've heard what they've been saying. 'Mrs Driscoll has had another theft from her shop tonight, Coco,' he says, making PATHETIC EXCUSES for what he is about to do. 'We can't let this continue.'

My eyes go narrow and hard and I shout at Mrs Driscoll. 'I bet you haven't got ONE BIT OF PROOF that it was Joe, have you?'

Her face is pinched and bitter and scarlet. 'We all know who does the thieving around here,' she hisses. 'And I saw him near my shop just an hour ago.'

'That doesn't mean he **STOLE** anything.' I say, still fuming. 'You just want someone to blame. Joe's got more taste than to steal the rubbish you sell in that **SCABBY** little shop of yours.'

Dad shouts at me then. He HARDLY EVER shouts at me so I'm a bit scared. 'Coco! Apologise to Mrs Driscoll this instant!'

But I'm not going to. NO WAY. Instead, I point at Mrs Driscoll. 'It's **HER** who should apologise.

She's blaming Joe for something he didn't do. He's **NOT** a thief.'

Before either of them can stop me I snatch the letter off Mrs Driscoll, tear it up, throw it on the floor and STAMP on it.

'Coco, go back to the cottage now!' Dad yells.

Witchy Driscoll folds her arms. Her lips go narrower and meaner than ever. 'It's no matter,' she says, her eyes like sharp grey needles. 'I've got plenty of copies at home. I'll just add another name to it, *your* name, young lady.'

Mum and Dad are in a **FURY WITH FRILLS ON**. There's no reasoning with them. I refuse to write to Mrs Driscoll and apologise for shouting and tearing up her horrible letter. If I do that it will be the same as saying that she's right about Joe, and I'll **NEVER** do that.

My punishment is NO COMPUTER TIME that night and I get sent upstairs to THINK about what I've done. Luckily, I've brought the bloomers with the lace bottoms home to work on, so I sit in my bedroom and hand-sew the lace around the ankles. I get a REALLY stiff neck from hunching over but I don't do any of the kind of THINKING Mum and Dad want me to do. Instead I just think about how **MEAN** Witchy Driscoll is and how her insides must be made of something **BLACK** and **POISONOUS**. And then I think about how empty I feel without Joe as a friend and how TERRIFYING life will be if he pairs up with Ruby. I feel scooped out but like I'm full of cold, heavy mashed potatoes at the same time.

I'm allowed to come downstairs later. Dad is drying up the fish-and-chip plates. I sort my felt pens into a rainbow on the table.

'So, are you ready to apologise?' he asks.

'No,' I say, with my **MADE OF STEEL** face on, looking straight at him, 'because I'm right and she's **WRONG**.'

Dad sighs, like he's exhausted, and rubs a plate very hard with a tea towel. 'You were *very* wrong to be so rude about Mrs Driscoll's shop.'

'But it **IS** scabby,' I say, 'and Joe **WOULDN'T** touch her stuff.'

Dad sighs again and shakes his head. 'There are some things that you just don't say out loud to people, Coco. It's very hurtful.'

'And I find it very **HURTFUL** that my friend Joe is getting a bad reputation because of a gossipy, lentil-brained sour-face who hates **EVERYONE**. He's a kinder, more gentle and more intelligent person than Mrs Driscoll will **EVER** be, and I'm standing by him.'

Mum concentrates on scrubbing a big saucepan that has been soaking for a couple of days. She has that *you-are-wasting-your-time* look on her face. She knows that I'm about five million times more stubborn than the average donkey but Dad insists on continuing to argue with me. I can see that he's close to giving up though and, eventually, one of his BIG FINAL SIGHS comes out.

'OK. Well, I admire your loyalty,' he says. 'I just hope you're right, young lady, or you could be heading for a lot of trouble hanging around with that boy. Don't expect me to come to the police station and bail you out when you get arrested for being his partner in crime.'

I put my head in my hands.

'We're not Bonnie and Clyde, Dad. He's just a nice boy who I sit with on the bus.'

Dad rubs the tea towel extra hard around the bottom of another plate. 'We'll see how *nice* he turns out to be, won't we?' he says, 'We'll just wait and see, young lady.' Then he drops the plate on the floor and it breaks into twenty zillion pieces – and he swears a lot.

I take myself off to bed RIDICULOUSLY early just to get away from Mum and Dad. I'm not sleepy so I look at costume pictures from *Gone with the Wind* in one of my big books and draw the chiffon dress with a green velvet ribbon around the waist that Scarlett O'Hara wears for a party. The party happens before the war, when Scarlett is still rich and spoiled.

You'd think that Scarlett would be a better, kinder sort of person after she has lived through a horrible war. For a long time she:

a) is almost starving

b) has nothing nice to wear

c) has to work really hard in the fields instead of going to parties

d) sees lots of people get killed, including her friends.

Well, it didn't work for Scarlett. The war is really long, so she has YEARS and YEARS to get a grip on herself and change, but she's even more CRUEL and GRABBY and SELFISH at the end of the story than at the beginning. I don't like Scarlett O'Hara AT ALL; I certainly wouldn't want to be friends with her, but Vivien Leigh, the BRILLIANT actress who played her, did get to wear some INCREDIBLE dresses.

In my dreams that night Ruby turns into Scarlett O'Hara. She steals my dress with the hooped petticoat AND she takes the prize money for the best design AND she takes my friend Joe and makes him HATE me. When I complain to her in the dream she just swings around in my big, hooped skirt and flips me away with her hand, saying,

'Fiddle-di-dee'

which is EXACTLY what Scarlett O'Hara says when she doesn't give a FROG'S FART about other people.

15

The next day is Saturday, the last day of the project. I wake up feeling like I've been in a wrestling match with a FAT BEAR. I'm EXHAUSTED from dreaming. It's like I haven't slept at all – I'm aching and GLUM on the inside.

Luckily, Mum is scrambling eggs when I stagger down for breakfast. Mum's scrambled eggs aren't the same as Dad's scromlettes but they are fine in an emergency. Dad joins us. This doesn't happen often at breakfast time so maybe Mum isn't as cross with him as usual – perhaps she's even starting to love him again a little bit. This seems like a good moment to plant the idea of going to Café Candela so I run off and rummage in my bag until I find the card Lennox gave me and prop it up between the salt and pepper pots without Mum seeing me. This is easy because she is concentrating on the eggs.

Dad is frowning at a bill from the people who are fixing the barn roof.

'Are you going to be here every breakfast time now?' I ask Dad, trying to sound like it isn't all that important to me.

Dad doesn't get a chance to answer me before Mum says a very definite, 'No!'

End of conversation. I nudge the salt and pepper pots with the card wedged between them a bit closer to Dad. This time he notices what I'm doing and I signal with big staring eyes towards the card. He looks puzzled, then realises I'm trying to pass him something. He picks up the card, reads it and smiles at me – just a tiny, quick smile so that Mum doesn't notice – then slips it into his back jeans pocket. I THINK I have planted a USEFUL seed of POTENTIAL romance.

Mum and Dad don't mention Mrs Driscoll at breakfast because they're too busy FRETTING about the barn roof. I can tell that they're stressing already this morning because Dad puts too much salt on his eggs. He keeps picking up the salt and grinding on a bit more, like he's forgotten that he's already done it.

Mum has lost count of how many eggs she's cooked. She keeps piling more and more onto my plate until I shout, 'STOP, enough eggs! I won't have another poo until Christmas if I eat that lot!' because everyone knows that too many eggs in your system makes your poo stop moving, like a train stuck in a tunnel.

I set off for the bus stop a bit early, to avoid DEATH BY EGG BLOCKAGE and also because I am pretty STRESSO myself after that dream and I need some oxygen. The picture of Ruby taking EVERYTHING and just flicking me away with a

'Fiddle-di-dee'

pops into my head again and again as I walk.

The rain stopped in the night but it is still humid. It needs to POUR down for about a month to make the air fresh and breezy again.

There's no sign of Joe on the bus. Perhaps he's avoiding me COMPLETELY, or else he's hoping that Ruby will beat me up because he's so angry with me. Well, no…maybe not. Joe isn't nasty like that.

I sit near the driver again. There's a man sitting next to me who sleeps for most of the journey, which is good because I'm not feeling chatty or cheerful. Ruby and Becky get on but don't sit together. I only know this because I can see them in the big mirror that the driver uses. It's beginning to look like Becky is definitely TRYING to get away from Ruby.

Ruby doesn't hit me with a bag 'accidentally' or elbow me in the ear or even look at me as she goes past. Maybe this has something to do with her row with Joe last night. The same questions come back to me. What could he have said? What did they argue about? And how come she was in Heckaby ANYWAY when she lives down here, in Tollworth? The only way I'll ever find out is if Joe speaks to me again, and that feels a bit unlikely RIGHT AT THIS MOMENT.

When we arrive Mrs Allen is flapping a bit because this is our last day. She gathers us for a meeting.

'Now, I need you all to crack on independently today,' she announces. 'Mr Carter will be here this morning but he will need to spend most of his time with Janna and Emmy. You older ones know what you need to do. I have to be absent this morning. A family emergency has come up. I'm sorry, it's a bit of a nuisance, but I'll be back as soon as possible this afternoon. Any questions?'

We shake our heads. Mrs Allen claps her big hands, 'Excellent. Where's Joe? Anyone know?'

Ruby speaks up. Her words are directed to Mrs Allen but her eyes are on me. 'I saw him last night, Mrs Allen. I think his dad's ill so he's got to look after his little brothers today.'

She is expecting it to be BIG NEWS to me that she was with Joe yesterday evening but I smile at her in a jolly, friendly and UTTERLY SARCASTIC way and say, 'Oh yes, what did you make of Heckaby's Chinese takeaway, Ruby?'

Ruby gives a little gasp and the grin drops off her face. I can almost hear it hit the floor with a S<small>P</small>L<small>OP</small>PI<small>NG</small> sound. Now she KNOWS that I saw her having a SPAT-O-MATIC row with Joe and I can see by her face that she has just declared war on me ALL OVER AGAIN.

Ruby waits until just after lunch to grab her chance. She catches me when I nip out to get a drink from the vending machine. I turn around from picking up my carton of juice and she's standing **RIGHT IN MY PERSONAL SPACE AGAIN** with a face like **SOUR LEMONS**. I am **SCARED STIFF** but I manage not to show it.

'So you spy on people, do you?' she starts. 'How else would you know that I was outside the Chinese takeaway last night, *nosy brat?*'

'I was buying fish and chips across the road, actually,' I say, trying to sound calm and collected, 'and you weren't **EXACTLY** having that **MASSIVE VERBAL DING-DONG** in private, were you?'

'That's none of your business, *flap-ears,*' she says, and tries to slap the side of my head just like she did before. But, even though I'm really shocked and scared, I manage to grab her wrist. I don't know what to do with it now I've got hold of it so I let it go again and push her away from me. She comes right back at me with her teeth showing and her fists ready.

'I said you'd be in hospital,' she hisses, 'and it looks like *today* is the day.'

She is just about to lay into me when Mrs Allen stumbles into the corridor, hot and puffing and laden with bags of fabric and tools. She looks like she's been to a jumble sale, not to attend a family emergency.

'Sorry, girls,' she gasps, 'I couldn't get back any earlier. Everything going well?'

'Fine, thank you,' I say cheerfully, knowing that it will annoy Ruby if I sound happy. 'We're just getting a drink.'

'Jolly good,' says Mrs Allen, and disappears into the art room.

Ruby is **FUMING**. She's missed her chance to hospitalise me by a **MILLISECOND**. Instead she spits words at me.

'I'm going to make you wish you'd never come to this school. You won't last the first week.'

And she **STOMPS** back into the art room in her FRANKLY HIDEOUS, pink, sparkle-covered trainers.

Mrs Allen calls us all together AGAIN. 'OK, gang! Listen up!' she says, waving us towards her. 'I have to give you some information about next week. As you all know, it will be the first week of term.'

GENERAL GROANS.

'You'll be allowed to come and make finishing touches to your projects at *lunchtimes* until no later than *Thursday*,' she announces. 'Got that? *Thursday lunchtime* is the *final* day for tinkering with finishing touches. After that *all* your work will be put on display in the foyer until half term. Any questions?'

I have LOTS of questions, like:

a) How am I **ever** going to cope with the first week of a brand-new school

b) **and** the pressure of finishing my costume

c) **and** avoid **attempts on my life** by Ruby?

But they all stay inside my head, whirling round and round and making me sick with fear.

Thankfully, I HAVE to concentrate like mad in the last couple of hours of the day so that my costume is NEARLY done. I'll have to save FULL-SCALE PANIC for later.

Mum picks me up on her way back from the DIY shop, so at least I don't have to get the bus home but I have to share the car with a selection of paintbrushes, buckets, squeezy mop heads, two flat-pack bookshelves and a bedside lamp.

'Aren't we giving Joe a lift?' she asks.

'No,' I snap. 'He wasn't here today. He's finished his work. But don't be too pleased, he's still my friend. He's just busy on his allotment.'

And yes, I know this is mostly lies because:

a) He **hasn't** quite finished

b) He probably **isn't** my friend at the moment

c) I don't have a **clue** where he **really** is.

But I'm not going to let my parents know that, am I?

♥

Just to top my life off with a GORILLA POO, things at home get EVEN WORSE from the moment I'm through the front door.

Dad is in the cottage having a cup of tea when Mum and I stagger in with her shopping. Mum must've started letting Dad come into the cottage when she isn't here. Has she given him his own key? This is definitely GOOD NEWS in my parents' relationship, but Dad's face looks like he is about to deliver very BAD NEWS.

He asks me and Mum to leave the shopping and sit down a minute. His face is grey and serious so neither of us argues. I am expecting him to tell us that someone has died but it isn't that, it's WORSE.

'Cordelia, I've just heard that Joe Grover was taken to the police station this morning,' he says in a flat voice.

My panic bells start ringing. 'What's happened? Is he OK?'

Dad clears his throat. 'It looks like Mrs Driscoll is going to press charges this time. He's not going to get off with a warning.'

Mum sighs. 'Oh dear, *silly* boy.'

Dad gives me a serious look. 'You *mustn't* hang out with him any more, Coco. I know you think he wouldn't do these things but you might just have to admit that you've been mistaken about him. He needs to sort himself out. You'll get a bad reputation very quickly if you're seen with a known troublemaker. And it's not just *your* reputation that's at stake here. Your mum and I are trying to build a business and we have to stay friendly with the whole village or they won't want to be our customers.'

My fists are screwed up tight under the table. 'That's all you really care about, isn't it?' I shout. 'You don't care about the **TRUTH**, you only care about your business. You **KNOW** Mrs Driscoll is just a big tub of **POISON** who is spreading lies about Joe but you **DAREN'T** stand up to her because she might spread lies about **YOU**, and that would stop people in the village wanting to be your customers. How **COULD** you be such **WIMPS?!** You're **OUTRAGEOUS!**'

NATURALLY, I storm off and **BOIL** quietly in my tiny bedroom. But then I start wondering about Joe. What if I don't know him as well as I think I do? Is it possible that he HAS been taking things? What if it isn't just 'tat' that he's been picking up and reusing for his allotment? It's hard to believe that he'd steal so much as a MOUSE DROPPING from that manky old shop but HOW COME he's always been around when SOMEONE is stealing? It doesn't look good. I want to hear HIM tell me the truth and I know EXACTLY where he'll be.

'Where d'you think you're going?' Mum asks when she sees me pulling on her wellies. She is checking the plug on the bedside lamp that she's just bought, while Dad tries to fit one of the flat-pack bookshelves together. His face is red and there are bolts and random bits of wood all over the kitchen table.

'Just out for a walk,' I say.

'Oh no you're not, young lady. I want you right here every evening until this business is sorted out. I'm not having you blamed for this trouble, too.'

'So now I'm **GROUNDED**? What for?'

'For your *own protection*,' Mum says and Dad nods his agreement with her.

NATURALLY I FLOUNCE back upstairs again, shouting, 'You are both **OUTRAGEOUS!** I am a **PRISONER IN MY OWN HOME!**'

Later on, Mum and Dad are in the barn, making plans for the cinema. I COULD sneak out and see if Joe is at his allotment but I'd be in SO MUCH TROUBLE if I did that I decide it's best to wait until tomorrow morning to talk to him. I don't want to risk losing any more computer time because I'll DIE if I don't communicate with Dru soon.

I text Joe:

Hve u bn arrested? Whts hppning?

Then I do lots of drawing to keep myself busy while I wait for a reply. I keep checking my phone – nothing. I WISH Joe would turn up on the doorstep and ask me to walk to the bridge with him, like he did before, even though I wouldn't be allowed to go. I just want to see him and know that he's OK. If my life were a film, that's what would happen. But, of course, it doesn't happen. Real life isn't like films.

I try to take my mind off it by watching *The Barefoot Contessa*. Ava Gardner is the star in it. Her costumes are extra-extra beautiful but the story is SO sad at the end. When she finally marries the man she loves it turns out that he was badly injured in the war and they can't have any children. I think it was a bit mean of him not to tell her this BEFORE they got married. Then I watch a bit of *Casablanca*, which is in black and white. The actress in it, Ingrid Bergman, wears mostly white and pale-coloured clothes with a few twinkly bits. She's in love with a man called Rick who runs a bar and a casino. The story happens during the Second World War and, although it's probably one of the most glamorous films in the history of FILM-WORLD, there are lots of sad people in it. They are all trying to escape from the Nazis, selling everything they have and leaving their homes to get away. People get separated from their families and some of them die before they escape, from sadness or being shot by spies.

To try and cheer myself up a bit I watch some of *The Sound of Music* with Julie Andrews. She plays a nun in this film so her outfits aren't very glam but there are some good songs and I sing along because no one is listening to my TRULY TERRIBLE voice. I only usually sing quietly in the bath but when the house is empty I sing LOUDLY. I don't THINK Mum and Dad can hear me from the barn.

But GUESS WHAT? I realise that *The Sound of Music* is a war story, TOO, and that Julie Andrews has to help a man and his SEVEN children escape to safety. War seems to be in loads of my favourite films – someone is always fighting a war, or having things go wrong in their lives because of a war.

Before bedtime I'm allowed back on the computer for a quick communication with Dru. It feels like ages since I was banned from it for refusing to apologise to Witchy Driscoll. Dru is home from her camping expedition and I manage to catch her online. Perhaps she can explain things.

★ Cordelia to Dru

Hi. Are you there? How was camping? Want to hear my latest GLOOMY OBSERVATIONS OF HUMANITY?

★ Dru to Cordelia

```
Camping was fine. There were no snakes
and my tent didn't leak. Tell me your
obs.
```

★ Cordelia to Dru

Why does every glamorous film ever made seem to have a war in the background?

★ Dru to Cordelia

```
I know, it's weird! I'll ask my mom,
wait there, she's just outside my room.
```

While I'm waiting for Dru I have a think, staring at the funny stains on the ceiling of the cottage. It seems to me that there is WAR in my films and a WAR with Ruby at the Scrap Project and I'm also fighting a MINI-WAR with that spiky red demon inside myself when I try not to lose my temper with Ruby and do stupid things.

★ **Dru** to Cordelia

Mom says that if you have something
terrible happening in a story, like a
war, you can show that no matter how
scary and desperate things get there
can always be a happy ending if we
are brave.

★ **Cordelia** to Dru

That makes sense. I like that explanation.

★ **Dru** to Cordelia

NEWS ALERT: There's a plague of tiny
frogs in our back yard after the
thunderstorm. I have to go and help
clear them out of the drains. We have
a frog-blockage!

★ **Cordelia** to Dru

But I haven't had a chance to tell you all my
news.

I type it all for her to read later. I write about
Ruby wrecking Gregor and Lennox's work
and Joe's terrible reaction to my USEFUL
INTERFERENCE and about seeing him having a

row with Ruby when I was queuing for chips. I tell her about Joe being arrested and how I haven't had the IMPORTANT CONVERSATION with him yet because everything has got so complicated – and I write about his brother dying, which makes me cry even thinking about it, and how his life is SO sad and how I don't believe ONE WORD of the rumours about him.

Then I suddenly have what Mum calls A BIT OF A MOMENT. I realise that it's time I sorted out some of these problems by myself and told Dru the SOLUTIONS instead of dumping all my *weeping woes* on her and expecting her to tell me what to do. I am such a *Whingeing Winnie* and it HAS to STOP. Other kids have their parents to moan at, of course, but mine are too busy to listen so I'm using poor old Dru instead.

I finish by PROMISING her that this is my FINAL MOAN and that I'll sort things out and then tell her THE HAPPY ENDING because, like her mum says, there can always be a happy ending if we are brave.

16

On Sunday morning my new school uniform is hanging up on the back of the door in our tiny kitchen. It looks like a dead person and every time I glance at it, it reminds me of the HUGE UNAVOIDABLE-NESS of tomorrow – the first day of term and, INEVITABLY, torture by Ruby. I can't eat my breakfast because of the fear WHIZZING round my insides.

Mum and Dad are busy measuring things in the outhouses. They obviously need to concentrate. I go out and lean on the door post, trying to look pale.

'I think I'm getting claustrophobia,' I tell them, 'and I've got a headache. Can't I go and get some fresh air?'

'Don't interrupt, Coco,' Mum snaps, raising a hand but not looking up from where she is holding the end of a tape measure against the wall. 'You can see we're busy. We have to work out where to put the power sockets in here.'

Dad taps at a calculator and doesn't seem to notice me. Mum eventually looks up. Perhaps I succeeded in turning pale or perhaps they just want me out of the way again because she sighs and says, 'You can go out for ONE HOUR and no more.'

I promise not to be any longer and I can tell by Mum's face that there'll be a DING–SPAT of an argument if I am. I throw on her wellies and Dad's waterproof jacket again and stomp off towards the bridge, texting Joe as I walk.

CN I CM 2 UR ALLTMNT RGHT NW, PLS? ND 2 TLK Cx

He doesn't reply straight away so I hang around at the bridge for a while. I stare into the stream, just like Joe and I did the other evening before the kiss THAT SHOULD NOT HAVE HAPPENED. The water has risen since then and twigs swim past quickly, bumping the stones then disappearing under the shadows of trees. Looking into water normally makes me feel calm but I'm too full of madly-anxious-heart-thumping worry about the things we have to talk about to feel even a tiny bit relaxed.

After a few minutes I look back along the high street and see Mrs Driscoll at an upstairs window above her shop, watching me. I'm QUITE tempted to make a rude sign at her for being so nosy but I don't because she looks ever so sad and pathetic all on her own in that big room. She is still watching when Joe texts back.

CRS U CN. C U SN. ALLTMNT 26, THRGH GTE NR CHRCH & STRGHT ON.

Phew! At least he didn't say, 'No, clear off.' So he probably doesn't HATE me completely. But that could all change because we need to have more than one IMPORTANT CONVERSATION now. I have so many questions for him AND so much that I need to explain. I try rehearsing a few speeches as I walk to the allotments but the words get as jumbled as bramble bushes so I give up and concentrate on BREATHING DEEPLY AND FEELING BRAVE.

Joe is rescuing waterlogged lettuces when I eventually find his allotment amongst all the others. Allotment number 26 is a secret world behind a battered blue door. Everything is lush, green and dripping, and smells fresh. It's peaceful in a way that wraps itself around you and makes you feel safe as soon as you step into it.

When he hears me come in Joe looks up at the dark clouds and waves me inside his little shed. My face must show that I have URGENT and SERIOUS stuff to say and that I'm not going to let him sulk with me any more. The FIRST thing I intend to discuss with him is his trip to the police station and whether he DID steal anything. But it doesn't work out that way around.

'I'm glad you've come,' he says.

And I BURST into tears and blurt out the stuff that REALLY matters through a great big dribble of snotty tears.

Joe hands me a slightly muddy packet of hankies and listens patiently while I BLATHER on about how I like him SO much as a friend but I just don't want a boyfriend AT ALL at the moment and how I've been scared STIFF that if I don't want to be his girlfriend he might turn against me instead of protecting me from Ruby. I tell him that I KNOW I've done a TERRIBLE thing, leading him on like that, and ask if he'll EVER forgive me and could he EVER be friends with such a SELFISH TOAD-GIRL as me because I'm TRULY, REALLY, MADLY SORRY, SORRY, SORRY?!! BLAH, BLAH, BLATHER, BLATHER.

He lets me get it all out before he says anything.

If we were in a film I would make a wonderful speech at this point about LOVE and LIFE and DESTINY, but real life isn't like that, that's one thing I DO know. Real life is quite often about having pink eyes and a runny nose from crying and feeling stupid or hurt or like you hate yourself. In real life you HAVE to try REALLY HARD to find the right words to use because no one has written them down for you to learn, like in films.

The only words I can dig out of my dribbly head are:

'Sorry,' and,

'I'm sorry,' and,

'I'm REALLY sorry,' and,

'I'm SO sorry,' and,

'I bet you HATE me now.'

I soak the paper hankies but Joe finds some more and I soak them, too. I am a complete HOSE NOSE for about fifteen minutes and I just KNOW that my face looks like a plate of raw mince.

When he can finally get a word in Joe smiles and says, 'Isn't it supposed to be me that's crying? I'm the one who's just been *dumped*.'

Even though he's smiling, his eyes look sad. 'Of

course I'll still be your friend!' he says. 'Honestly, Cordelia! What do you think I'm like? You must have a really low opinion of me. I wouldn't have wanted to kiss you if I didn't want to be your friend as well as your boyfriend. What sort of creep would want to go out with someone they didn't actually like as a friend?'

RELIEF! I can't tell you how happy I am just knowing that he doesn't DESPISE me.

I haven't said anything about the police, or stealing, or my parents, or Mrs Driscoll, or the row I saw him having with Ruby yet. We need a pause first.

'Would you like some tea?' Joe asks, with brilliant timing.

I nod. 'Yes please. And I'm sorry if I interfered between you and Lennox and Gregor. I really did think I was helping.'

Joe shakes his head. 'No, *I'm* sorry about that. I was just being proud and macho. You did a good thing. Thank you.'

'So we're properly friends and everything's OK?' I ask, just to make sure.

Joe laughs quietly. 'Properly,' he says.

I watch him pour some tea out of a flask. He

passes it to me. The shed smells of old wood and soil. It isn't horrid, though. It's comforting and dry in here. Gardening tools are hanging up neatly on nails around the wooden walls and there's a little shelf with seedlings in trays under the tiny window. There's just enough space for two wooden chairs and a teeny table where the big blue thermos flask stands next to an open packet of digestive biscuits and two books about organic gardening. I get the feeling that no one comes here except Joe.

When I've sipped my tea and paused enough I start IMPORTANT CONVERSATION NUMBER TWO.

'Now that we're friends again are you going to tell me what's going on?' I ask this straight out even though I'm still a bit worried that he'll go silent and sulky on me again. I keep sipping my tea and sit back in my chair. It's a bit wobbly. Both chairs are wobbly and so is the teeny table. Joe knows what I'm talking about but he doesn't answer straight away. He holds out the packet of digestive biscuits first and I take one.

'What's going on about what?' he says.

I answer with a bit of an impatient huff but also a little smile because I know that he knows

EXACTLY what I mean and he's teasing me. 'Don't try to be MYSTERIOUS, Joe. It's all over the village. The other day Ruby called you a thief and now my dad says you're in trouble for stealing from Driscoll's and that it's not the first time. I KNOW you were taken to the police station yesterday but I don't BELIEVE what people are saying about you – I'll still be your friend, anyway, even if it IS true. I don't think I could STAND not having you as my friend, Joe.'

He is grinning. HOW could he be so totally UNFAZED by such a SCARY LIFE EVENT as being arrested?

'OK.' He settles into his chair. 'Here's the truth. I've never stolen anything *in my life* except the stuff out of skips, but that was an accident – I didn't know I was supposed to ask first. I didn't take *anything* from Driscoll's or the Akbars', not last time or this time, or *any* time. I was just in the wrong place. I just happened to be at the *scene of the crime*, as they say.

I watch his eyes for signs of a lie but don't see one. 'I believe you,' I say, without needing to think about it for more than a nanosecond. I am SUPER-CERTAIN that I'd know if he was bluffing. He's just too nice and open and ordinary to be a good liar. 'But what does Deadly Driscoll say you stole?' I ask. 'And when are you supposed to have done this VILLAINOUS ROBBERY?'

'Friday night,' he says, taking another biscuit and offering them to me again. 'She says that three bags of Bentley's Liquorice Dibbles and a posh box of chocolates got taken.'

My voice squeaks out quite loudly because this is such a RIDICULOUS idea, 'But you don't even EAT chocolates and sweets and stuff!' I say. 'You just chew carrots!'

Joe gives his usual shrug. 'Yep, I know. These digestives are my only junk food, but Mrs Driscoll doesn't know that, does she?'

I dunk my second biscuit as a little lightbulb starts glowing in the back of my brain. It gets brighter and brighter. 'Did you say Liquorice Dibbles?'

Joe gives another shrug. 'Yes, but I don't think the police care what *kind* of sweets they were, just that they didn't belong to me. I told them that I *hate* liquorice, but they weren't going to believe that, were they? What's your point anyway?'

'I think I've just worked something out,' I say.

I press the replay button in my brain as I get my thoughts straight.

a) The sweets went missing on Friday, just before Joe and Ruby had their row outside the takeaway.

b) On Saturday Ruby yelled into my personal space as we stood by the vending machine.

c) When she spat those words at me they were **liquorice-smelling words!**

It all falls into place with a ground-shaking CLANG! I make sure that I am looking straight at Joe so that he can't hide anything.

'It was Ruby, wasn't it?' I say, my eyes bogglingly wide. 'That's why you were having a row outside the Chinese takeaway.'

Joe looks a bit shocked. 'How did you know about that?'

207

I wave my hand. 'Doesn't matter. I was queuing for chips. I saw you. She was the thief last time as well, wasn't she? How many times have you taken the blame for her stealing stuff?'

I can tell that I'm BING-BANG ON THE TRUTH BUTTON because Joe pauses, looks down and then mumbles, 'Well…but…'

'But **NOTHING**. Why don't you **TELL** someone? You don't have to take the blame for her **MORONIC BEHAVIOUR**.'

But there's obviously something I don't know and it all comes out then, in his little shed with cups of tea out of a flask and digestive crumbs on the floor between our feet. I finish my second, soggy biscuit as he tells me.

'I can't let her get into trouble,' he begins, sitting back with a heavy sigh, 'because her dad would batter her black and blue. Where d'you think she got that black eye?'

Joe tells me that Ruby often walks over to Heckaby in the evenings just to get away from her dad. 'When she gets home, he's ready to wallop her for the slightest reason,' he explains. 'That's why her behaviour is so crazy.'

More light bulbs come on as he explains a bit more.

'She usually texts me and asks to meet up,' he explains. 'But when we go into the shops together, she keeps nicking stuff. I never know she's done it until afterwards.'

'Is that what you were fighting about outside the takeaway?' I ask.

Joe nods. 'I was angry with her for taking more stuff. I said that if she didn't leave you alone I'd tell someone about the stealing. I thought she'd make a deal with me but she didn't – she just *exploded* and said that no one would believe me, anyway, because they all think I'm a thief. She's not stupid, she knows how to twist things around like that, and I couldn't really tell on her knowing that her dad might *seriously* hurt her. I couldn't do that to anyone. Could you?'

I shake my head. 'No, I don't think I could.'

Ruby's life suddenly looks SAD and BLEAK.

'She steals and hits people and bullies them,' Joe says, 'because she's never learned how to make friends or how to behave normally. How could she with a dad like *that*? Her mum cleared off ages ago. Last year she missed loads of school because of *mysterious injuries*.'

My thoughts are tangled up like ten-foot weeds.

Until now, I've never even wondered what Ruby's life might be like and I would NEVER have guessed that she went home every day to a violent ogre of a dad.

'Is that why Mrs Allen is so soft on her?' I ask. 'Does she know what Ruby's dad's like?'

Joe nods. 'Probably. She must *suspect* that someone hits her, and I'm sure Becky knows but Ruby won't talk to the teachers about it because she's so scared of him. But until she tells an adult no one can really do anything to help.'

Maybe I've been clever working out that Ruby's the thief, but I didn't work out what her BIG LIFE PROBLEM is, did I? Cordelia Codd, you are NOT as smart as you think.

Joe walks back through the village with me even though it's out of his way and he has a heavy wheelbarrow full of waterlogged salad to push. I get him to say goodbye before we reach my door so that Mum and Dad don't see him. He gives me a little hug and says, 'My offer is still open, by the way, but only for a little while. I like you a lot, Cordelia, but there are plenty more girls at Wellminster.'

I nod. 'Fair enough,' I say, although my BIG FAT EGO is a bit bruised by this. Isn't he supposed to be lovesick and brokenhearted for a few weeks, at least? I hate myself all over again for even THINKING such a thing.

'And,' he says, giving my shoulders a gentle little shake, 'Don't worry about Ruby. I'll still protect you from her if I'm needed.'

'Thanks, Joe.'

When I reach to the Jug and Monkey I glance back, hoping to give him a wave, but he's already rounded the curve in the road and is out of sight.

17

I write to Dru and remember to ask about HER stuff first, instead of blurting out all my own news. Is she still scooping up frogs, I wonder? Has her home returned to anything like normal?

There's no reply because it's only one o'clock in the afternoon here, which makes it about five in the morning over there.

Lunch is a quick sandwich and a bag of crisps because Mum and Dad are expecting a plumber. 'On SUNDAY! HONESTLY! Don't they have days off?' I ask as they scoff their cheese and pickle butties at ninety miles an hour.

'It's an emergency,' Mum explains. 'There's a leak in the pub toilets.'

I don't want to think about leaky toilets while I'm eating so I don't ask any more.

As soon as they've gone off to get ready for the plumber I go back on the computer. No one has told me that I can't because they are too concerned about leaky loos. Tomorrow is the first day of school and I have to talk to SOMEONE.

Dru is up now, even though it must still be SQUINTY-EYES time in Seattle.

★ **Dru** to Cordelia

The frogs are still around. I told my big sister Jess that she should kiss one and see if it turns into a handsome prince. I shouldn't have said that because she has this ugh-phobia thing about frogs and she threw up on the carpet.

★ **Cordelia** to Dru

Oh yuck! Poor Jess!

As promised, I have good news, but not quite the **HAPPY ENDING** I expected. Joe and I had a big talk **THIS VERY MORNING**. He wasn't angry, but I cried like a squeezed-out bath sponge.

★ **Dru** to Cordelia

I'm so proud of you I could burst! Well done!!
You're still friends, then?

★ **Cordelia** to Dru

Absolutely!

I tell Dru the whole, entire conversation that Joe and I had in the shed and about my ACCURATE deduction regarding the Liquorice Dibbles, and my not so brilliant realisation that Ruby has a HIDEOUS monster for a dad.

But I still can't help hating her until I'm ALL SHADES OF PURPLE because she's caused SO MUCH upset and HURT at the Scrap Project.

I've promised Joe I won't tell anyone. He says everyone deserves a second chance, and some people, like Ruby, need LOTS of chances because they're SO MESSED UP. If I was in charge the Ruby MacPhersons of this world wouldn't get ANY chances.

★ **Dru** to Cordelia

Thank goodness you're not Boss of the World!

I hope Ruby gets help with that nightmare dad, and quickly. No wonder her behaviour is WEIRD IN EVERY WAY.

I have to run. More frogs to catch.

Bye! xx

I am just writing Bye! when the computer goes
black and the lights go out.

♥

Mum and Dad have managed to bring Heckaby to a
COMPLETE standstill with a bit of dodgy wiring.
The electrician must have connected something
all wrong yesterday and when Mum plugged her
hairdryer in, PING! The power went out from here
to the far end of the high street.

It was the first time that Mum had taken a break
long enough to wash her hair in DAYS – she was
trying to grab a shower before the plumber arrived.

And I don't know HOW people in the village
KNOW that the problem started at our place but
they are PRACTICALLY QUEUING UP to
knock on the door and complain.

The first person to turn up is Mr Clench from the
Copper Kettle Tea Room. He is a podgy man who is
usually quite smiley, but not today. Today he looks
like a BIG FAT EXPLODING RASPBERRY
SPONGE CAKE!

'I can't make tea without a boiler,' he says,

sounding like a bit of a BOILER himself. Mum is on the doorstep apologising LIKE MAD, doing her best grovelling act and looking a bit of a mess with her hair only dry on one side. Then Mike from Mike's Bikes comes along, with Mr Akbar from the newsagent's.

'I've got no lights in the workshop,' says Mike. 'How long is it going to be?'

'We can't open the cash register without electricity,' says Mr Akbar. 'It's hopeless. What are you going to do?'

While Mum does her best to stop a riot breaking out Dad is on his mobile phone having a STRONG WORD with the electrician. He looks EXASPERATED.

When the power went off Dad was clearing stuff out of the cellar underneath the pub. The plumber was late and Dad complained that he 'might as well get on with something' while he's waiting. So he was already in a bad mood but now he's got an **ANGRY MOB** on the doorstep AND a hopeless electrician on the phone AND he's covered in black smudges of soot because the cellar used to be a coal store.

I stay at the top of the stairs, peeking down at all

this action. After a few minutes Dad comes off the phone and goes to the door to tell everyone that the electrician is in Wellminster and will be here in less than an hour.

'An **HOUR!**' they all shout, like this is **JUST NOT GOOD ENOUGH** and they will all die unless the electricity is fixed **IMMEDIATELY** by Dad waving a magic wand. HONESTLY, adults are so UNREASONABLE sometimes.

Dreaded Driscoll arrives, of course, with her finger pointing and her evil eye fixed on Mum. I see Mr Akbar, Mike and Mr Clench all take a step back as she gets closer, like she is FEARED BY ALL. She screeches at Mum. 'You're a bad lot, you are. You move in here, disrupting us with your dirty building work, and send your brat round to smash my eggs. You're bad news, you lot.'

Dad isn't having THAT. He steps forward and folds his arms across his chest. 'That's quite unnecessary, Mrs Driscoll,' he says in his I'm-just-about-controlling-my-temper sort of voice. 'We're trying to make an honest living and you don't seem to like change, that's all.'

'I don't like not being able to watch the telly on a Sunday afternoon is what I don't like,' Witchy

Driscoll shouts, 'and I don't like having to clean up the mess your brat makes of my shop, her and her *thieving friends*.'

Dad shows her the palm of his hand, gently but firmly. I can tell that he is REALLY STRUGGLING to keep his cool. 'That's enough, Mrs Driscoll. We'll go back inside now and sort this out as soon as possible. We can only apologise and promise we'll do our best to get things put right quickly. Now, if you'll all EXCUSE us. I'll send the electrician to each of you to make sure everything's OK.'

'And I'll make sure he sends you the bill,' shouts Mrs Driscoll. The others nod and grunt to show that they agree with her.

'Yes, yes, of course,' Dad says, trying to sound cheery. 'Don't worry about that. Goodbye.'

When he's closed the door Dad leans against it and gives a huge sigh. He runs his hands over his head. It's like rubbing a shaved tennis ball and I think he's forgotten that he's been down the sooty cellar because now he has black smears all over his face and his baldy patch.

♥

So now Mum and Dad have a bad reputation with most of the village. They've got into everyone's BAD BOOKS but it has nothing to do with me hanging out with Joe, it's because of a rubbish electrician.

I decide to get busy, to try to forget that the start of school is looming over me like a guillotine. Thinking about it will just get me into a TSUNAMI-SIZED PANIC so, when the queue of complainers has left, I find a torch and start rummaging in the outhouses for useful stuff. It's still daylight but the clouds make it gloomy and there are some dark, spidery corners in the outhouses that I want to avoid. I spot a few wooden crates like the ones Janna and Emmy used to make their bookshelves and I want DESPERATELY to rescue them for my new bedroom.

We have three little outhouses joined together. They are built of red bricks with proper tiled roofs and concrete floors so they are good, dry spaces for storing things. Eventually, we're going to use them to keep the big freezers in for the restaurant and to store cleaning equipment, big tins of olive oil and tomatoes and all sorts of stuff that there isn't space for inside. The last outhouse in the row is having a new concrete floor put in because the old one cracked and weeds grew up through it. The builders poured the new cement yesterday and I've been given STRICT INSTRUCTIONS not to go ANYWHERE near it because it will take at least two days to set properly. The middle outhouse is empty and clean but the first one, where I'm searching, is still piled high with junk that is heading for the skip. Dad says it is all going to be thrown out tomorrow so I have to be SNAPPITY-QUICK about it if I want to rescue useful bits and pieces.

I've already pulled out two crates and put them down in the yard when I see little Mina wandering in through our gate. She's on one of her 'strolls'. I'll just finish pulling out the next crate and then I'll take her home. If I get Mina back safely Mr Akbar might not be so cross with Mum and Dad about the electricity. Mina noses around outside Dad's caravan and then toddles over to see what I'm doing.

'Hi Mina,' I call.

I keep chatting to her so that she knows I've seen her and maybe she won't scream so much when I try to take her home. At the same time, I am tugging on a car tyre that is in the way of an old lawnmower, that is in the way of a tin bucket, that is in the way of those lovely, perfect wooden crates that I am DETERMINED to rescue for my bedroom.

'You look very nice today, Mina. Is that a new dress?' I ask her, half turning to look at her and half concentrating on pulling the tyre out of the way.

Mina nods and strokes the front of her marzipan-yellow sequinned dress.

'Are you going somewhere special?' I ask, as I lift the rusty lawnmower out of the way. I am SO nearly there. I can almost reach the crates. Mina grins.

'Wedding,' she says.

'Oh, lovely,' I reply. Not that I really think weddings are PARTICULARLY lovely, I am just trying to keep her attention. I've been to LOTS of weddings and they're mostly ALL THE SAME. You get thrown together with kids who are much younger than you who you don't know AT ALL but are APPARENTLY related to you in some distant way, and you're expected to get along with them and ENTERTAIN each other. DISMAL.

I've moved the tyre and the lawnmower and the bucket and I have a good grip on one of the crates now. I need to lean across an old bicycle frame but I KNOW I can lift the crate over if I just

CONCENTRATE for a moment…and THAT'S when it happens.

I hear a dull SPLAPPING sort of sound, then there's a tiny pause, then an **ALMIGHTY SCREAM**. I drop the crate and run to the last outhouse. Mina has fallen face down into the wet cement. It looks like she's tried to get up but has slipped again and rolled over. She is fully coated, like a big blob of marzipan, in dark grey half-set concrete. **HOW** am I going to explain **THIS?** I lean into the outhouse, grab her hand and pull her out of the gloop. It makes a loud sucking sound. We have to hurry through the yard and along the high street to the newsagent's because I don't want her to set hard before her parents can get her dress off and clean her up – but she HOWLS all the way.

The shop bell PONG-PINGS when I go in. Mr Akbar opens the door to the sitting room behind the counter. Loads of Mina's family are in there. They are all dressed in their best wedding clothes and are chattering away happily. Mr Akbar's eyes nearly pop out when he sees Mina, then his voice goes up like a lion roaring. Mina is still sobbing and now she's dripping cement onto the shop floor. She points at me.

'She push…push me,' she says between big gulps of air.

WHAT a little traitor! I will never trust a toddler again! They are sophisticated and **TREACHEROUS** under their angelic faces.

'Oh no!' I say, very quickly and quite loudly, pointing back at her. 'You fell, I didn't push you.'

But Mina screams. 'SHE PUSH, SHE PUSH!'

By this time the whole family are up and in the shop, staring at Mina. Mrs Akbar shoves her way through, sees the mess Mina is in and claps her hand over her mouth in horror before having a good old yell at me.

'What have you done? Why did you do this to her?!' she yells.

I start trying to explain. 'She just wandered into the yard…' I say, but no one is listening. The whole family are gasping and shouting at me and being GENERALLY DRAMATIC. Mrs Akbar looks like her head is going to go KA-BOOM! with stress, so I run out of the shop and back home. They probably already think that I am some kind of GANGSTER for hanging out with Joe, and that my parents are deliberately sabotaging their power supply, and now they think I've done this to their baby daughter.

223

I JUST KNOW that the gossip will be all over
Heckaby in less than an hour. I can almost hear it –
'THAT TERRIBLE GIRL pushed poor little Mina
into some cement! They're a dreadful family!'

The electricity isn't back on until almost bedtime.
The Akbars must've cleaned Mina up and gone off
to their wedding because none of them come round
that night to tell my parents the BRUTAL thing I've
APPARENTLY done to their little angel-child.

This should give me a chance to tell Mum and
Dad what REALLY happened before the Akbars
get to them, but they are so busy arguing with the
electrician and then deciding what they want the
builders to do on Monday morning, and agreeing
which bills should be paid first and which left until
later that I can't get A WORD IN EDGEWAYS,
not even at dinner time.

I finish rescuing the crates and put them all in
the big empty space that will be my new bedroom
and try not to think about Mina, or about the whole
village believing we are some sort of criminal family.

At least I'm friends with Joe again, but now I

have to keep the DARK AND COMPLICATED SECRET about Ruby's dad.

I NEED to tell Dru what's happened, even though I've promised not to dump my troubles on her again. I tell her about Mina and the cement and I can't keep off the subject of school.

★ **Cordelia** to Dru

...I've got the creeping terrors **CRAWLING** all over me about tomorrow. Just because I know **WHY** Ruby's being **DERANGED** doesn't mean she's going to stop being that way, does it? She'll be waiting for me tomorrow!!

★ **Dru** to Cordelia

TELL SOMEONE who can do something about it. Joe is really sweet for trying to protect her but you have to protect yourself, too. Meanwhile, remember that you are going to be **THE GREATEST COSTUME DESIGNER IN THE HISTORY OF CINEMA.** One day in the not-too-distant future you will be seeing your fantastic costumes on the screen and Ruby will be

F...O...R...G...O...T...T...E...N.

That's option one.

Option two is:

Ruby keeps making you miserable. You lose your confidence and your friends and are so scared of going to school that you flunk everything and never get to be any kind of designer or anything. You end up flipping burgers for a living and marry a boring man and have boring children and eventually, tragically die of boredom and disappointment. You choose.

★ **Cordelia** to Dru

You're right **AGAIN**. I can't live without you. Don't ever go off the radar.

★ **Dru** to Cordelia

No chance of that but tomorrow we're going to Aunt Zillah's.

And mysteriously, our frogs have disappeared. I hope they don't move back in while we're away or Jess will probably move out.

ALSO I'm being sent on a science camp
for geeks after we've been to Aunt
Zillah's. Jess gets to stay longer
than me by her pool. I feel a BIG
protest coming on.

★ **Cordelia** to Dru

A pool! Bliss!! We just have puddles! Have a
good time!

Love ya!! xx

A good telling off from Dru always cheers me up.
It gives me a little burst of energy so, up in my not-
quite-ready-bedroom, I stack the crates against one
wall, then another wall, then another, until I've tried
them EVERY POSSIBLE way. I arrange them on
top of one another, then next to each other, then
back on top of each other again until, eventually, I've
decided how I want them. Next, I take them back
out to the yard, borrow some work gloves and heavy
sandpaper from a pile that Dad has left down in the
hall and sand and sand and SAND the crates like a
mad girl until well after anything like bedtime. I put
all my anger and upset into it. It's great therapy.

There is a good side to having parents who are

227

too busy to notice that you haven't gone to bed – even when it's the day before school starts. You can sometimes stay up for HOURS doing strange, obsessive things, like sanding down wooden crates until your arms are about to drop off and you collapse into bed, EXHAUSTED, which is exactly what I do.

When it's very late I creep back to my tiny bedroom in the cottage, past the kitchen where Mum and Dad are shuffling papers. They jump when I stick my head round the door and say goodnight.

'Oh, my goodness, Coco. Are you still up?' says Mum, looking at the clock.

'Most parents check,' I say, to make a POINT.

Mum and Dad look at each other then make a big fuss about apologising and giving me extra big hugs. They don't seem to notice that I'm covered in sawdust.

'Big day tomorrow,' says Dad.

'You have NO idea,' I say.

My school bag is packed. I have my sports kit ready, too, and my uniform is now in my bedroom, hanging on the back of the door – still looking like a corpse.

I find a big piece of drawing paper and a fat felt pen and write my BIG LIFE VISION again:

I am going to be
the **greatest** costume designer
in the history of cinema!

I stick it to the wall opposite the end of my bed with sticky tape, which I'm not supposed to do because of the wallpaper but it IS an emergency, then I hop back under the covers and lie, staring at it. The streetlight outside shines onto it through a crack in the curtain.

By reminding myself of what I am aiming for in the future, all the troubles I have right now look a TINY bit smaller. I fall asleep remembering what Dru told me. 'One day Ruby will be

f...o...r...g...o...t...t...e...n.'

18

But **OH MY GRIM GODFATHERS**, she isn't
f...o...r...g...o...t...t...e...n
in the morning!

When I wake up, as if the **COLD FEAR** wasn't
bad enough, my arms ache and my hair is stiff with
sawdust from all the sanding I did last night.

I drag myself out of bed and have a quick shower.
Downstairs, it seems Mum has been up for hours.
She is bouncy and cheery and her jabbering gives
me a headache. I feel too sick to eat breakfast.
That's two breakfasts I haven't eaten. I NEVER
miss breakfast so I know this is probably **TERMINAL
TERROR** setting in. I keep trying to think ONLY
about good things, like my Scrap Project skirt and
how good it looks. Then I try to think about the
beautiful costumes in *Gone with the Wind* and any
film I can remember just to keep LOVELINESS in
my head instead of the MEGA-UGLY day that is
waiting for me.

Mum is so happy to have the electricity on again and so nervous and excited about getting me off to school (and out of the way) that she is oblivious to my LESS THAN CHEERFUL expression. I TRY to think of a way to tell her that I am PROBABLY going to die in my first week but when she's in one of these BUBBLESOME MORNING MOODS she just talks and talks all chirpily and doesn't listen. It usually means that she's drunk too much coffee.

Mum is interrupted by the doorbell. She must know who it is because she gives me her don't-argue-with-me look and says, 'Stay in here, please, Coco.'

Further DOLLOPS OF DREAD fall on me like cowpats when I hear Mrs Akbar's voice.

'Could you please keep control of your daughter as there was an incident with little Mina yesterday.'

'Her daughter' means me, of course. Should I go to the doorstep and stand in front of Mrs Akbar with my arms folded giving her a HARD LOOK that says, 'WE BOTH KNOW IT WASN'T MY FAULT'?

If I had more energy I would, despite Mum telling me to stay put. Instead, I listen and let my temper **RISE TO BOILING POINT** as I **TRY** to choke down some of my cereal.

Mum is doing her grovelling act again. 'Oh, I see, well, I'll certainly have a word with Cordelia. I'm sorry if she caused you any bother.'

Mrs Akbar whines and tuts. 'Mina's dress is ruined.'

I send a telepathic message to Mum's brain. **DON'T** you **DARE** offer to replace it!

'Well, of course,' Mum says, ever-so-politely, 'if it was Cordelia's fault, she'll replace it out of her own pocket money.'

WHAT?! I am **SO** tempted to go to the door and **SHOUT**. My self-control at this point is **IMPRESSIVE**.

'I should think so,' says Mrs Akbar, 'and please make sure your gate is locked. Anyone could wander in.'

'Yes, of course. I'm so sorry about that,' says Mum.

Mum comes back into the kitchen and sees my **HORRIFIED** face. My cereal is now just a stiff gloop in the bowl.

'**MUM!** What are you **DOING?**'

She puts a finger to her lips. 'I know, I know, I know all about it. Lily from the chip shop saw you trying to help Mina yesterday. She called by when you were still asleep this morning to warn me that there might be trouble. I *know* you didn't do it, I'm just trying to keep the neighbours sweet.'

'Then you're being a **COWARD**,' I say. 'And what d'you **MEAN**, I'll replace it with my pocket money? I'll throw myself into a pit of snakes before I'll do that.'

'Mrs Akbar knows *perfectly well* that it wasn't your fault,' Mum says. 'She just needs to blame someone. Let it go, Coco.'

LET IT GO?

LET IT GO.

Where have I heard that before?

'Someone should tell her to look after Mina properly,' I snap back.

'Mrs Akbar does her best,' Mum explains, 'but Mina would be a handful for anyone.'

'**SO!** Does that mean I should let people accuse me of things I haven't done?' I say. 'Is that **LETTING IT GO?** Because, if it is, I'm not playing that game.'

Mum sits down and pours me some juice. 'No, Coco, that's absolutely *not* what I'm saying you should do. We just don't want to have any more conflict with the neighbours at the moment, not after the electricity business. If I'm going to get planning permission for the cinema I can't go upsetting people. They could all write to the council and get the cinema stopped, you know?' She clicks her fingers. 'Just like that.'

Yes, I do know. I know that the cinema is Mum's BIG DREAM PROJECT.

'And, anyway,' she says. 'It sounds like Lily from the chip shop likes us, even if no one else does.'

'Lily is sticking up for us,' I point out, 'despite what the gossips in the village are saying, just like I'm sticking up for Joe despite what you believe about him.'

Mum sighs and gives me a look that means, 'That's different and we won't discuss it now.' But I know I've scored a BIG FAT point for Joe.

Mum takes me to school because it's the first proper day and because she has to go to the DIY shop in Wellminster, anyway, so she's driving that way.

I slouch down in the front seat and peek out of the window. All the school kids I see are wearing the same white, short-sleeved shirt and black trousers as me. Most of them have their blue sweatshirts tied around their middles because the weather is still too warm and sticky to put them on properly. There are all sorts of kids, every shape and size and skin colour. Some have sticky-up hairstyles, others have scraped-back ponytails. Some of the boys have long, straggly hair, and some have it almost shaved. Some kids have backpacks, others are carrying dazzly, bling-covered handbags. Most of them are wearing trainers but a few have Doc Martens, and some are ACTUALLY tottering to school on clacky high heels – I bet THAT'S against the rules! But the thing I notice most is that they ALL look like they've got loads of friends, and I HAVEN'T.

Mum is chattering like a budgie and now the rain is starting again and there's the HIDEOUS screechy-squeak of the windscreen wipers to put up with as well – they're scraping from side to side, like fingernails scratching on metal. I slap my hands over my ears and close my eyes, wishing that I could fall asleep and wake up somewhere else, ANYWHERE else, even the middle of a desert or a jungle full of creepy-crawlies.

The kids outside start hunching up against the rain. Some pull waterproofs on. A few have brollies. Brightly coloured umbrellas are the ONLY cheerful thing about this dismal morning.

We're getting really close to school now. I TRY to tell myself that I will probably make at least TWO

new friends by the end of the day and that I'll feel
COMPLETELY differently about my life by home
time, but when Mum drops me near the gates and
drives off with a quick wave all I feel is that this is

THE END

FINIS

FIN

as they say in films.

I have a letter from the school in my pocket that
says Years 7, 8 and 9 should all gather in the Main
Hall. There are signposts to it so it's easy to find. At
the door to the hall a friendly lady with glasses on
a chain round her neck asks me my name and year.
She ticks me off a list and then shows me which row
to sit in. I'm one of the early ones (Mum's timing).
The hall fills up around me. I see Joe and want to
wave to him but I don't want to embarrass him in
front of his mates, so I don't. My tummy turns over
when Ruby comes in and sits at the end of the row
behind me. I don't think she spots me and I slide
down in my chair a bit to try and be less visible.
I keep very still, listening to everyone chattering

and finding their friends. When the hall is full, Mr
Okenden, the headteacher, welcomes us and says the
usual headteacher-ish things about working hard and
being proud of our school. Then we have to go off
and find our tutor groups. I wait until Ruby has gone
before I set off.

Wellminster looks different when it's crawling
with kids, like a massive anthill. The letter tells
me which registration group and room to go to.
I find it easily enough because there are signposts
everywhere. I shuffle up the concrete stairs next to
the hall behind lots of other kids, and along the wide
top corridor.

Room 2b is a bog-standard classroom with lots
of tables for two people, all facing the front. The
window at the side looks out over the muddy sports
field. I sit halfway back and watch quietly as the
chairs are taken.

The seat next to mine stays empty and I suppose I
should've guessed it would happen – in walks Ruby,
looking like she's ready to FIGHT her way through
the first term. Becky comes in after her with two other
girls. They must be her proper friends because she sits
with them and doesn't go anywhere near Ruby.

Ruby walks straight up to me and stands right

next to my table. I pretend to be looking in my bag for something. My fingers are trembling a bit. She stays by my table until I can't pretend to search in my bag any longer and I have to look up. She just gives me an EVIL GRIN to let me know that she still has BUSINESS with me and then moves to a table at the back.

I know it's STEREOTYPING but why ARE the kids who sit at the back ALWAYS the ones who either want trouble, or a good sleep, or to spend the lesson sending text messages? If they knew what a cliché they are, maybe they'd do something different.

I'm glad Ruby sits where I can't see her because, if I concentrate on what the teacher is saying, I can forget – for a few seconds at a time – that she's in the room.

Our form tutor is Mr Carter – the same Mr Carter who helped at the Scrap Project. At least I THINK it's the same man but he's a lot more old-fashioned and scary-looking in term-time, with his grey jacket and tie. He doesn't say, 'Hello,' and he COMPLETELY ignores any kids who come in late.

'I'm going to call the register,' he says at last. 'Answer when you hear your name. You should be listening to me and nothing else.'

Mr Carter doesn't look up and he doesn't give anyone a second chance if they don't answer right away, he just growls, '*Too slow*, you're marked late.' At the end of the register he just says, 'If you *arrived* late or weren't *listening* then you are *marked* late. No excuses. I'm *now* going to give you a *timetable*. The *timetable* will *vary* for some of you so *listen* for variations. I will *also* give you a *homework* diary. Do *not* lose *either* of these.'

I write my name on my homework diary, which is a DEEPLY UNINTERESTING shade of grey, and look very closely at the timetable. This is just a calendar printed off a computer on a sheet of white paper.

Mr Carter: this new, strange, unrecognisable, Mr Carter – or perhaps it's his STRICT ROBOT TWIN – is speaking again and I DAREN'T miss anything.

'The timetable will *begin* with the *first* lesson today. *Look* at your timetables *now* and work out *what* you will be doing and *where* you will be doing it. Aled Coombes? Tell me where you will be.'

A skinny boy in the row next to mine is looking frantically at his timetable. I can feel his panic. It makes my own heart thump. 'Erm…erm…

ur…where am I?' he mumbles. 'Sorry, got it, yes, English in room 2S.'

Mr Carter doesn't say whether he's right or not but moves on. 'Alice Fong?'

Alice is on the front row. She looks nervous and pushes her glasses up the bridge of her nose. 'Also English, but in 2T,' she says quickly.

Mr Carter swings round and points to a very tall boy with the worst case of spots I've ever seen. 'Jamie McCallister?'

Jamie dithers a bit. The room is TENSE as we all wait for him to be shouted at. His answer isn't very confident and comes out as a question. 'Um…let me see, err…Physics in 2W?'

Mr Carter looks disgusted. '*Physics?!* No, boy. If you have **Physics** on a **Monday** then you have the timetable *upside down.* Turn it around, turn it *around*, for heaven's sake!'

Jamie does a bit of a twizzle with his paper. 'Sorry, yes, err…oh, English in 2T, like Alice.'

Several voices in the class make an 'oooooh' sound and I hear Ruby say, 'Just like Alice! How sweeeeet!'

She says this out loud, which means that she's either very brave or VERY stupid. I wait for Mr

Carter to explode in her direction, but he doesn't, he ignores her. He ignores all the other *oooohs* in the room, too. This seems to be how Mr Carter deals with TWITS – he just ignores them, they are BENEATH HIS RADAR, unworthy of attention. He sails over them like a big old-fashioned ship floating over little fish. I hope I'm nowhere near when he starts firing his cannons!

'Right. You should all understand the timetable now,' Mr Carter says, but quite a few kids are scratching their heads. 'English for *everyone* this morning. You will mostly be doing the same subjects at the same time, but in different groups. This is *nothing,* I repeat, *nothing* to do with ability. You will be re-grouped on results later in the year. Any questions?'

As if anyone would DARE ask.

I've got English, like everyone else, and I'm in 2T. From my timetable I can see that English is followed by History in 2F, then a library period after lunch, followed by games. THANK GOODNESS I brought my sports kit.

Mr Carter gives out a map of the school, saying, 'This is just in case any of you are new, or have *lost* your sense of direction in the holidays.'

Is THAT all the help new kids get here? Mr Carter tells us all to make our way to our first lesson and be back here for afternoon registration at 1.15 *PROMPT.* I hope the signposts are good or some of us may never be seen again.

I'm just about to dive for the corridor to put as much distance between myself and Ruby as possible when he calls, 'Ruby, Becky, Cordelia. *See me* for a moment before you go…'

So I have to hang around and stand RIGHT next to her.

'You three are all involved in the Scrap Project, aren't you?' says Mr Carter, looking over his glasses at us.

We all nod.

'You can go to the art room at lunchtimes until *Thursday*, remember. I think Mrs Allen has told you already but she has asked me to *remind* you. So, if you have any finishing touches to do, *that's* the time. That's all I had to tell you.' He waves us away like flies. 'Off you go…oh, and good luck.'

I mutter a 'thank you' to Mr Carter and dash for the corridor. I keep moving quickly and make it to the next room safely. Phew!

19

Ruby doesn't come in to my English group –
JUBILATION! – but Becky does, and she sits
next to a smiley, plump girl whose name I don't
know. Alice Fong sits with someone who is
obviously her best mate because they are chatting
and giggling, and I'm left with an empty space
again, until a girl with long dark hair who doesn't
speak sits next to me. She looks MAJORLY
MISERABLE. I smile and say, 'Hi.' She just grunts.
This is all the conversation I can get out of her.
I can't be bothered trying to make friends with
DEPRESSING people so I decide to ignore her
and she ignores me. How am I going to make new
friends if I only get LEFTOVER people to sit
next to?

Our proper English teacher isn't here. How can
a teacher NOT be there on the first day of term?!
The stand-in teacher is Miss Wallcott. She explains
that Mr Gurniman, our REAL English teacher, has

got delayed at an airport in the Far East because of 'an unexpected adventure' and will be back in a couple of days.

'Will he be on the news, Miss?' asks tall, spotty Jamie who had his timetable upside down.

'Gosh! I hope not,' says Miss Wallcott, with a little smile. One of the boys whistles from the back of the room. Miss Wallcott looks about the same age as Dru's big sister, Jess, who is nineteen, but I suppose she must be quite a lot more than that. I think she's a tiny bit scared of us but she's so sweet and pretty-looking that most of the boys behave well and go pink when she asks them a question. It's like she's cast some sort of SPOOKY SPELL on the class.

We start reading *Carrie's War* by Nina Bawden, taking it in turns to read out loud. Even though it's a story told by a girl, the whole class, boys included, are completely gripped by the end of the lesson. The story really makes you think about how families got split up and messed about during the Second World War and how hard it was for kids who were evacuated to the countryside because they had to go and live with people they didn't know and who weren't always kind to them.

Thanks to Miss Wallcott, lunchtime arrives quickly, then I race to the art room to check on my costume. Joe arrives a little while after me, smiling, and asks how I'm getting on.

'OK so far,' I say, but my voice sounds a bit tight and squeaky because I'm nothing LIKE relaxed. I'm SO glad he got to the art room before Ruby. Joe nods at my work, which is still hanging on Griselda where I left it on Saturday.

'Will you get finished by Thursday?' he asks.

'Yes, I think so,' I say, stroking the skirt and inspecting it closely. 'I've just got to go around and sew the hem up, then iron it. It's a long way around the hemline though, about four metres of little stitches by hand, so I've got to hurry up.'

There's just the two of us in the art room for a while. Joe is still mounting his diagrams and photos onto a display board because, of course, he can't bring a whole greenhouse made from a bunk bed all the way to school. Everyone else has nearly finished their projects.

Becky's armour looks amazing, Lennox's cushions are SUMPTUOUS and Gregor's lampshades are OUTRAGEOUSLY ARTY. Janna and Emmy's bookcases are SHINY and BRIGHT and SMOOTH – they've even put some books on them to show how well they work. Ruby's necklace isn't quite finished but it looks like she only has to mount it onto a board that she's covered with black velvet. That means she could be here any minute, which spoils the lovely feeling of peace and quiet as Joe and I get on with our work quietly and nibble our lunches.

We aren't really supposed to eat in the art room but we hide our sandwiches as soon as Mrs Allen pops in, waving and smiling and 'helloooing' to us. Ruby is right behind her, helping to carry boxes of craft materials. WHAT A CREEP! Ruby looks at Joe, then at me and obviously doesn't like the idea that we've been in here working peacefully and happily together because her face drops like a bag of pebbles. One second she's wearing a goody-goody grin for Mrs Allen, the next it's a vicious scowl directed straight at me. At least she won't ATTACK while Mrs Allen AND Joe are in the room.

That first lunchtime works out OK because Ruby doesn't take long to finish her work. I hear her telling Mrs Allen that she is going off to talk to someone about the netball team. I can't IMAGINE her playing in ANY kind of team. Team sports involve getting along with other people so I just can't see her managing THAT.

Before I know it, it's time to go for afternoon registration and I'm about a third of the way around the hemline with my tiniest stitches. I think I'm on target to be finished by Thursday as long as nothing holds me back and I CONCENTRATE.

Mr Carter takes the afternoon register. Then Miss Wallcott comes in. Perhaps we're ALL getting a bit of a crush on her because everyone looks at her gooey-eyed, like she's a beautiful bunch of flowers, or a new puppy. Next to her, Mr Carter looks like a piece of old wooden furniture with creaky hinges. Even he seems to be under her spooky spell though because he isn't nearly so grumpy with us as he was in the morning.

Ruby is sitting way behind me again and I'm doing quite a good job of pretending she's not there. In fact, I begin to wonder if she's lost interest in me until something HARD hits the back of my head. It stings – REALLY stings. I let out a little 'ouch' and put my hand on the place where it hit, just behind my ear. When I check, there's a dab of blood on my hand. I look down I see a sharp little stone on the floor under the next row of desks. I'm **NOT** going to turn around. I am **NOT** going to let her see that my face is screwed up with the pain. I get a paper hanky from my bag and hold it on the place that's cut. Do I tell someone now? Do I pick up that pebble and take my blood-spotted hanky to show Mr Carter and Miss Wallcott? But how can I PROVE that Ruby threw it? I bottle the anger up inside me again and tell myself that she's just a girl with a dad who beats the stuffing out of her, that she's frightened and MESSED UP INSIDE, but that doesn't stop her being a bully and a cheat and a liar, does it? It doesn't make me want to say, 'Poor Ruby, she can't help it.' I still hate her until I'm *CRIMSON AND SCARLET WITH RAGE*.

For the library session Miss Wallcott separates us into two groups. I'm in Group 1. Ruby and Becky are both in Group 2. Oh JOY! Miss Wallcott takes half the class at a time to see the new library. My group is the first to go with her. It includes Alice, Jamie and Aled.

The 'new' library is in a temporary classroom. Most schools seem to have these. They're very boring-looking buildings, like boxes with windows. This one seems to have been dropped in a forgotten corner of the school grounds, beyond the sports block and across the yard where the bins are kept. Weeds and tree roots are growing up through cracks in the tarmac here and I can hear the rattle of pans and chatter of voices coming from the school kitchen nearby.

From the outside the new library looks PRETTY DISAPPOINTING but inside it's ANOTHER WORLD. There are rows and rows of old wooden shelves and big, circular tables with books spread out on them. MASSIVE vases sit at the centre of the tables, filled with giant silk poppies. There are comfortable old chairs with tasselled cushions to sit on. The walls are covered with maps and star charts and posters that explain things like the insides of volcanoes and the parts of skeletons. The windows have green blinds that can be pulled down with a cord and, best of all, right in the middle of the floor, there's an old-fashioned black stove with a chimney pipe that goes all the way up and out through the roof. It has a metal guard around it and a circle of big leather armchairs. We all sit down on these and point our toes towards the stove, pretending to warm them because it's not cold enough to light it yet.

'Is it a museum?' asks the plump girl who was sitting with Becky earlier. Her name is Penny.

Miss Wallcott gives a little laugh. 'No. A lot of the things are quite old but it's a proper library for you to use.'

'Where did you get all this old stuff?' asks Penny.

'Well,' says Miss Wallcott. 'The school was given some money by a very generous lady who lives in Wellminster. She was sad to see the old library in town close down and asked us to help her save some of its contents. We came up with the idea of creating a quiet space for the students at Wellminster to read or do their homework in peace.'

Brilliant, I think to myself. It's a recycled library! It's 'tatting' on a GRAND scale. I wonder if Joe has seen it yet.

'Kids will wreck it, Miss,' says Aled, screwing his face up. 'They'll nick the books and scratch the tables.'

'Shut up, Aled,' says Jamie, looking irritated. 'It's a good idea. I want to know when it's going to open. I need a place to get some brain-rest.'

'It'll be open after school for a couple of hours, Monday to Thursday,' says Miss Wallcott, 'starting next week.'

She steps across and puts a hand on the big, flat wooden counter. 'When you arrive, anything you have that makes a noise: music players, phones, any gadgets *at all*, get put in a plastic bag with your name on it and stored in a locker for you. This is a *gadget free zone*. No phone calls, no web browsing, no music, no gizmos of any kind.'

'What's the point of that?' says Aled, looking a bit panicked, as if it would be like having his entire brain unplugged.

'Shut up, Aled,' say several kids at once this time.

The idea of peace and quiet is VERY appealing to young people, despite what grown-ups might think. It means that we can get away from nagging parents and obnoxious brothers and sisters if we're unlucky enough to have them or, in my case, noisy builders.

'It's like a place for head space, isn't it, Miss?' says Penny.

'Exactly,' says Miss Wallcott.

'That's what you should call it, Miss,' says a girl at the back. 'The Head Space, not the library.'

Miss Walcott's eyes light up. 'Brilliant idea, Jamila, I'll suggest that to the committee.'

We're given a task to do to help us find our way

around. We have to find a book that we think looks interesting and look at it for a while, trying out the chairs and tables and lamps. Then we tell someone a little bit about why we chose our book using VERY QUIET VOICES, and they tell us about theirs. After this we swap and put the other person's book back in EXACTLY the right place by looking at the little numbers on the spine and matching them to the numbers on the shelves. I am paired with Aled.

'This is a graphic novel about James Bond when he was still at school,' Aled tells me. He needs to practise his LIBRARY WHISPER because his voice is quite loud.

I flick through it. It's like a thick comic. I like the way it looks, loads of exciting pictures. I've never read a graphic novel before and I make a mental note to investigate them.

'What's yours, then?' he asks, in a properly quiet voice this time, but not very enthusiastically.

'Costumes. I like costumes.' I know my face lights up like I'm a costume-geek (is there such a thing?) but I don't care. 'That's what I'm going to do when I leave school.'

'What? Sewing and stuff?' is all Aled can say.

'Yes, well…' I get ready to educate him, in a

whisper, about costumes. I give a little cough. 'You have to design the costumes first but you can't do that until you've researched them. Then you have to create patterns and find the right fabrics, too. It's not just sewing.'

Aled yawns without covering his mouth. He's got a really big mouth. 'Oh, right,' he says, when his yawn eventually finishes. Clearly, Aled has no interest in costumes. Never mind! We're all different, I SUPPOSE.

I take Aled's spy-boy book and find the right place to put it on the shelves marked FICTION A-Z by AUTHOR. Penny is nearby, sliding Jamila's book back into place. She notices me and looks around before whispering, 'I can't speak to you. Ruby says no one's allowed to be your friend, but you seem really nice to me. Everyone **HATES** Ruby.'

And she scuttles back to the group that is gathering near the counter. Ruby is stopping me from making friends with **ANYONE**. How **DARE** she try to **CONTROL MY LIFE** and how am I **EVER** going to shift this **RUBY BLOCKAGE?**

20

The next lesson is games. As soon as I walk into the changing room and set eyes on Miss Brudge I have a terrible feeling that we're going to be taken out to do some sort of military-style-fitness-circuit-training. She looks as strong as a tank and like she might eat bullets for breakfast but she has VERY clear skin and long shiny hair – I guess from being so healthy and sporty. Her thick, brown ponytail isn't a high, bouncy one. Instead, it's caught in an elastic at the back of her neck, so it doesn't move much. And, yes, she's REALLY, HONESTLY called Miss Brudge, which is somewhere between Fridge and Budge and which has GOT to win the UGLY NAME OF THE CENTURY AWARD.

When I've finished changing and stuffed my clothes into a locker I look down to check the laces on my trainers – I had to use bits of wormy old string that are COMPLETELY different lengths.

Going for an FW (Final Wee) halfway through

changing for games was a BAD MISTAKE. Never leave your games kit unattended. When I came back and went to put my trainers on, the laces had gone. Naturally, I couldn't prove who'd taken them. I explained to Miss Brudge that they 'seemed to be missing' and asked politely if she had any spares I could borrow.

'I see' she said, her dark, beady eyes laser-beaming around the changing room like a spy in one of Aled's books. She obviously knew that laces don't fall out ON THEIR OWN and was scanning the changing room for evidence.

Ruby was already in her immaculate pale blue kit, looking angelic and keen to go outside and be sporty. Pale blue! HONESTLY! What a STUPID colour for games kit. It always gets mucky and sweaty, doesn't it? Chocolate brown would be better, or bottle green. Why don't grown-ups think these things through?

Anyway, after detecting nothing with her X-ray vision, Miss Brudge reached into a big drawer in a desk near the door. The drawer was bursting with lost property. There were so many hair elastics and slides and mobile phones and belts and lip balms in that drawer that she could've opened a small shop.

She pulled out two conkers on strings, then took a big pair of scissors that looked like you could shear a sheep with them and snipped the strings off the conkers.

'There you go. Make do with those for now,' was all she said, and handed the shrivelled strings to me.

So now I'm trotting out towards the field, which is soggy from all the rain, and I'm praying that she doesn't make us actually go ON the grass or we'll all sink like the Titanic. I'm very conscious of the tatty strings in my trainers. One is JUST long enough to tie in a bow and the other is trailing on the ground. This is NOT a stylish look. Being humiliated by Ruby like this is almost **WORSE** than getting a good slap in the face. I'm just thinking that I'm doing very well at controlling my need for revenge when she jogs past me in her expensive-looking running shoes and says, 'Not got enough money for laces, Cordelia? What a shame!'

We are told to warm up by running along the length of the playing field but THANKFULLY to stay off the grass, which Miss Brudge describes in a shouty voice as a *'QUAGMIRE'*. Good word, QUAGMIRE. I must write it down. We have to jog all the way along to the metal fence where the school grounds end and then back to where she's standing. Girls and boys have to go together.

A few super-sporty kids sprint off ahead. A lot of the boys hang behind the slower girls, probably to get a look at our bums in our games shorts. I don't like this feeling AT ALL and the boys make some very rude comments. Most of the boys have got scrawny legs like canaries, and some have got pretty lardy backsides, so I don't think they should be saying ANYTHING about the girls' legs and bums. Some of the girls shout things back but we all keep jogging and puffing along because if Miss Brudge tells you to *'KEEP MOVING'*, you don't dare stand still. When my group – about twenty-five of the NORMAL and STRAGGLER-SPEED kids – is halfway along the length of the field, the SPORTY SPRINTERS are already on their way back and whizz past us.

Ruby jogs at the front of our big group, clearly quite happy to show off her backside to everyone behind her. Seeing her prancing along makes me hate her even more. There's a HUGE puddle coming up on her left, at the edge of the QUAGMIRE. I find an extra burst of energy and catch up with her because I'm not SUCH a bad runner when I can be bothered to try. She's so surprised to see me right alongside her that she doesn't have time to react before I shove her sideways. She *squelches* into the big puddle but the mud underneath it is deeper and more slippery than I imagined and she skids straight over onto her bum, so hard that her head flies back and even her HAIR goes into the *squish*. Her games kit doesn't look so immaculate now. But, **OH CORDELIA, YOU TWIT!** What will Joe think of that? I've done **EXACTLY** the wrong thing, I've let the spiky red demon get control of me again, and now the war will just go **ON AND ON**, won't it?

Ruby doesn't get on the bus that evening, which is a relief. I don't know how she is getting home and, of course, I don't **CARE**.

I sit with Joe and confess what I did to Ruby. It feels best to do this straight away because I don't want him to find out from someone else, like last time.

IMMEDIATELY, I regret telling him because he's **FURIOUS** with me, even though I tell him about her throwing the sharp pebble at the back of my head and stealing my laces and about Penny telling me that no one is allowed to speak to me **BY ORDER OF RUBY**.

'Look,' I say, feeling more than a little bit **MIFFED** myself, by now. 'I know all that stuff with Ruby's dad is **HIDEOUS** but I'm not going to let her make my life Hell any longer. Why should she spread her misery around?'

'I keep telling you to just keep away from her and she won't bother you,' Joe insists.

I'm getting **SERIOUSLY CROSS** with him now. 'That's just a complete pile of **TOAD PLOP**, Joe.' I say. 'OK, it was stupid to push her in the mud, that makes me just as mean and stupid as her, but I've got to do **SOMETHING**. I'm not going to spend my life running away from her. I'm going to tell one of the teachers **THIS WEEK** if she doesn't back off. I've had enough. And, frankly,' I say, sounding a bit like a line in *Gone with the Wind,*

'I don't give a damn about what happens to her at home.'

Joe frowns deeply and crosses his arms. 'How can you be so cruel, Cordelia? You know what'll happen if her dad finds out.'

I come straight back at him. 'How can **YOU** be so cruel that you keep telling me to put up with her nastiness? How can **YOU** be so **STUPID?** I **KNOW** you're right about the revenge thing and how it just keeps the fight going on and on and isn't helpful. I **KNOW** that bit, and I'm **TRYING** not to do it but protecting her from getting into trouble **ISN'T** going to change **ANYTHING**. She'll **NEVER** bother trying to get along with people if she doesn't **HAVE** to. She'll carry on being a complete **MOO** as long as there's a soft touch like you who'll take all the blame and keep all her secrets, and generally be a **BIG, DOZY CUSHION** for her. Or maybe you're just *vain* and you like the fact that she fancies you, even though she's a bucket of **PUS AND POISON**. Maybe you **LIKE** the idea that she's jealous of us being friends because it's **FLATTERING** or something weird and twisted like that. Well, she needn't be jealous any more because until you **WISE** up, I'm **NOT** your friend, Joe Grover. So go to your allotment and plant **THAT** idea.'

I move to another seat and IGNORE HIS EXISTENCE whilst also biting my lip a lot and worrying about what I'm going to do NOW, after all that SPEECHIFYING. But I don't look back when I get off the bus, not even a tiny glance in his direction. I'm holding my breath to keep the tears in.

At home, Mum is talking to Mrs Akbar on the phone and trying to wash salad at the same time.

'Yes, we've definitely spoken to Cordelia, Mrs Akbar, but it *does* seem that Mina just wandered in and slipped into the concrete.'

I can't quite make out Mrs Akbar's words but it's clear she's having a good old rant down the phone line.

'No…no…of course I'm not saying that Mina is a liar,' says Mum when Mrs Akbar stops to breathe. 'But little girls sometimes say things so that they won't get into trouble, don't they?'

I hear Mrs Akbar's voice going through the ceiling!

Mum rolls her eyes and sighs and gives me a TIRED sort of half-smile. The table is covered with papers, bills, adverts, plans and letters, as usual. Why is my family so HOPELESSLY CHAOTIC?!

I run up to my room and burst into tears, letting it ALL out. I don't fall asleep after my sob but just lie there, feeling like I've been wrestling with a fat bear again. Eventually, I wash my face and get on the computer to write it all down for Dru – but I don't send it. I MUSTN'T go back to offloading all my worries on her.

We all sit down later, to have Mum's lovely pasta and sauce and a crispy salad. The food smells so good that I feel better just breathing in the herb and tomato wafts coming from my plate. Mum and Dad want to hear all about my first day at school. **CAN'T THEY SEE** that my eyelids are swollen from crying? They look like a pair of round, pink mushroom tops. I can't possibly look like I've had a HAPPY CLAPPY day, can I? Maybe they know there's something wrong but they're waiting for me to tell them in my own time. I hope so, because I decide that **NOW** is the time.

'Ruby threw a pebble at my head,' I start saying, out of the blue, 'and it cut me, and then she stole my laces…'

But I don't think they even hear me because my voice is drowned out by a LOUD knock at the door that makes us all jump. Dad answers it and, OH! MIGHTY DOG DROPS! It's Mrs Driscoll again! She fires her sharp little mouth at Dad like a machine gun without even bothering to say hello first.

'These lorries are making too much mud,' she rattles. 'When's it going to stop? This building nonsense of yours, when's it going to end? Eh? It's a disgrace, mucky-ing up the whole village with a mess like this.'

And on…and on…and ON she goes. Dad invites Mrs Driscoll in for a tour of the building works so that he and Mum can explain all the improvements they are making. He's being SO polite to her that it makes me want to **VOMIT**. Mum and Dad both have to leave their pasta to go cold in the kitchen while they deal with Mrs Driscoll. They'll be trying to persuade her that it'll be a good thing for Heckaby to have a gastro-pub and a cinema because more people will want to visit this DUMP OF A PLACE if they make it a bit LESS of a dump. Some people might even want to LIVE here, which would bring more customers to her MANKY little shop.

Personally, I think Mum and Dad are wasting their time. Witchy Driscoll would probably rather saw off her own leg with a nail file than change her mind about something.

So I eat my dinner on my own, which is not

exactly fun. I won't be able to get near Mum and Dad for ages now, and when I do they'll have forgotten that they wanted to know about my first day. GREAT – I DON'T THINK.

After my lonely dinner I watch a film that I discovered when I was peeking into the boxes of DVDs waiting to be unpacked. I hadn't noticed this one in Mum and Dad's collection before, but then they do have about five ZILLION films so it's not surprising that I missed one. As soon as I saw the big crinoline skirts on the cover I knew I had to watch it.

The film is Italian. It's called *The Leopard* and it is a big helping of gorgeousness in frock-form. It is also one of the LONGEST films I've ever seen, nearly as long as *Dr Zhivago* but not as long as *Gone with the Wind*. I skip through some of the scenes, even though they have lovely Italian countryside and beautiful old houses, because I want to get to the parts with the best costumes.

The star is called Claudia Cardinale. She has long dark hair and looks like Snow White. The best scene is a big posh ball at an enormous villa. I use my pencil crayons and pastels to try and copy the colours of the ball gowns. I make rough skirt shapes all over a big sheet of paper and then smudge colours onto them in patches and swirls using my pastel sticks. I make the shapes look like a room full of skirts swinging and swishing around.

In the film there are lilacs and greens, oranges, pinks, all kinds of blue, and chocolate and peach colours. Some dresses are frilly, some are plain, some have stripes and others have flowers. Some dresses are more than one colour. The women have ringlets and flowers in their hair and the dresses are trimmed with lace that's cream and coffee, caramel and strawberry-coloured. They are all carrying little pouch bags that match their dresses. They must have been SO HOT dancing in those heavy skirts with corsets squeezing them round the middle. A lot of the time they have to sit down and fan themselves. There is so much fan-flapping going on that the room sometimes looks like it's full of frilly butterflies. The men wear blue and gold uniforms because there is a war going on (another film with a war in it!).

Before I know it Mum is calling to remind me that it's 'nearly bedtime'. At least she remembered to remind me tonight.

21

Joe and I don't speak on the bus the next morning. I'm still cross with him for not respecting the fact that I'm having a VERY HARD TIME coping with Ruby. I sit quite near him, though, so that when she gets on it looks like we're still friends and she doesn't try anything.

In both Maths and History I have to share a table with the depressed girl again. She's wearing very dark nail polish today and is hiding her face behind her long hair again, like yesterday. I've sat next to her in three lessons so far but I'm still not sure what she looks like and it's only when our Maths teacher, Mr Brascombe, asks her a question that I find out her name is Samantha.

'Samantha Tuttington. Recap for us, please,' he asks. 'The difference between an obtuse and an acute angle is?'

Samantha looks up by moving her eyes but not lifting her chin, as if her neck doesn't work properly.

She shakes her head very slightly.

'No? Anyone?' asks Mr Brascombe, throwing his arms open to the whole class because, CLEARLY, he's not going to get a dazzling response from Samantha. He was probably just checking that she's still alive under her hair.

Mr Brascombe is quite EXPRESSIVE for a maths teacher. He waves his arms about and walks around a lot. At a guess, I'd say that he's about as old as Miss Wallcott, which means he doesn't look much older than the biggest kids in school. He wears a shirt with no collar and trendy shoes. I'm glad the teachers in our school aren't all expected to wear ties and suits, like in my last place, Beckmere. It's a school, not a BANK, for heaven's sake! Children are human beings, not numbers in a savings account. I think uniforms are fine for kids, so that their mums and dads don't have to spend loads of money on clothes, but it makes the teachers look like they are just supervising an exam factory when they dress like business people. It doesn't make you feel like they CARE about you, but like they want to PROCESS you, like a cheque, or a frozen pea.

Maths is generally something I stumble through in an AVERAGE-ACHIEVEMENT-BUT-QUITE-

BORED sort of way. I can measure stuff and guess lengths and widths quite accurately because I've spent such a long time looking at fabrics in John Lewis and on market stalls when I'm out with Mum. Angles are quite interesting, too, because those are going to be handy when I want to cut my own patterns for sewing, but most of the maths we're taught doesn't seem to have a PURPOSE. The teachers don't really explain what it's FOR. Why would I want to know how to solve an equation just so that I can solve an equation? I expect these things are very useful for SOMETHING, but they haven't told us WHAT exactly, so my brain doesn't know where to store them. An equation is like a dress with no hanger, it just flops onto the floor of my brain and lies there.

History is easier to cope with because it's full of stories, and stories need costumes, don't they? AND we have lovely Miss Wallcott.

I decide to like History before the lesson has even started. But it gets even better. We're looking at portraits of very posh, important people from the 15th and 16th centuries. They didn't have cameras or newspapers to tell people how important they were in those days, so they had portraits painted instead. When Queen Elizabeth I had her portrait done she wanted people to know how powerful and wealthy she was so she wore her best clothes, all covered in jewels, and LOADS of make-up to cover her terrible skin as well as a wig to hide her baldy head – I think she had a disease that made her hair drop out. Then she had ships and oceans and maps painted in the background to make it look like she owned EVERYTHING.

We look very carefully at the clothes in the portraits and Miss Wallcott tells us how rare and expensive the fabrics would've been. She has brought in a piece of ACTUAL Elizabethan fabric that she's borrowed from a museum. It used to be part of a dress worn by a rich lady and now it has to be kept in a glass case to protect it.

Miss Wallcott stands it on one of the desks so that we can take turns looking. We aren't allowed to touch the case it's in, but we can all get close and have a peek at it through a magnifying glass.

'This is to show you just how detailed the clothes of the time could be,' she says. 'There were no sewing machines, of course, so every tiny stitch had to be done by hand.'

♥

At the end of the class I BEG her for ONE MORE LOOK. She smiles. 'You really like it, don't you, Cordelia?' she says. 'OK. Just a quick second look.'

The fabric is dark green silk covered in tiny pearls and red garnets. It is criss-crossed with gold and silver thread.

'It must've taken AGES to make,' I say, staring through the magnifying glass like Sherlock Holmes looking for clues.

'Weeks and weeks, probably,' says Miss Wallcott, 'and with no electric light to help them see.'

I tell Miss Wallcott that I love costumes and am going to be a great costume designer one day. I don't feel silly telling her and she listens without laughing or making any comments about how difficult that will be. She just says, 'Oh, I *see*. That's why you're so interested. Do you sew things at home?'

'I'm starting to,' I say. 'Mostly I draw. I copy from films and books. I practise a lot.'

Miss Wallcott's face is twinkly and interested. 'That's brilliant, Cordelia,' she says.

And I feel like she means it. So that's when I realise that Miss Wallcott is the teacher I'm going to tell about Ruby. She'll listen. I KNOW she'll listen. I'll get my courage up and I'll tell her TOMORROW, when I'm sure about what I'm going to say.

At lunchtime, before I go to the art room, I check out the school canteen. I told Mum and Dad that I think I should give it a try. They are happy to make sandwiches when they've got time, or for me to make my own, but I want to see what sort of *gloop* they serve here. It might turn out to be better than I expect.

Going to the canteen means being quite brave because I haven't got anyone to sit with. I'm not speaking to Joe until he apologises, or at least says something kind to me, and Ruby is bound to show up. This means I am VULNERABLE TO ATTACK.

I queue up and get a tray. I can choose between oily chips or grey mashed potatoes with pale-coloured beans or alien-green mushy peas. The drinks are a yellowy-brownish milk shake or thin orange squash. There isn't a salad leaf in sight. I go for chips, beans and a milk shake. My lunch is mostly BEIGE. The food is worse than I expected, not better.

There's an empty seat by the window so I start to make my way over. I don't spot Ruby. She comes at me from the side, walking quickly, and 'accidentally' bumps me **VERY HARD**. Beige food flies up in the air and lands ALL OVER two younger kids sitting nearby. My milkshake hits the floor, sending honey-and-banana liquid splattering over twenty people's legs. They all scream at the same time. My metal tray hits the floor tiles, followed by my cutlery, in a great

CLANGING, BOUNCING CLATTER.

Everyone cheers at the noise, as if it's the lunchtime entertainment. Ruby keeps walking.

IT'S A HIT-AND-RUN LUNCH-TRAYING!!

I am **CRIMSON** with shock, fury
and **COMPLETE HUMILIATION**. I am
also LUNCHLESS and surrounded by people
who are laughing at me or who want to kill me
because I've coated them in bean and banana-
flavoured stickiness.

I MAY NEVER BE ABLE TO SET FOOT IN THE CANTEEN AGAIN!

I run out of the door and head for the art room.
Joe isn't there, which is a shame because I want to
shout at him, **'LOOK WHAT SHE'S DONE NOW!'**
It's a relief that Ruby's necklace is finished so she
probably won't come in.

I get on with my sewing, concentrating as I work
my way around the long, long hemline of my skirt. I
try to do tiny stitches, like on the Elizabethan fabric.

Concentrating helps me to calm down a bit, breathe normally again and push back my tears – but the calm feeling doesn't last.

At afternoon registration I spot a note going around all the desks. Eventually it lands on mine. It's obvious that SHE has spent ages designing it on a computer because she's used loads of different fonts and colours to make it **BLARE** out, right in everyone's faces. It says

Joe Grover
AND
Cordelia Codd...

in BRIGHT red letters on LUMINOUS lime-green paper. Underneath our names there's a list of some things that Joe and Cordelia **CERTAINLY DO NOT DO, NEVER HAVE DONE, AND NEVER WILL DO**.

It's one of the rudest things I've EVER read. You can use your imagination because I'm NOT repeating

ANY of them. I screw the note up but then think again. I flatten it out, fold it and keep it as evidence. It will be a good example of Ruby's nastiness to show to Miss Wallcott...if I don't DIE of embarrassment when she sees it.

On the bus that afternoon I sit near the driver again in case of trouble but I needn't have bothered. Ruby walks past my seat without seeing me this time because everyone is rushing to get on the bus and out of the rain. Joe looks at me but I look away and he moves down the bus to sit somewhere else.

The rain is so heavy now and the sky so black with thunderclouds that no one bothers to bully anyone else, they're all too busy watching for lightning flashes and shrieking every time the bus goes through a flood-puddle on the road. It's a cloudburst, a total DOWNPOUR, it's AMAZING, but I'm stuck in a miserable bubble in my head after Ruby's note and the hit-and-run lunch-traying, and I can't get myself to join in with the general excitement.

The ford near the village is deeper than I've seen it before. The driver goes through very slowly so that his engine doesn't get soaked. When I sprint along the splashy pavement and into the cottage Mum is upstairs moving her bed and putting buckets out on the floor. She looks EXHAUSTED.

'What's up?' I ask, still puffing and panting from running through the rain.

'The roof's leaking,' she says. 'Can you check your room? Dad's phoning the builders. Here, take a couple of buckets.'

My bedroom ceiling has a huge, dark damp patch in the corner and there's a drip near the top of the bed. I put the bucket in the right place to catch it and start stripping the sheets so they don't get wet, then I prop the mattress up so it's not under the drips. Wow! Mattresses are HEAVY, aren't they?

Mum chucks a roll of plastic bin liners in through my door. 'Stuff your sheets and clothes in one of these, and bring them downstairs,' she calls, 'then grab some things for tonight and tomorrow. We'll have to squeeze into the caravan with Dad.'

We can't stay in the restaurant because the paint is still drying on the walls and it smells of weird chemicals, and we can't sleep upstairs above the restaurant where our new flat is because it's still dusty and draughty.

Dinner is a quick sandwich and then we all have to *squidge* up and share Dad's scruffy little tin can of a caravan. Mum and Dad are pretty stressed by the time we pile in with our bed linen and overnight 'essentials'. The caravan isn't really big enough for one person, never mind THREE. It smells of toast and socks and aftershave and rust all mixed together. It's TRULY TERRIBLE!

Mum and Dad start snapping and niggling at each other about tiny, UNIMPORTANT things, like where we should sit and where's the best place to put things.

When they start arguing over why there aren't any teabags, I've had enough.

'Can you two PLEASE save your energy for things that ACTUALLY MATTER?' I STRONGLY SUGGEST.

They ignore me, of course. Then it explodes into a FULL-BLOWN argument between them inside this overstuffed bean can. They fight about why there isn't any milk and who got mud on Mum's blanket and why the floor is sticky. Dad turns on the microscopic telly and starts watching sport. Mum says he's being antisocial and thinks we should play Monopoly or Scrabble or Pictionary or something before bed. Dad doesn't fancy this. Mum gets annoyed because he's *just not trying*. I can feel myself getting more and more scared. When they fight like this I don't know if Dad will be here in the morning or if we'll have to move again or WHAT'S going to happen. Eventually I grab my blanket and my bag with my overnight 'essentials' and open the door.

'I cannot **STAND** listening to you two **ANY LONGER**,' I shout. '**STOP IT!**'

For a moment they both SHUT UP.

I put out my hand for the keys. 'I want to sleep upstairs,' I say to Mum, because I can't bear to look at Dad or I'll cry. 'I'm not sharing with you two while you're like this. I'd rather risk getting **HYPOTHERMIA** upstairs.'

I think they suddenly realise how UNBEARABLE and SELFISH they're being because Mum hands me the keys, saying, 'I'm *so* sorry, Coco,' and lets me go up to sleep on the dusty floorboards in my new room.

It's not too bad up here. I have Mum's yoga mat to lie on and at least it's quiet, apart from the SKY-RATTLING thunderstorms.

In the morning I find Mum curled up on one of the benches in the pub. She must've got fed up, too, and risked being poisoned by paint fumes rather than spend the night near Dad.

We're both sitting in the kitchen, staring into cups of tea. We have bags under our eyes and stiff shoulders from sleeping in funny positions.

'Everything will be OK, Coco,' Mum says, stirring her tea slowly.

'I know,' I say. 'I know the roof will get fixed and the cinema and the restaurant will get going and everything. I know all THAT stuff will be OK. But are you and Dad EVER going to be proper friends again?' Then I hear myself sounding like Joe. 'You've got to stop throwing the hurt backwards and forwards at each other.'

22

There's no chance of getting into school in the morning. The stream that runs past the village has overflowed. The gardens are all flooded and the gutters along the high street are racing with fast, muddy rivers of rainwater. That means the allotments will be flooded, too. Poor Joe. Mum makes some phone calls and it looks like I won't get back to school until tomorrow at the earliest, if the rain stops. No one who lives this side of the ford and the stream can get out of Heckaby at the moment, and no one on the other side can get in.

At first I think GREAT – no school means NO RUBY. But I quickly remember that I still have a load of the hemline to sew on my skirt. Today is Wednesday. Thursday is the deadline. I'll never get the skirt finished. It will go into the exhibition still uneven and wobbly around the bottom. I'll NEVER win the prize with a wobbly hemline, will I? *DISASTER! UNAVOIDABLE DISASTER!*

Getting busy is the best way to stop a TOTAL PANIC-PANTS ATTACK. There's nothing I can do about the skirt and the exhibition. I just have to LET IT GO for today, which isn't easy for a CONTROL FREAK like me.

Dad is busy measuring for carpets and curtains upstairs. I can hear him clumping around on the floorboards and Mum is rescuing more clothes and towels and bed linen from the leaking roof by stuffing them all in bin liners. At least they've stopped fighting for now.

For the whole morning I sit in the empty restaurant. The paint fumes have cleared so it's safe. I have all my drawing things with me and Mr Belly is curled up beside me. It's too wet to go hunting for mice so I think he's decided it's an official C.D.O. (Cat's Day Off). It's quiet in here for the first time EVER since we arrived because the builders can't get into the village. Lovely!

I'm copying from a big book about costumes that I borrowed from the town library in Wellminster. We joined the library as soon as we moved here but Mum hasn't had time to take me there much. She says that I can get the bus and go by myself if I want but I'm scared to, just in case I bump into Ruby when I'm out on my own.

I'm working on a picture from a film called *The Bride of Frankenstein,* which was made in 1935. It's black and white and I'm using different pencils to make shadows and light and spookiness. The thunderstorm, which stopped for a little while at breakfast time, has started roaring and booming over the village again, so it feels like a perfect day for monster costumes.

In the picture, the bride in *The Bride of Frankenstein* is an actress called Elsa Lanchester. She's wearing a long white dress with HUGE shoulder pads. The sleeves are bandages, wrapped round and round, all the way to her fingertips. I'm thinking what a brilliant Halloween costume it would be and that I could probably make it from an old bed sheet when Mum pops her head through the door.

'Mrs Allen rang from school about the Scrap Project,' she calls.

I jump up. 'Yes? What did she say?'

Mr Belly looks annoyed at being disturbed. Mum is casual, like it's just a crumb, A TINY CRUMBLET of unimportant news that she's giving me. 'Mrs Allen says don't worry at all about your costume. She says that a girl called Ruby has offered to finish it off for you. That's kind of her, isn't it?'

And Mum rushes away to carry on with her jobs without any idea that my heart has stopped beating and I **AM NOT BREATHING!** Mum's words are like a FAT MUD PIE that just hit me on the side of the head and knocked me COMPLETELY OVER. After what feels like about twenty minutes but is probably only a few seconds – or else I'd be dead – I manage to gasp a big gulp of air in, and then breathe out again, squeaking, 'What? No! She can't…she mustn't touch it… No!'

Mum can't hear me, of course, so as soon as my legs will respond I race after her shouting, **'HAVE YOU GOT THE NUMBER?!** I need to call Mrs Allen! Ruby **MUSTN'T** touch my work. She **MUSTN'T!'**

I chase Mum into the cottage, where she's now surrounded by black bin liners full of our stuff, listening out for more drips coming from upstairs and putting piles of letters and papers into plastic folders to keep them dry.

'Sorry, Coco. Mrs Allen said she'd be busy teaching for the rest of the day so just asked me to pass the message on. What's the matter?'

283

My top **BLOWS** like a whale's spout. 'What's the **MATTER?** What's the **MATTER?** If you'd **EVER** sit still long enough for me to tell you, you'd know exactly what's the **MATTER!** I've tried to tell you about Ruby but you're so **OBSESSED** with your decorating and building stuff that you won't **LISTEN** to me.'

Mum looks up, 'Are you sure you're not over-dramatising a bit, Coco?' she says calmly. 'You do get a bit passionate about things sometimes.'

And I burst into **PASSIONATE** tears…**AGAIN**.

Mum stops shuffling things around. She looks at me, blinks and seems a bit surprised. Has she JUST realised that I NEED TO TALK? I am almost **HYSTERICAL** (this means wildly uncontrolled). I should not have to be **WILDLY UNCONTROLLED** with upset and completely **FLOODING** with tears before anyone **LISTENS** to me.

Mum says, 'I think we'd better sit down a minute,' then she passes me a box of hankies and makes us some tea, and gets some ginger biscuits for us to dunk. She pushes all her papers into a pile so that most of the kitchen table is clear, then she listens to the WHOLE LONG SAGA.

I tell her about Ruby slapping me and her being jealous because of Joe…and Joe being my only friend…and the stuff she planted in my bag so I looked like a thief but Mrs Allen being too soft to do anything…and what Ruby did to my hooped petticoat and Lennox and Gregor's work…and Mrs Allen STILL not doing anything…and how Ruby threw a stone at me and won't let other girls speak to me…and about her stealing the laces from my trainers and the hit-and-run lunch-traying…and how I have to sit near the driver on the bus in case she attacks me and that I am now POWERLESS to stop Ruby DESTROYING my lovely work.

When I stop to catch my breath Mum calls Dad in for an URGENT FAMILY CONFERENCE. Dad is sulky at first because Mum was so bossy with him last night but when he sees Mum's serious face and realises that the conference is about MY NEEDS, not his and Mum's, or the restaurant or the cinema, he leaves his sulkiness behind and comes in to join us. Then I tell them both THE WHOLE THING ALL OVER AGAIN and they both listen even though Mum has already heard it.

When I've finished telling them I'm VERY tired and ALL CRIED OUT. It's past lunchtime – too late to stop Ruby doing whatever she's going to do to my beautiful skirt and petticoat. Mum and Dad are gazing at me with sad eyes that are pink from dust and stress and lack of sleep.

'I don't know what to say, Coco,' Dad starts. 'We've been a bit too wrapped up in the house.' He keeps running his hand over the place where his hair used to be.

Mum strokes my hand and says, 'We're *really* sorry, Coco, you do know that, don't you?' Her hair is messy, but still beautiful, like always.

I nod, because I DO know that they're sorry. They look SO sorry for DEEPLY NEGLECTING me that their faces make me want to cry again.

'Shall I make a scromlette,' Dad asks me, 'and we can talk some more?'

'Yes, please,' I say, 'as long as I don't have to go to Driscoll's for the eggs.'

That makes us all laugh a little bit, but you can tell that we've all just had an EMOTIONAL CRASH. We must look like the most EXHAUSTED family in the universe.

Dad makes a MASSIVE, creamy, mushroom scromlette and we sit in the empty restaurant going over all the details again and again, eating lots to make us feel better, and Mr Belly gets some biscuits to keep him happy.

When I've calmed down and am full of scromlette I'm not cross with them any more because it's obvious how TERRIBLE they feel about being too busy to notice my traumas.

I don't tell them that I've fallen out with Joe again. Joe and I have to sort that out between ourselves. And, besides, they still believe the nasty gossip about him, don't they? And I don't tell them that it was Ruby who stole from Driscoll's Discount and the newsagent's. That's for Joe to sort out, not me. He has to decide that it's time to stop being a softie. I can't MAKE him do that, can I? What I CAN do is decide that I'm not going to let Ruby bully me any more. To make her stop I'll have to get some adults involved now and if that means that her dad finds out that she's a bully then maybe she'll start asking some adults for help too, to sort HIM out.

Mum and Dad want to call the headteacher, Mr Okenden, that afternoon and arrange to speak with him as soon as they can get to the school, but I tell them that I want to talk to one of the teachers myself first and ask her to help me sort it out. Of course, I'm thinking of Miss Wallcott. Dad frowns at this idea but I think Mum understands when I say, 'I need to be able to TELL you what's going on, and I MIGHT need you to come into school, but not yet. Let me see if the teachers can help first.'

The rain carries on battering us all afternoon. I go up to my new bedroom and lie on Mum's yoga mat, under my duvet, with all my clothes still on. I must be really exhausted from crying, because I CONK OUT completely with Mr Belly purring beside me.

When I wake up it's STILL raining, and I can hear shouting and doors banging and footsteps hurrying around. The voices sound frightened. I hear 'hospital', 'water', 'Mina', 'Joe', and I suddenly SNAP-CHANGE from being half asleep and dreamy to SCARED STIFF.

I run downstairs into the weirdest scene EVER. Little Mina is sitting next to Joe on one of the pub benches, BAWLING HER EYES OUT. Joe is silent and looking down at the floor. Water is draining off both of them, all over the new cushions.

Mum is rushing about saying 'blankets', 'hot bath', 'wrap them up', and grabbing anything she can find to put over them. Mina keeps *yowling* and *screaming.* It's a horrible, *brain-piercing* sound and I want her to **SHUT UP** because she looks

OK to me, just a bit soggy and cold, but Joe doesn't look OK AT ALL. He starts shaking.

Joe's dad is there, trying to comfort Mina and rub Joe's back at the same time. When he turns to say something to my dad I can see that he's as white as milk and really scared. Dad is at the bar pouring brandy.

'He's in shock,' Dad says. 'Give him a nip of this.'

Joe's dad gets Joe to sip the brandy. Mum brings a load of blankets and wraps Joe and Mina up. Joe coughs and shivers and looks confused and dizzy and hasn't stopped shaking. Mum throws another blanket over him and another over Mina and then runs out calling that she's going to fetch Mina's parents. I don't know what to do. I don't want to be a useless WET LETTUCE in what is obviously a DEEP CRISIS, but then Joe looks up and sees me. His face is pale green. I run to the kitchen for a bucket and come back just in time for him to throw a HUGE CHUNDERING PUKE into it. Wow! Yuck! Poor Joe! And I know then that I could NEVER be a nurse. Joe mumbles into the bucket, 'I'm sorry, Cordelia. You were right, I'm too soft with Ruby.'

'Well,' I say, holding the bucket towards him and

trying not to look at its contents. 'Never mind that now. Let's talk about it later, shall we? After you've had a bath and brushed your teeth.'

But Mina and Joe need to be seen by a doctor. They have to be taken to the hospital in a helicopter because the ambulance can't get through the flood water. Joe's dad and Mina's sister, Maryam, go with them. The helicopter has to land in the primary school car park where the whipping of the blades sends puddles splashing up like sea-spray. The noise is DEAFENING.

Men and women in heavy, serious rescue gear take Joe and Mina off as quickly as possible. Maryam carries Mina. Joe says that he can walk to the helicopter and that he feels much better after his big puke-up session but when he stands up one of his legs hurts so much that he groans and then passes out. I've NEVER been so worried about another person IN MY ENTIRE LIFE. It really scares me when he is carried off on a stretcher EXTRA FAST by the rescue people.

As the helicopter takes off I'm trembling so much that Dad offers me a brandy but Mum says, 'Don't you dare give her alcohol, John! I'll put the kettle on and make some chamomile tea.'

I cling on to Dad saying, 'Is Joe going to be OK? Is he OK?'

Dad hugs me back really tightly and says, 'Yes, absolutely, I promise, Coco.'

It seems that most of the village comes back to the pub then and Dad lights the open fire to dry everyone out. Even though it isn't cold, lots of us are shivering with shock and dampness. Dad gives everyone who wants one a free drink and they all swap stories about what they THINK happened, although nobody REALLY knows yet. All Mum and Dad can tell them is that Joe staggered to our doorstep in the middle of the storm carrying Mina, so traumatised and exhausted that he couldn't speak. Mum called the ambulance and went to tell Mina's family while Dad called Joe's dad, who ran down here as fast as he could. It's probably the WEIRDEST night Heckaby has ever seen.

It's nearly dark when everyone has gone. Mum and Dad clear up the pub, then we sit in the tiny cottage kitchen and play Monopoly until bedtime to take our minds off it all. We eat crisps and cheese and crackers instead of proper dinner and Mum and Dad drink some wine while I have chamomile tea and then a big glass of hot milk.

Dad and Mum keep telling me that Joe is going to be fine. Dad jokes that having a helicopter land on the playground is probably the most exciting thing to happen in Heckaby since the Normans invaded in 1066. This makes Mum giggle. She looks pretty when she giggles and I see Dad gaze at her a bit sad and soppy for a moment, like he wishes she would fall in love with him again. I wish she would, too. But I think her heart is still a bit FRAGILE.

It's the first evening in MONTHS that they don't look at paperwork or talk about building stuff, and I've hardly thought about Ruby with everything that's happened. These are my best-of-all-times, when Mum and Dad are both here and we do something easy and relaxing and peaceful – except that I HATE it when I land on PARK LANE and have to pay Mum hundreds of pounds of my Monopoly money.

23

As soon as I'm awake in the morning my first thought is that Joe is in hospital and I want to visit him AS SOON AS POSSIBLE. Then Ruby comes crashing back into my head like a stampeding rhinoceros and I am filled with **GRUESOME** thoughts of what she will have done to my dress. Is it possible to be sick with worry **RIGHT TO THE ENDS OF YOUR HAIR?**

THAT'S how I feel.

It's Thursday. Deadline day. Jenny Grover calls Mum and I get taken to school in Jenny's Range Rover, which can go through massive puddles without a problem. I'll probably arrive near the end of registration because we all slept a bit late – but I have a note for Mr Carter asking him to MAKE AN ALLOWANCE because it's not every night that your friends get taken off in a helicopter.

Mum comes along and, of course, we both ask Jenny straight away about Joe. She tells us that his dad called from the hospital to say that he and Mina are going to be 100% fine but that they have both been EXTREMELY LUCKY. Mina calmed down and went to sleep eventually and Joe is still too tired and confused to tell us everything. All they know is that he jumped in the river to pull Mina out.

'Wow! He's a hero, isn't he?' I say. And they both agree.

'Does that mean people will be nice to him now and stop accusing him of stealing things?' I ask.

Mum raises her eyebrows at me in a way that says I should be quiet ON THAT SUBJECT but Jenny doesn't seem to mind.

'I certainly hope so,' she says. 'Why *anyone* would want to steal from Mrs Driscoll's horrid little shop I can't imagine.'

I giggle and gasp at the same time and look at Mum to see her reaction. I have to try REALLY HARD to stop myself from shouting at Mum, 'I TOLD YOU SO!' but somehow I manage. I have to ACTUALLY put my hand over my mouth to stop the words coming out.

Mum and Jenny talk about last night all the way to Wellminster. They are in the front of the car and I'm stuck in the back, sandwiched between Jenny's 'GORGEOUS PUMPKINS'. They are both chewing soggy biscuits and smiling at me. I miss most of the IMPORTANT INFORMATION that I could pick up by listening to Mum and Jenny because I have to concentrate on making sure THE GOBLIN PUMPKINS don't wipe their biscuit-and-dribble mash on my sleeves.

I hear Jenny say that Joe and Mina have to stay in hospital for some sort of tests. The nurses and doctors are checking that they didn't catch any deadly diseases from the river water, and Joe had to have X-rays and tetanus injections and stitches because he cut his leg on a supermarket trolley when he jumped in. And just to put icing on the POO CAKE for him, the flood water swept away his greenhouse. Poor Joe!

In assembly, Mr Okenden says LOVELY things about Joe. I don't now how he got the news so quickly – probably over some special headmaster BAT PHONE.

The whole school gives him a HUGE round of applause and I WISH he could hear the clapping.

Part of me does WONDER, a TINY bit, whether I made a mistake not wanting him as a

boyfriend. But I'm NOT going back on that decision,
it would just mess him around and, besides, he'll
be SURROUNDED by much prettier girls than
me as soon as he gets back. That's what it's like
for HEROES. And anyway, I keep telling myself,
'YOU'VE GOT THINGS TO DO, CORDELIA
CODD!' You can't be distracted by romance when
you're going to be

the *★ GREATEST ★* costume designer in the history of cinema.

After assembly, and all the lovely stuff about Joe,
there's double science to get through before I can
go anywhere NEAR the art room to find out what's
happened to my Scarlett O'Hara skirt. But, before
I know it, it's lunchtime and I'm racing down the
corridor to the art room.

RUBY MACPHERSON HAS PIMPED MY SKIRT!!

My mouth is hanging so far open with **OUTRAGE**
and disbelief that, if I **COULD** make my body move
one single step forward, I'd trip over my own bottom
teeth. But I'm paralysed, FROZEN, unable to shift
my limbs for SEVERAL...LONG...SECONDS.

My beautiful, Scarlett O'Hara-style hooped skirt in soft green is now COVERED in **GROTESQUE** strips of **GOLD BLING** sequins. **SEQUINS!!! FOR THE LOVE OF LULU!!!** And she's actually sewn **CHEESY PINK-GLITTER-COVERED CHRISTMAS BELLS** all around the hemline.

This is the absolute, final, **INTOLERABLE END.**

RUBY MACPHERSON MUST DIE!

Mrs Allen bustles in and chirps, 'Hello!' But she notices that I can't speak or move and comes to stand next to me. She looks at the skirt, then looks at me, then looks at the skirt again, sighs and says, 'Ruby's finishing touches aren't quite in the right style, are they, Cordelia?'

I am stifling a **WAR CRY** of **VENGEANCE**. It comes out as a squeak. 'No, not quite.'

I think Mrs Allen can see that I'm close to a **COMPLETE NERVOUS BREAKDOWN** because she says that she may be able to allow me extra time to 'make a few changes,' as she puts it.

'I'll see if I can get you out of the lesson before lunch tomorrow as well, so that you can work on it. Who would be teaching you?'

'Miss Brudge. Games,' is all I can say.

I am touching all the terrible things that have been sewn onto my skirt, tugging at them to test how easily I can take them off and put it right. My heart is in a puddle on the floor next to me. But I save my tears for later and just GET ON WITH IT. I have soon taken off half the cheesy pink balls and most of the strips of gold bling sequins. I am so busy that I don't have time to find Miss Wallcott to tell her about Ruby. My best revenge now is to make the skirt MORE LOVELY THAN EVER. Either that, or I will have to **FORCE** Ruby Macpherson to eat a ***FAT SEQUIN SANDWICH***.

By the end of lunchtime Mrs Allen has got me out of Games with Miss Brudge the next morning. This is a MIRACLE – DOUBLE HOORAYS for Mrs Allen. Perhaps she isn't so WET and USELESS after all. I promise her that I'll be here straight after morning break the next day and that I'll work VERY fast.

I still have quite a bit of rescuing to do but everyone else has finished their work. Joe has his lovely photo display to exhibit, even if his ACTUAL greenhouse is now several miles up the river.

Before I leave for afternoon registration I ask, 'Don't you think Ruby should be disqualified for this, Mrs Allen?'

Mrs Allen perches her big bum on the edge of my table and speaks softly. 'Ruby has some problems at home, Cordelia.'

I nod. 'I heard.'

'Although that doesn't excuse her behaviour I don't want her to be put off coming to the art room. It's a safe place for her here. Do you understand?'

I nod again. 'Yes, but…'

'But…' says Mrs Allen, finishing my sentence, 'that doesn't mean that there isn't a consequence for her actions. Unfortunately I was not able to supervise yesterday lunchtime or this would never have happened. I'm sorry about that. However, you can be sure that the judges will be aware of her behaviour and that her chances of winning are *greatly reduced*.'

I keep nodding but inside I'm cheering and thinking **RUBY MACPHERSON HASN'T A HOPE OF GETTING THE PRIZE!!**

The question now is: who WILL get it?

Jenny *and* Mum pick me up after school. They must be getting on better now because they've been together all day. They went to visit Joe at the hospital, Mum tells me, then dropped the 'gorgeous pumpkins' at nursery and went to the hairdressers. Mum has even had a manicure – I don't think she's ever done that before. She looks great! Perhaps she's making herself lovely for Dad – I hope so!

Jenny says that she and Mum have had a

GIRLS' DAY OFF. That's good, I think, but I wish my mum would have a girls' day off with ME sometimes. I'm a little bit jealous but I don't think about that TOO MUCH right now because I want to know about Joe.

'You can ask him all about it yourself,' Mum says. 'Dad is going to take you to visit him later, if you want.'

I can't wait, but I have a lot to tell Mum and Dad about today first. It is still stuck in my heart like a lump of cold cabbage.

They have obviously decided that they need to be extra careful with my feelings for a while and give me some attention because when we get home we all sit down and have a cup of tea and dunk ginger biscuits while they listen to me describing Ruby's latest piece of SABOTAGE *(sabotage = to deliberately destroy or obstruct).* Good word, I think. I also explain that I haven't had time to speak to a teacher yet, but that it's OK, I've got a plan to see Miss Wallcott as soon as my project is finished.

They seem a bit surprised at how much I have to tell them and how soft Mrs Allen is being but then I tell them about Ruby's dad, which I'm probably not supposed to but I HAVE to because it is now VITAL INFORMATION if they are going to understand things properly. Mum and Dad sigh a lot and roll their eyes as if they wish they'd known all this was going on. Well, it's their fault that they didn't know, isn't it? It's their fault but they couldn't really help it. It's just one of those things that there's no point blaming anyone for, I suppose. You just have to start making things better from where you are now. That's what Dru would say, I think. Maybe her wisdom is rubbing off on me – perhaps it's creeping over the internet and infecting me in a good way, with sensible thoughts.

Mum is strict with me but I know she's right when she says, 'This will stop, Coco. I *absolutely promise* it will. But if you haven't spoken to a teacher about it by next week, Dad and I are coming into school to see Mr Okenden.'

I manage not to cry again. Perhaps I'm getting tougher.

Dad has baked an extra special apple crumble for pudding, which would help anyone feel better AND, of course, I have seeing Joe to look forward to.

Before we leave for the hospital I just have time to tell Dru about our DRAMATIC NIGHT

OF RESCUE and Joe being a HERO. I tell her about what Ruby did to my skirt, too…and how she hasn't got a CHANCE of winning now but, sadly, neither has Joe because his greenhouse has been washed away. I remember to tell her that Mum and Dad are trying MUCH harder and are listening to me now AND that Mum has been making herself look lovely, which means there may be *romance in the air* between my parents.

There's no time to wait for a reply because Dad calls me to get in the car. The rain has FINALLY stopped. Dad drives extra carefully, though, because the roads are still splashy and slippery.

We find Joe lying in bed on a children's ward. His eyelids are heavy and he looks like he's lost loads of weight overnight. He's still too tired to sit up. Dad shakes hands with him and then goes to talk to Mr Grover in the corridor, leaving us together.

Joe manages a smile, and I know that we're friends again. No problem there. We like each other too much to fall out for very long. I tell him that he's the village hero now and show him the headline in the local paper.

HECKABY HERO:
Boy, 14, saves toddler from certain death

I read a bit to him where it says,

'Local allotment holder Joe Grover, aged just 14, jumped into the raging torrent without any thought for his personal safety.'

Then I get Joe to tell me the whole story until he's EXHAUSTED from talking.

It turns out – and this was COSMICALLY, MYSTICALLY lucky for Mina, that Joe was on his allotment on Wednesday evening, trying to rescue what was left of his waterlogged salad. He spotted her standing on the bank of the stream – only it wasn't a stream any more but a fast-moving river. She'd obviously wandered off from home again. Joe could see that she was in danger so he ran over to get her and take her home. But the muddy bank gave way before he got to her and she fell into the water and was swept along.

'I just jumped in,' he tells me, giving one of his shrugs. 'I think anyone would've done the same.'

'Everyone came to the pub after the helicopter left,' I tell him. 'They were all talking about it! I think they've completely forgotten that they were cross with Mum and Dad because of the electricity going off.'

I tell Joe how the whole village was **FUMING** with Mr and Mrs Akbar at first. 'They were all huffing and puffing and tutting and saying, "*Imagine letting a toddler like that out of your sight!*" But then Lily from the chip shop came in and shut them all up.'

'How come?' Joe asks.

'They were all sitting there, gossiping away and Lily said, "*You're all being a bit too harsh, actually, it's more complicated than you think.*" Then she told them all how she had just been to see Mrs Akbar and she is REALLY upset and embarrassed about the whole thing. Apparently, Mr Akbar got stuck in Wellminster, on the other side of the water, when the flood came. He couldn't get home. He was **FRANTIC** with worry because, Lily told them, Mrs Akbar has a heart problem that makes her fall asleep a lot and Maryam can't watch Mina AND look after her mum AND the shop AND do her homework all at the same time. "*THAT'S how come Mina manages to wander off,*" Lily told everyone straight and it really shut them up. Then they started to be a bit nicer about it and I think they felt ashamed for being so JUDGEMENTAL.

'And, of course, NOW that everyone KNOWS the problem, they can help out instead of just being huffy-puffy and superior and saying nasty things about the Akbars. They've all agreed that if ANYONE in the village sees Mina wandering around they'll just pick her up and take her straight back home, even if she kicks and screams, AND they'll check that Mrs Akbar is OK, too. And Mrs Akbar won't have to pretend it's someone else's fault when Mina gets into trouble any more. Now that everyone knows what the problem is they can help, in a friendly way. I think that's a good result, don't you Joe…Joe?'

But Joe's eyelids are closing and I'm not sure that he's heard most of what I just said. I suppose I was RATTLING ON a bit. So I just sit next to him quietly until Dad pops his head around the door to say we'd better go because Mum is stuck back at home with all the washing up.

Joe mumbles that he's mostly still tired because the hospital is too noisy to sleep and he can't wait to get home and go SPARK OUT for a few days. I think he might be being POLITE AND DIPLOMATIC because I'm sure it's my jabbering that's worn him out. I give him a little kiss on the cheek.

'I'm really proud that you're my friend, Joe,' I say.

He looks a bit embarrassed and says, 'Thanks, I'm just sorry that you had to hold the bucket and look at all my puke.'

I shrug, just like he does sometimes. 'If you can be brave enough to leap into a RAGING TORRENT and save someone's life then I think I should be able to cope with a bit of chucked-up river water.'

24

Mum and I sleep upstairs in the new flat again and in the morning both Mum and Dad drop me at school on their way to have coffee at Café Candela. This is BRILLIANT – my mum and dad are having a bit of time off together. It's ALMOST like a date. I can't wait to tell Lennox that they've been to his brother's café but I don't have time to look for him today.

I just have to get through one lesson and then I'm free to go to the art room for the rest of the morning and all of lunchtime. It's Maths, and I'm a bit late in because there's a queue in the girls' toilets and I needed an FW.

Because I'm the last one to arrive I can see that Ruby is sitting on her own and I realise that she probably ALWAYS sits on her own – I just haven't noticed because she sits way behind me. It looks like Penny was telling the truth: everyone *HATES* Ruby – they're all afraid of her but she can't MAKE people sit with her, can she? I don't let Ruby see me looking at her. I don't want her to know that I nearly died of **EXTREME UPSET** when I saw what she did to my skirt because that's exactly what she wants.

As soon as the bell goes for morning break my heart starts jumping because I realise that NOW, before I go to the art room, is the time to catch Miss Wallcott and tell her what Ruby has been doing. Mrs Allen might be able to make sure Ruby doesn't win the prize for her design but I still don't believe she will do anything to stop her from bullying me.

I hurry down the corridor and knock on the staffroom door quickly, before I have time to chicken out. A teacher who I don't know opens it and sounds like he's irritated that his coffee and chatting time has been interrupted by a pupil.

'Yes, what is it?'

'Is Miss Wallcott there, please?' I ask. 'It's quite urgent.'

He looks around the staffroom without letting go of the door, as if he's getting ready to shut it in my face.

'No. You'll have to try again at lunchtime,' he says, like he couldn't care less. He starts to close the door just as Miss Wallcott arrives, and says, 'Hello, Cordelia. Everything OK?'

The teacher I don't know disappears into the staff room.

'Sort of...well...not really,' I tell her. 'Can I talk to you?'

'Of course, Cordelia. Only, I've got a meeting now and then I'm away for the weekend. Will you be OK until Monday? I'll be in the Head Space straight after school finishes.'

I'm quite glad that I can delay it a bit. My thoughts have got a bit jumbled and I'm scared that Ruby is going to see me talking to her. I keep glancing from side to side, checking that she isn't coming up the corridor.

Miss Wallcott must think I'm being a bit weird.

'Yes, that'll be fine,' I say, nodding.

'Let's make it four o'clock on Monday, then?' Miss Wallcott says with a smile. 'We'll find a quiet corner.'

I write the appointment in my journal and she writes it in her diary. I feel much better knowing that I've made a time to see her but sick with the **COLD TERRORS** at what might happen when Ruby finds out I've spoken to a teacher about her. I feel like I've started something that I can't go back on. Will it end with me being in hospital, like Ruby said it would? I tell myself that I CAN'T think about POSSIBLE DEATH OR INJURY until the Scarlett O'Hara skirt is finished, but the fear sits at the back of my head, like a grouchy goblin hiding in a dark corner.

♥

By about eleven o'clock, the skirt is already looking much better. The pink-glitter-covered bells and strings of sequins have all been snipped off. This isn't hard to do because, HONESTLY, Ruby's sewing is RUBBISH. Her stitches are big and loopy and loose. I'd NEVER let her work for me. When I'm a great costume designer I'll only have BRILLIANT sewing experts in my team.

By the beginning of lunchtime I've almost sewn up the whole of the hemline. I'm in a state of DEEP CONCENTRATION, thinking that I only need A LITTLE BIT LONGER before I'm finished, when Mrs Allen makes me jump OUT OF MY SKIN by suddenly shouting from inside the store cupboard, 'Oh good heavens! I almost forgot Heliotrope!'

I catch my breath and call back, 'Are you OK, Mrs Allen?'

She bustles out. 'Yes, yes, dear. I have to pick my cat up from the vet. You'll be OK here for half an hour, won't you? It completely slipped my mind. Poor Heliotrope will be pining terribly.'

'I'll be fine,' I say, nodding. 'I'll just finish up. Thank you for the extra time.'

Mrs Allen has already grabbed her handbag. She glances up and down the nearly finished skirt. 'You've done a *very* good job, Cordelia. I hope the judges are impressed.'

And she whizzes off to get the unluckiest cat in the world, the cat that got the name HELIOTROPE. It sounds like a disease that cats die from, not a name. I can imagine someone saying, 'My cat died of a nasty heliotrope.' And, yes, I KNOW it's the name of a flower and supposed to sound pretty, but it just DOESN'T.

Finally, I finish the last little stitch around the hem, then – and I know I'm not supposed to do this UNSUPERVISED but I have no choice, I get the iron and ironing board out so that I can press it all over to finish it off PERFECTLY. I've done lots of ironing before at home, so it's no problem.

It's when I'm putting the ironing board down and it creaks and squeaks in a way that echoes around the art room that I realise I'm COMPLETELY alone. Somewhere down the corridor I can hear voices but there's no one very close by. Not only that, but I am completely alone in a room that contains EVERYONE'S scrap design projects, finished and ready for the exhibition.

In the far corner, Joe's photo board is propped up against the wall. Gregor's two best lampshades are hanging from the ceiling on super-thin strings and Lennox's cushion covers are in a neat pile. Janna and Emmy's bookcases are in another corner, next to the dummy wearing Becky's Roman centurion's armour and, over by the window, pinned onto a black velvet board in a perfect sweep of strings – one, two, three strings, each shorter than the last – is Ruby's beautiful blue-green, silver and turquoise recycled necklace. Oh dear! I can feel my spiky red demon popping up again.

The perfect opportunity to have **_DEVASTATING REVENGE_** on Ruby has been plonked in front of me. One **_SNIP_** of the scissors and all those lovely beads would be on the floor, rolling under cupboards, never to be seen again. She wouldn't **_EVER_** be able to prove that it was me.

I pick up the same scissors that I used to unpick her rubbishy stitches from my skirt. They're very small and very sharp. I could do this SO quickly. I look around the room. My skirt is finished and hanging up ready for the exhibition. It looks great and there's nothing else I need to do here. I could be sitting somewhere at the other end of school, eating my sandwich before Mrs Allen gets back.

I walk towards Ruby's necklace and gently lift up one of the strings of beads. It's a lovely necklace but I **HATE** it because **SHE** made it. I slip the blade of the scissors under the fishing wire connecting the beads and look around the room again, just to make double-triple and quadruple sure that I'm alone. That's when my eyes meet Joe's, smiling out from his photo board. He's leaning against the bunk bed frame before he turned it into a greenhouse. He's looking right at me, and I hear him saying, 'If we keep doing hurtful things back and forward, eventually everyone is hurt and everything is wrecked. Brave people are the ones who refuse to throw the hurt back.'

I take a deep breath, still holding the scissors there but looking at Joe, and I understand what he means now. This is a moment where I CHOOSE whether I'm going to be a person who tries to change the world or a person who is just part of the same old problems going round and round, back and forth. It might just be a necklace but it feels like I have my finger on a **BIG NUCLEAR BUTTON**.

It's THE MOST difficult thing I've EVER done, but I take the scissors away and step back from Ruby's necklace.

♥

I get through Friday afternoon SOMEHOW but I'm so tired now that I've finished the Scarlett O'Hara skirt that my eyelids are drowsy and droopy. Ruby doesn't appear in afternoon registration. She seems to miss quite a lot of school.

Mum and Dad pick me up at home time. They obviously went shopping after their trip to Café Candela because the car is full of boxes with light fittings in and there's a big carrier bag full of little test pots of paint and samples of wallpaper and curtain fabric. I can't wait to have a closer look at those.

'Did you get your skirt finished?' Mum asks as I climb in and arrange the bags around me.

'All done,' I say, then start rummaging in the boxes to check that they've bought the kind of light fittings I wanted. I'd quite like to forget ALL ABOUT the Scrap Design Project and Ruby and my appointment with Miss Wallcott for now but Mum asks, 'Have you arranged to speak to one of your teachers yet?

'Yes, I'm seeing Miss Wallcott after school on Monday,' I say.

'Well done, Coco,' Dad says. 'Let us know if you need us, won't you?'

I promise I will and I start to feel lighter than I did this morning, cheerful and not like I'm dragging a sack of stones around inside me. This is because:

a) My parents have spent all day together and still seem to be speaking to each other.

b) The Scarlett O'Hara skirt is finished and it feels good knowing that I've done my absolute, complete and utter best.

c) I found the courage to arrange to talk to Miss Wallcott.
d) I **didn't** take revenge on Ruby.

It's as if I'm suddenly more confident and my life feels a bit more UNDER CONTROL. That helps me to have a more relaxed weekend. Well, as relaxed as it gets at our house.

When we get home the roof of the cottage is being fixed. I don't mind that the builders are back – feeling GENERALLY more relaxed means the MASSIVE MESS we live in doesn't bother me quite so much. Mum calls to me over the top of a stuffed bin liner she's carrying out of the room. 'We've been invited up to the Grovers' for a little party tomorrow evening. Jenny says Joe will be back home by then. He's feeling a lot better.'

Mum isn't QUITE making sense.

'Are you sure you want to go?' I ask. 'You still believe he steals things, don't you?'

Mum puts down her bin liner and sighs. 'He has shown that he's an extremely brave young man, whatever else he may or *may not* have done. Your dad and I have agreed that he deserves a clean slate.'

'Does that mean you think he's OK?' I ask.

'Yes, that means we think he's *probably* OK,'

Mum says with a smile. 'Now, help me carry some of these bin liners.'

I think Mum has just demonstrated one of the ways that adults AVOID admitting that they have been COMPLETELY wrong about someone. This could make me INFURIATED but I won't tell her this and start an argument because I'm quite cheerful at the moment and I'm practising LETTING GO.

Saturday is a BIG REST DAY for all of us. We talk about which light fittings should go where and try out the little test pots of paint on my new bedroom walls and look at wallpaper for the landing. These are all lovely, creative things that don't feel like work so Mum and Dad are very UN-STRESSED for a change and, before we know it, it's time to go to Joe's party.

I can't wait to tell him about NOT cutting up Ruby's necklace, but when we get to his house it's FULL of people from the village and I HARDLY get a chance to talk to him. Mr and Mrs Grover are handing round lots of snacks and nibbles and pizza slices and the GOBLIN PUMPKINS are running about in their pyjamas. Mr Clench from the tea room and Mike from Mike's Bikes are there, and Vera from the hairdressers. Mr and Mrs Akbar have closed the newsagent's early to come along, but Mina has been left at home with her big sister, Maryam, because she's still a bit tired after falling in the river.

Lily from the chip shop brings her boyfriend, Jason, and Mrs Kwan from the takeaway comes with a big plate of spring rolls that everyone dives on because her spring rolls are FAMOUSLY crispy.

But MOST HAPPY-MAKING OF ALL is that Joe's mum has come up from London. She is as tall as a statue and has big, kind eyes. She's very beautiful and everyone says that they can see where Joe gets his good looks from, which makes them both go pink in the cheeks. She spends a lot of time talking to Joe's dad but Joe manages to introduce us and I chat to her about school and tell her that Joe got a round of applause in assembly. Joe puts his arm around her from time to time and gives her a little squeeze. He must miss her *SO* much.

The house is packed and no one is grumpy or

gossipy. Why do people need something almost
TRAGIC and terrible to happen, like Joe and Mina
nearly drowning, before they get together and
realise that their neighbours are OK? It's another
one of those stupid things about the world.

I see Dad chatting with Joe later, when I'm
tucking into another spring roll and telling Lily
about my Scarlett O'Hara dress. I hear Dad tell
him that he can come and look in our skips for
stuff for his allotment ANY TIME HE WANTS,
which makes Joe's face light up. Dad says that we've
probably got enough old wood for him to build a
whole new greenhouse and a shed as well.

The only person who doesn't come is Mrs
Driscoll, but I'm not sure that Joe would want
her there, anyway, not after the horrible things
she said about him. It's a bit sad really, because
she must be ever so lonely, stuck inside her
MISERABLENESS. I don't suppose anyone will
back her up and help her to get Joe into trouble
with the police now. Maybe she'll give up writing
nasty letters. Maybe she'll LET IT GO.

It's quite late when we get home and I just have
time to fill Dru in on the latest happenings before
bed. I tell her about having to repair my costume

and how I DIDN'T cut Ruby's necklace and about
Joe being a hero and my dad really liking him now. I
tell her about Joe's party and especially about his mum
being there but I don't manage to wait and see if she
sends a reply because my eyes just WON'T stay open.

I lie under my duvet on Mum's yoga mat wishing
that Dru was here, having a sleepover in my empty
bedroom with just the bare floorboards and the moon
outside like a huge penny. I miss her and, although
I can see that lots of the kids at my new school are
quite nice, I wonder if I'll EVER make a friend as
special as Dru again.

Mum creeps into the room quietly and settles
down into her bed, which is a line of sofa cushions
with a sleeping bag on top. We aren't going to try
sharing the caravan with Dad again. It's better to stay
in here and avoid arguments.

'I don't mind that you and Dad aren't living
together properly,' I say.

Mum's voice reaches me through the darkness.

'Thank you, Coco,' she says.

'I mean,' I continue, 'I think I'd rather have Dad
nearby than under the exact same roof if you two are
going to fight like babies.'

'I'm sorry, Coco. We've both been a bit stressed,'

Mum says. 'Although today was good, wasn't it?'

'Yes, today was good,' I agree. 'But maybe you and Dad need a bit of SPACE between you while you're setting up this business. Otherwise you'll argue and mess that up as well as your relationship.'

I've been a bit too DIRECT, I know, but I'm tired and it just slipped out. Mum coughs and shuffles, and rolls over to face me. I can just make out her wide-open eyes shining in the dark.

'Is that what you think, Coco? That we've messed up our relationship?' Mum asks, sounding hurt.

'Well, not COMPLETELY,' I tell her, feeling SO sorry that I said it, 'but I wish every day was like today. Most of the time you're blaming each other for everything that goes wrong. You've got to start being friends again.'

'We *are* friends, Coco, the best friends in the *world*, I promise you,' she says, leaning towards me a little bit, 'but we just *forget* sometimes, when we're really busy.'

I think I've said enough so I shut up and let Mum go to sleep, and I lie there thinking that it's weird but my parents are definitely happier with at least two walls between them most of the time. And it's not like I have to travel miles to see my dad, like some kids do. We even sit down and eat together most days. Perhaps it's better this way for now, and I'll just have to keep learning the dreaded P word. PATIENCE.

I get a reply from Dru in the morning with photos of her and Jess messing around in her aunt Zillah's swimming pool. There's another girl there, too. She has short, dark hair and a big smile. She and Dru are wearing the same swimsuits. Dru looks different, tanned and taller and her hair – that used to be so frizzy – is in smooth, bouncy curls. She looks really happy and that makes me a bit sad. We are both changing so much but she seems to be changing quicker than me AND she has a new friend. This gives me a sharp, stabbing feeling somewhere just above my tummy because I want Dru and me to be like we were before she left, but I know that's not going to happen. She sounds just the same, though.

★ **Dru** to Cordelia

```
What a story!! I knew this Joe would
turn out to be a good guy. And now
```

he's friends with your dad! That's what Aunt Zillah would call **EXTRA GRAVY** on your **DUMPLINGS**.

AND you get a triple-gold-star-peace-award from me for not wrecking Ruby MacFearsome's work when you had the chance. I'm **SOOOOOOO!!** proud of you.

I've sent a photo of my friend, Esther. She's going to science-geek camp with me next week.

Good luck with the Scrap Design competition!! I should be able to email from camp.

Must take a final dip in the pool now.

Dru xxx

25

On Monday Joe is back in school and the Lord
Mayor comes to shake his hand in a special
assembly, so this time he hears the applause.

The Lord Mayor gives Joe lots of great presents
that people have sent him. He has a ton of vouchers
for free trips to the cinema in Wellminster and
loads of book tokens from the manager of the big
book shop. The Italian restaurant has offered him
dinner for his whole family, and the sports shop has
promised him a free pair of trendy swimming shorts
and some goggles, which some people might think
is a pretty bad joke considering Joe nearly drowned.
But it's all brilliant and it's SO lovely seeing him
smile and have everyone cheering him as he leaves
the stage – still limping a bit because of his stitches.

When the Lord Mayor and Joe sit down Mr
Okenden comes on stage and stands behind the
podium with an envelope. My tummy swirls and
burns because I know what's coming.

'We're now going to have the results of the
Scrap Design Project,' he says, turning the big white
envelope over and over in his hands so that we are
all watching it VERY closely, as if we're hypnotised.
He makes a LONG speech to tell all the kids what
the Scrap Design Project was about, then he starts
describing all the entries and who made them, and
what year each of us is in. It's nice to hear my name
and have kind things said about my costume but
it makes me even more nervous and I get TENSE
AND TIGHT AND TWISTY on the inside. Then
he tells us who the judges are and reads a long list of
names of people that no one has heard of but who
are, apparently, our Parent Association. He reminds
everyone that the entries will be on display in the
main foyer until half term. He goes on and on
AND ON, so while he's doing this I look around
for the others.

Lennox is a couple of rows behind. He pulls
a silly face at me and makes me giggle. Gregor is
sitting next to him, looking cool as a cucumber. I
can't see Janna and Emmy because they're probably
sitting at the front with the other year seven kids,
but I think I catch sight of Emmy's mad bunches
bobbing on top of her head. Becky is in the same

row as me. Her knees are jiggling up and down with impatience. Ruby is at the end of our row. Her arms are crossed and she's sucking her teeth, as if she's SUPER CONFIDENT that it's her name in the envelope and she can't wait to see the look of disappointment on our faces when it's read out.

FINALLY, FINALLY, when I don't think I can stand the tension ONE SECOND LONGER, Mr Okenden stops jabbering and opens the envelope. My heart is beating about five thousand times faster than normal. Mr Okenden looks at the white card inside. He smiles and nods, then looks out across the hall.

'The £100 prize for the best Scrap Design this year goes to…' He pauses, like it's a cheesy contest on television. I HATE it when they do that. Someone near the back makes a drum roll sound and the whole hall starts giggling. Even Mr Okenden can't help smiling. 'The prize goes to… Becky Freemantle.'

There are cheers and whoops and applause and I think I also hear a gasp of horror from Ruby's direction but I DAREN'T look at her. Joe is clapping. I look behind me and see Lennox and Gregor clapping, too. I see Becky going up on stage to collect her prize and I remember that hers WAS, after all, a brilliant idea that looked great and I find myself clapping too and thinking RUBY DIDN'T WIN! HOORAY! I'm applauding like mad now, but I know that it's not for the right reasons. I'm clapping with RELIEF that it's all over and JOY that Ruby didn't win rather than because I'm happy for Becky, but I can't help it. Am I being a bad loser? I don't know. I catch sight of Ruby, who isn't EVEN clapping. She's looking at the floor, shaking her head and still sucking her teeth. At least I'm not THAT BAD. How can Ruby NOT be even a little bit pleased for Becky? But I think we all know that Ruby will **NEVER FORGIVE** Becky for winning.

By morning break time that day it's obvious that Ruby has turned her bullying radar on Becky. But Becky and her friends hit back at Ruby. They throw stuff across the classroom at each other and say loads of **REALLY MEAN** things.

In the art room that afternoon Ruby steals Becky's new pencil case, so Becky chucks Ruby's trainers out of the window. At home time I walk past the bus queue on my way to meet Miss Wallcott and see Ruby start shoving Becky, so Becky starts shoving back and then there's a **MASSIVE** shouting match between lots of people who join in. They look like a pack of **HYENAS** snarling at each other – it's all **DEEPLY UNDIGNIFIED**. The swearing and pushing goes on and on and back and forth, and it's ALL just a BIG FAT WASTE of time and energy. But they stop COMPLETELY AND INSTANTLY when they see Miss Brudge marching towards them with a face that says 'I-will-CRUSH-you'.

Can you IMAGINE what her detentions must be like? She probably makes kids jog round the playing field for a week with no food or water.

But Becky and Ruby are deadly enemies now and their fighting is probably
TO BE CONTINUED…

When I sit down with Miss Wallcott in a quiet corner of the Head Space I'm shaking a bit. It feels completely like the RIGHT THING to do but that doesn't mean it's easy. I manage to tell her the whole story without crying.

Miss Wallcott is a CHAMPION LISTENER. She gives me all her attention for ages and ages and our meeting ends with her PROMISING, 'I *will* be speaking to Ruby as soon as she arrives at school tomorrow and I *will* be speaking to Mr Carter and Mrs Allen to make sure that they understand how serious this is.'

'But how will you stop her hitting me again?' I ask. 'And how will you stop her telling the other girls not to be friends with me?'

Miss Wallcott sighs and says, 'We can't watch her all the time, Cordelia, but after I've spoken to her she'll understand that serious action will be taken if she doesn't stop.'

I leave the Head Space feeling like this will only work IF Miss Wallcott does what she says she will. But you never know with teachers. She might be a BIG WEEDY DISAPPOINTMENT like Mrs Allen or she might actually DO something. I have to just TRUST her and WAIT AND SEE if Ruby backs off.

Ruby's bullying of me actually ends in a WEIRD and UNEXPECTED kind of way. She is so busy being **SUPER NASTY** towards Becky that she doesn't seem to be interested in putting me in hospital any more. She mostly ignores me. It's as if she just needs someone, **ANYONE**, to be horrible to, and now it's Becky's turn to get picked on.

Ruby doesn't change her behaviour, just her TARGET. But then she even stops picking on Becky because she's absent from school for quite a few days and no one knows where she is.

I tell Mum and Dad that the trouble at school has blown away and disappeared since the end of the Scrap Design Project, which is sort of true.

School days have settled down into a routine. I know what my lesson timetable is and I've sort of got used to having an empty seat next to me. Even though the other kids speak to me now they all have their own special friends already, so I'm still a bit of an odd-girl-out. Joe and I are still great friends but he is usually surrounded by ADORING FANS now that he's a hero so we don't get to chat very often.

I expected to feel MISERABLE if I didn't win the prize, but all I feel is a little bit disappointed. I'll get over it. My big ego is just slightly bruised, that's all. And I wanted to win for the wrong reason, didn't

I? I wanted to win so that Ruby didn't, so there's NO WAY that I deserved the prize.

The skirt and petticoat look great, and that's what matters. Mrs Allen has displayed our work beautifully in big glass cases in the school entrance. Parents and kids are saying lots of nice things about them and visitors have written lovely comments in a special book that Mrs Allen put out. Gregor and Lennox have ACTUALLY started selling their work to the teachers.

There's more good news, too! GREAT news, in fact, and I've been able to report these happy-making things to Dru. I'm much less of a MOANING-PANTS now.

★ **Cordelia** to Dru

How goes the science camp?

I promised to send good news and now here are two more **HELPINGS OF HAPPINESS**.

The most important thing is that Ruby has **BACKED OFF**.

I tell her about Becky winning the prize and how Ruby dumped her nastiness on her for a while, but now she's disappeared. And, of course, I tell her about Joe getting presents for his heroism and the Lord Mayor visiting.

But now – how's **THIS** for an **EXCITING DEVELOPMENT...**

My second favourite teacher at the moment (numero uno is still Miss Wallcott) is our Drama teacher, Mr Gampy. He's organising a big Halloween Ball at school to raise money for books to go in the Head Space, and he's asked me to help make the costumes. **JOY AND RAPTURE!!!**

★ **Dru** to Cordelia

FANTASTIC news about the Halloween Ball. Please, please **SEND PHOTOS** when it gets going.

Science camp is **SURPRISINGLY** good fun – lots of interesting stuff to do and plenty of staring at wriggly things down microscopes.

Then Dad calls me for dinner and I have to send Love in buckets xxx and leave Dru, which is a bit INTERRUPTY but my tummy is rumbling so I don't mind too much.

♥

By the beginning of the third week of term I've got
used to not FEARING FOR MY LIFE every day,
even on the bus.

I visit the Head Space most days after school, to
look through costume books and do my homework
away from the building noise at home. It's BLISS!
I'm in there now, sitting at a big wooden table with
books spread out around me, drawing ideas for the
Halloween Ball.

It's almost closing time and most of the kids have
gone. All I can hear is my pencil making lines on
my sketchbook and a boy turning the pages of a
giant atlas on the next table. I'm looking at a photo
of a beautiful actor called Fenella Fielding in a funny
horror film called *Carry on Screaming*. She's wearing
the most amazingly glamorous wicked-lady dress
in red velvet. I'm just trying to draw the lovely long,
skinny sleeves on her dress when I start to hear
Ruby's voice whispering from behind a bookcase. I'm
not COMPLETELY sure that it's her at first because
she hasn't been seen in school for a while. I stand up

and peek around the shelf. Yes, it's DEFINITELY her, and she's with Miss Wallcott!

The first thing I notice is that Ruby has another **HUMUNGOUS** black eye. She's sniffing and sobbing into a pile of paper hankies and struggling to get her words out. The boy who was looking at the atlas is leaving. Perhaps Ruby and Miss Wallcott think everyone has gone.

I take a step back behind the bookshelf and listen. Is that bad? I don't know, but I can't RESIST. Ruby says, 'I daren't go home any more. He really hurt my arm this time.'

Then Miss Wallcott says, 'This cannot continue, Ruby. We must take this up with Mr Okenden immediately.' She speaks very softly so I don't hear everything but I catch, 'We'll make some phone calls,' and, 'people to help you,' and, 'a doctor,' and, 'might be broken.'

And then Ruby says, through great big snotty sniffs, 'He says he'll kill me if I tell anyone, and he *would*.' So, of course, I KNOW that Ruby is talking about her dad and I suddenly feel SO sorry for her, but really glad at the same time because this means she's FINALLY getting some help.

I don't say ANYTHING TO ANYONE because

I know I wasn't supposed to hear all that. Ruby doesn't come in for another couple of days but when she does come back her face isn't quite so BOSSY AND SCARY-looking, just tired and still bruised, AND she actually smiles at a few people before sitting very quietly in her usual place at the back. After school she gets a different bus home so I don't see her.

On our bus, Joe sits with me and tells me that Ruby has finally got some help, and that she's staying with her auntie in Wellminster. He says that it looks like her dad isn't EVEN going to be allowed to visit Ruby any more unless there's someone with her who she feels safe with, so he can't hurt her.

I really am GENUINELY pleased for Ruby, even though I still don't want to be her friend and I can't pretend that I think she's nice, but it's good that she's safe from her ogre of a dad. And I'm NOT trying to take the credit for it but after I told Miss Wallcott what Ruby was doing, Miss Wallcott did have A WORD with Ruby. Maybe their talk started with a telling off but PERHAPS they also talked about why Ruby behaves so badly – that MIGHT have made it easier for Ruby to ask her for help. Well, anyway, I'd like to think I had SOMETHING to do with Ruby getting things sorted out.

Things are relaxed and chatty between Joe and me. And JUST THINK, if I were his girlfriend I'd always be worried about what I look like when I'm talking to him. I'd probably stress and fret all the time about whether he thought I looked pretty and what I should wear. When you're just friends with a boy it's much more fun than being a girlfriend – there's no PRESSURE.

On the Wednesday of the third week of term a new girl joins our registration group. She has very short whitey-blonde hair, dark skin like Joe's and big round glasses, and is wearing shiny black Doc Marten boots. My first thought is that this girl has STYLE. My second thought follows very quickly: 'What sort of a time is THIS to turn up at school? WEDNESDAY of the THIRD week!' Her family must be totally DISORGANISED to let that happen. My third thought isn't so grumpy – I notice that she's got her stuff in a REALLY INTERESTING bag. It's just like the one that Mary Poppins has in the film, but a bit smaller. No one else has a bag like that in school.

Then I see her name on a book that she's just taken out of this VERY INTERESTING BAG.

Fiona Kidney.

Weird name. I can see it clearly because she's just sat herself next to me without EVEN asking me if the space is free, which it is, of course, because I still don't have a best friend, but that's not the POINT.

Before I even say, 'Hi!' I ask about her name, which is REALLY rude of me, I know, but I'm so surprised to have someone sitting next to me that I temporarily forget my manners.

'How come you're named after a major body organ?' I ask, and she just laughs and points to where I've written

Cordelia Codd

in big fancy letters on the front of my notebook.

'The same reason you're named after a fish,' she says. 'It just *IS*. Live with it!'

And I like the way she pulls her face, as if she doesn't care a **BIG BADGER'S BURP** what anyone thinks of her name. It makes me smile. She sees that I'm smiling and smiles back. We don't say anything else in registration because Mr Carter is in a bad mood, which means he is **BEYOND SCARY**.

After registration we have a library session and we can choose between the ordinary library and the Head Space. The Head Space is so popular that they are already opening it during school hours, not just the evenings.

As soon as Mr Carter says that we can leave I decide to risk being COMPLETELY REJECTED by Fiona and speak to her a bit more.

'We can go to the Head Space next instead of the ordinary library,' I say, hoping I don't sound like a girl who's desperate for a friend. 'Have you been there yet?'

She shakes her head. 'What's that?'

'I'll show you,' I say, and off we go.

We talk in the corridor on the way. 'How come you're starting so late in the term?' I ask her, as we nudge and shuffle our way through the crowds of kids.

'My mum and dad just split up,' Fiona says, 'so Mum and I have come to stay with my gran.'

'Did you mind moving schools?' I ask.

'Yes, I minded **A LOT**,' she says, rolling her eyes and pulling a **DISGUSTED** face. 'We lived in Birmingham. There's all sorts of stuff going on there. This place is like a *very boring* dream.'

I give a big nod of sympathy. 'I like your bag,' I say.

When she tells me she got it from a vintage shop near the bus station my eyes pop out all BOGGLY. 'We have a vintage shop in Wellminster?' I ask.

'Yeah,' she says, as if she means *have you been living on the thirteenth moon of Jupiter or something?* 'Of course we have a vintage shop. Everywhere has one tucked away somewhere, even Wellminster.'

I'm VERY impressed and I can't hide this. 'You've only been here for five minutes and you've already found a vintage shop? Will you show me it?' I ask, knowing that there's a SERIOUS risk of her telling me to PLOP OFF and find it myself. This is, after all, only the first conversation we've had and we could fall out straight away.

'Yeah, no problem,' she says, sounding, I THINK, a little bit like she's pleased that I'm interested. 'I'm going on Saturday if you want to come along.'

'Great,' I say, trying to sound like I go shopping with LOADS of friends EVERY weekend when in fact I haven't been anywhere without Mum or Dad since we moved here.

We get to the Head Space and stand amongst all the wood and books and leather chairs and plants. There is peace and stillness here. Fiona breathes in the smell. 'It's like a library in an old film,' she says. 'I love it. I love old films. Do you?'

And I just **_KNOW, ABSOLUTELY, IMMEDIATELY AND DEFINITELY_** that Fiona Kidney and I are going to get along JUST EXTRA-EXTRA-FINE.

ACKNOWLEDGEMENTS

A huge THANK YOU to all those who have
worked hard to get the second Cordelia Codd
adventure out into the world.

Thanks also to Professor Toni Noble and
Professor Helen McGrath from Australia, and to
the Resilience team at The Young Foundation in
Bethnal Green for their brilliant work helping to
build emotionally strong and happy children.

Hi! Cordelia here!

These are my **TOP TIPS** for **TAMING** your **TEMPER**. They might get you through those **DISASTROUS** days.

Feeling **ANGRY**?

★ Breathe in and out three times **SLOWLY** before you say **ANYTHING**.

Why? Because strange breathing is better than **SCREAMING**. No one takes you seriously when you **SCREAM** about things.

★ Walk away and, **AS SOON AS POSSIBLE**, do something that **BURNS** energy – netball, drama, swimming, a bike ride, a run around the block!

Why? Because **ANYTHING** that gets your body moving will send **HAPPY-MAKING** chemicals to your brain. This is a **SCIENTIFIC FACT**.

★ Walk away and take an **EXTENDED THINKING BREAK**. Write down **WHY** things feel **OUTRAGEOUSLY UNFAIR**. Ask an adult you trust to **LISTEN** while you read it out. Then talk about it.

Why? Because talking about **STUFF** is what **INTELLIGENT** people do. Using **VIOLENCE** or taking sneaky **REVENGE** is **STRICTLY** for the **PRIMITIVE AND BRAINLESS** – and it gets you into trouble... I know this because I **SOMETIMES FAIL** and do the **BRAINLESS** thing.

So, remember:

GET CALM – breathe, walk, exercise.

GET THINKING – but not worrying. Write stuff down if it helps.

GET TALKING – to an adult you trust or a sensible friend.

When you've done this don't forget to **GET LISTENING** – be prepared to learn things about yourself that you **DON'T** like. Maybe you're **NOT QUITE PERFECT** but that's OK, no one is, and we can all improve.

Love
Cordelia
xx

Hi, Cordelia here again!

Being **BOTHERED** by **BULLIES**? Check out these hints. They may not work **MIRACULOUSLY** but they will certainly help.

Remember! It is **NEVER** your fault if you are bullied. You are just **UNLUCKY** at the moment. The bully is the one behaving **BADLY**. Even if you are different from other kids, it is your **RIGHT** to be different. You even have the right to be a **WEIRD GEEKY FREAK**, if you want.

Don't **FEEL** confident? Well, you can still **LOOK** confident. Practise these **GOOD HABITS** so that you don't look like you can be **PUSHED AROUND**.

★ Stand tall

★ Smile

★ Look into people's eyes

★ Speak clearly and give your **OWN** opinions, not what people **WANT** to hear.

★ Ask an adult you trust or a sensible friend to tell you if you have any **NERVOUS** habits: nail-biting, scratching yourself, fidgeting etc, and practise **NOT DOING THESE** so that you don't look like a **SCARED BUNNY RABBIT**.

★ Find an adult you can talk to and **TELL THEM**. Don't be scared that the bully will **GET** you for telling. They probably won't **DARE**. If the adult doesn't **ACT FAST**, find another adult to tell. Pester them until they **PROTECT** you – that's their **JOB**!

Everyone deserves a **BIG, HAPPY LIFE**!

Love
Cordelia
xx

A **Q&A** with **CLAIRE O'BRIEN**,
author of

CORDELIA CODD

FRANKLY, RUBY,
I DON'T GIVE A DAMN!

If you were an animal, what would you be?

❤ I like the idea of being a tiger, or a monkey
that could swing through the treetops, but
a 'friend' told me I would probably be a
chihuahua.

What was the worst job you ever did before you
became a writer?

❤ Putting grated cheese into flan cases in a
factory...boring!

If you were an athlete, what sport would you choose?

❤ The pole vault because I love the idea of going upside down on a big, bendy stick then falling onto a massive cushion.

What is the best place you have ever been on holiday?

❤ Venice was very special. It felt like walking around inside a painting.

If you could visit somewhere you've never been, where would you go?

❤ Norway, in winter, to see the Northern Lights. It's on my 'must see' list.

What do you think is the world's greatest invention?

❤ The bicycle, definitely!

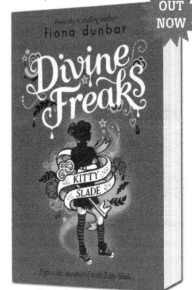